High praise for
NARCISSUS NOBODY
by Gina Yates

THE HIGHLY ENJOYABLE debut by the youngest daughter of Richard Yates lands as keen-eyed and poignant, largely thanks to its appealing misfit protagonist, Hope Townsend. . . . [Gina] Yates shines with smart, witty prose and painfully accurate descriptions of human awkwardness . . . Compusively readable work.

> *PUBLISHERS WEEKLY*

GINA YATES—DAUGHTER of the American master Richard Yates—is further proof that writing talent is often a genetic phenomenon. *Narcissus Nobody* is a charming tale of wayward young adulthood and the vicissitudes of love at any time in life.

> BLAKE BAILEY, author, *A Tragic Honesty: The Life and Work of Richard Yates*

ONE OF THE best novels I've read in years. A delightfully hilarious, gorgeously written, and emotionally complex story of one woman's journey to self-discovery and self-acceptance. Yates's unforgettable cast of lovable misfits will win your heart. A remarkable debut!

> ANDREW PORTER, author, *The Theory of Light and Matter*

GINA YATES's *Narcissus Nobody* is an engaging brew of witty wisecracks, colorful characters, and surprising heart. A novel that's both fun and funny and dances to its own playful and unconventional drumbeat.

> AARON HAMBURGER, author, *Nirvana Is Here*

NARCISSUS
NOBODY

NARCISSUS NOBODY

A NOVEL

GINA YATES

THREE ROOMS PRESS
New York, NY

Narcissus Nobody
BY Gina Yates

© 2021 by Three Rooms Press

This is a work of fiction. Names, characters, businesses, places, events, and incidents are either the products of the author's imaginations or used in a fictitious manner. Any resemblance to actual persons, living or dead, or actual events is purely coincidental.

ISBN 978-1-953103-00-0 (trade paperback original)
ISBN 978-1-953103-01-7 (Epub)
Library of Congress Control Number: 2020949600

TRP-086

First edition
Publication Date: April 13, 2021

BISAC category code
FIC044000 FICTION / Women
FIC076000 FICTION / Feminist
FIC019000 FICTION / Literary

COVER DESIGN:
Victoria Black, www.thevictoriablack.com

INTERIOR DESIGN:
KG Design International, www.katgeorges.com

DISTRIBUTED BY:
PGW/Ingram: www.pgw.com

Three Rooms Press
New York, NY
www.threeroomspress.com
info@threeroomspress.com

*With gratitude to my mom and dad,
and hope for all Earth's animals.*

"I thought this was so big I could say whatever I meant. I guess you can't, ever. I guess there isn't ever anything big enough for that."

—DOROTHY PARKER—

NARCISSUS
NOBODY

ONE

EXCERPT FROM *BLINK AND YOU'LL MISS IT: Oregon's Secret Roadside Attractions.*

Though considered an eyesore by Ashbrook locals, a statue dubbed "Origami Man" has earned a cult following among off-the-beaten-path tourists. The five-foot sculpture, made mostly of scrap metal objects wrapped with copper wire, mysteriously appeared on a country road near the town's outskirts in the weeks following the death of its most famous native son, controversial author Brooks Nixon. It perches among the tall weeds like a mythical man-beast: part prairie raccoon, part post-apocalyptic robot, its scheming eyes belying a smile as serene as the Buddha's.

From the road, one immediately notices what appear to be crumpled pieces of wastepaper stuck all over its protruding shards. They are origami animals—present when the sculpture first appeared—which visitors have continued to replace in the years since. For the origami-challenged, a family-owned gas station up the road has capitalized on the tradition, selling a menagerie of sloppily folded cranes, frogs, and elephants to leave as offerings.

No artist has ever taken credit for the tribute, and no one really knows how it got there. Many have theorized that Nixon, whose mother was Japanese, constructed it before his death and arranged for its secret installation, just to leave one last riddle for the world to puzzle over. The fact that it sits on land the author owned adds merit to that case.

A quote engraved in stone brings one more layer to the mystery; though ascribed to Nixon, no one has ever positively verified its source.

"LOVE, LIKE DEATH, IS NO BIG DEAL."
Brooks "Narcissus" Nixon, June 7, 1951–April 4th, 2012

* * *

LATE SPRING, 1992
SAN LAZARO, CALIFORNIA

HOPE TOWNSEND WOULD FOREVER SINGLE OUT "Message to the World" as the most treasured knickknack in her entire collection— and the best part, she would muse half-jokingly, was that she would've overlooked it if it weren't for her dogs. The credit for the find always went to Biscuit, as he was the one who first sniffed around it and began tentatively lifting his leg. In all fairness, though, Peaches did drag them all to the yard sale when she went after that bird.

"Peaches! Leave it!"

Nathan shook his head and mumbled something indiscernible, while Midnight trotted along next to him looking almost as smug. "You should get that mutt a choke chain."

Hope glared sideways at him. "Careful what you say, my friend, or *you'll* be getting a choke chain."

The yellow lark swirled through an overgrown lot and around two oddly placed houses, but before it disappeared, all three dogs— and Hope herself—encountered a vision that seized their attention. Atop rows of rickety card tables and weathered blankets, heaps of indiscriminate clutter beckoned to them like a lost city of gold.

All of them except Nathan, of course; "Yippee, a gar*bage* sale," he grumbled, well within earshot of the event's proprietor. He just had to spoil everyone else's fun, as usual.

Hope nudged him and pointed at a tumbledown shed spilling over with electronics—that should keep him busy for a while. At least he could pretend to assess the value of a few dusty computers and VCRs before ultimately dismissing them all as worthless. She began pawing over a table of books as the guy selling it all, a scraggly old hippie dude in a lawn chair, tipped his sombrero at her. "Paperbacks are fifty cents each."

"Awesome!" She hoped by letting her genuine enthusiasm shine through she could counteract Nathan's unforgivable rudeness.

There were two things fitting her tastes in that sinkhole of faded reading materials: "A Guide to Vegan Junk Food" and "Herbal Mood Remedies A-Z." (She might even own both books already, but what the hell, she could afford to gamble a dollar.) While fumbling for her coin purse, she felt Biscuit's tug; thankfully (and as it would turn out, fatefully) she picked up the object he intended to pee on right before he completed the act.

"Found that little gem in a dumpster about five years ago," the homeowner bragged, apparently feeling relaxed enough in her presence to pull out a neon orange bong and light it.

She raised her eyebrows and nodded, mirroring his energy, though she hadn't yet discerned what the redwood carving was supposed to represent. Tipping it over, she noticed a title: "Message to the World" and a date, October '74. Only after she'd squinted and gone "mmm" did it hit her: she'd been studying a meticulously carved life-size hand—complete with veins, knuckles, and fingernail ridges—its middle finger held erect.

"Mmm . . . I think I might need this."

"What're ya waiting for then? Two bucks and it's yours."

"Sold."

He didn't notice her passing him the money; his eyes had narrowed to black slits for a deeply savored drag. "I'll even throw in a couple more books for ya if ya want. Ain't got a clue what half of 'em are anyway. My shrink says I buy stuff I don't need to fill an emotional void."

She wedged the bill into his bong-gripped hand. "Lucky for you, *my* emotional void's still got plenty of room in it."

He stood up with a gravelly laugh and led her to a kiddie pool containing, she realized, volumes upon volumes of obscure drivel she had absolutely no interest in. But there was no turning back now; she could always cut up whatever she took, make a collage with it or use it to line the rabbit's cage.

One book stood out immediately from the rest with its glossy bright cover and crisp, untouched pages. The name Brooks Nixon meant nothing to her, but she did recognize the guy's face: she'd seen him on Donahue once a few years back. It was in tenth grade; she had feigned a crippling migraine to escape the hollow, starched zippiness of Spirit Week. But the mob-like zeal of that mostly female talk show audience—fervor for some numb-nuts and his hypomanic portrayal of all men as sex-crazed androids with zero self-awareness or control—had filled her with as much revulsion as the canned pep she was trying to avoid. *This is worse than a genuine migraine,* she remembered thinking.

The longer she stood there, the more covers started catching her eye. She picked up a book of Hummel postcards; *old ladies love this shit,* she remembered. Bringing this to the nursing home would be like bringing a lockpick into a prison. She'd try anything to make her workday go by a little faster, not to mention distract them from their wretched lives. Too bad Mavis would be too out of it to care.

"Find a treasure in there, did ya?"

A couple of them, she started to say. But when she looked up, she realized he'd meant the question for Nathan; her grumpy companion had just emerged from the shed carrying a bright red boombox.

"That depends on what you're asking for it."

"I'll go twenty-five on that one. It's a Panasonic."

"Pfft! Seriously? I'll give you ten."

"All right, I'll take twenty, but I can't go any lower. That's a nice piece of equipment there. You don't see too many red ones."

"Yeah, it *is* red . . . but without a CD player it's kind of useless. Cassettes are gonna be obsolete by 1995."

"Twenty's firm, sorry."

"I can't do twenty." He dropped the player carelessly atop a tray of dried flowers and turned to Hope. "You ready?"

"I guess so." She sighed, stepped up from the pool, and followed, but made sure to glance back at their host and shrug.

"You gonna take these off my hands, Miss?" he asked, gesturing hopefully at the last two books she had touched.

"Well, okay, if you insist." She placed another dollar on the table. "Thanks. And here's a token of my appreciation."

The man gave her a perplexed look. "A toke?" Then he looked down at the table and laughed. "Oh, a *token*! Thank you very much, ma'am. You have yourself a wonderful day."

"You too."

Nathan didn't speak to her until they'd gone almost two blocks; apparently something about the failed exchange had left him in a pouty mood. But he eventually snapped out of it to inquire about her purchases.

"I'm gonna put it on my mantle," she proclaimed of the statuette, holding it out in front of him and making slow baton-like movements so he could appreciate its craftsmanship from every angle.

"Cool. Is it signed? Oh, here it is . . . Matthew—"

"No, that's not the artist, it's the title. See? It says, 'Message to the World.'"

"Oh, I see . . . some psychopath made this in the loony bin before he offed himself. How lovely."

Hope lowered her head and groaned. "*You would* assume that. A person doesn't have to be crazy to express their emotions, you know. And you don't have to be suicidal to want to tell the world to fuck off."

He chuckled. "Spoken like an expert. Well, anyway . . . without a signature, it can't have much value."

"It has *value* to *me* because I *like* it. I paid *two dollars* for it."

"Yeah but I'm just saying . . . oh, never mind."

Hope was happy to let the subject drop. They'd had other versions of this argument a million times; he saw her inattention to financial matters as a sign of flakiness, while she found his rigid materialism offensive. He stirred it up so often because it illustrated his point in their larger ongoing spat, the one where he claimed they would never make it as a "real" couple. And that tired old squabble did not need rehashing.

Nathan pulled an unnecessarily high-tech sport watch from his pocket. "So, what time are you supposed to punch in at the Decrepit Gardens today?"

His mockery of her place of employment usually made her laugh—and she did appreciate his attempt to lighten things—but this time she could barely manage to roll her eyes.

He put the watch away and cleared his throat. "Sorry about that. I meant to say, 'What time does your shift begin at the Faded Forest?'"

She turned her head to hide the reluctant grin he'd drawn out. "About five minutes ago. But it's not like it matters. Mavis doesn't know the difference. As long as I'm there to turn on *The Price is Right* at eleven, she'll be fine."

"Ah. Well . . . do you want a ride?"

His offer made the knot in her stomach loosen a little, as she'd worried he might not make it. She didn't need disappointment over his lack of courtesy adding to the mounting stress over her supreme lateness.

Without warning, Biscuit made a lunge for a greasy discarded chicken wing in the grass. Hope jerked him away from it, and her forcefulness drew looks of disapproval from two passing joggers. She didn't know which stung worse: their misguided cruelty-shaming or Nathan's face when he saw the shiny paperback that plummeted out from beneath her arm.

"You can't be serious," he groaned. "Is that the informercial dipshit who says men can be trained like dogs?"

"I don't know what *you're* so worried about," Hope said, kicking the chicken wing into the gutter as Peaches got hopelessly tangled up in her leash. "I mean, I obviously suck at dog training, so."

Nathan laughed a little, but not enough to let her off the hook completely. From a core deep within her seethed the rage she usually managed to keep contained, accompanied by an almost visceral urge to knee him in the crotch. If he'd tried treating that boombox-seller with the tiniest amount of dignity, she wanted to say, she wouldn't have felt compelled to guilt-buy all these hideous, unwanted items. She opened her mouth to say as much, but then she remembered the ride.

Her tardiness had now veered into official truancy territory. It took her another twenty minutes to get all the animals situated, and by the time he got her to the parking lot of the unfortunately named Pale Willows Retirement Village, she'd opted to try and sneak in the side door to avoid being noticed.

"All right, here we are—Bland Acres Declining Community. What time are you getting off?"

"Six-thirty."

He yanked up the emergency brake and rushed out to open the door for her, making a valiant effort to improve her deteriorating mood. "Call me," he said, swirling his long brown hair into the hood of his sweatshirt. "There's still half a bottle of that . . . um . . . that gooey stuff left. And I'll let you handcuff me to the kitchen chair again if you wear those . . . you know . . . those little presents I got you."

He had such a hopeful look on his face; to tell him what she really thought of his edible vanilla massage oil and steel nipple clamps would have been like telling a six-year-old Disneyland just burned down.

"Will you give me a ride home?"

"Oh, okay. Sure."

Just then a kitchen staffer emerged carrying a large trash bag and Hope made use of the opportunity to hold the door and slip in through it. "Okay, see ya later then."

"Later."

Even though she'd worked in that gloomy, gray behemoth of a building for nearly a year, she often still felt like an invisible presence in its paradoxically warm halls. Hired privately by the family of Alzheimer's patient Mavis Bradly through a classified ad ("no experience necessary"/"kind heart a must"), she existed to give one-on-one companionship to Mavis alone, a function that had apparently earned her nothing but droopy indifference from the overworked clock-watchers around her.

The interior hallways of the prison-like structure were not without their charm, though; whoever had done the decorating here had at least made some effort to create points of interest. The pictures hanging between the residents' rooms all had a certain air of naiveté and humor to them. Hope so adored one painting—a portrait of a raccoon dressed in a suit and tie—that she'd often fantasized about taking it. Even the couches outside the elevator exuded a certain midcentury modern flair. (But that could've easily just meant that they'd been there for ages.) Either way the place had much more appeal than the sterile golf course community clear across the country in Florida where her parents—barely even fifty—had recently relocated. Without a doubt, Hope concluded, this would be a much better spot to waste away in.

Unlike the weary staff, most residents of Pale Willows Retirement Village treated Hope with earnest wide-eyed recognition. Even that catatonic wheelchair-bound gent from the fifth floor—the one she only ever saw when she rushed up there to steal coffee from the staff room—usually managed to raise his eyebrows and nod at her. More than likely, her long, dark-hued dresses distinguished her from the teal blur of scrubs and unreadable nametags. Her makeup probably helped, too; she always wore dark lipstick, as though to underline everything she said so people would know she meant it. And she traced her eyes with coal, so they had to look into them rather than simply check their own reflections.

And she didn't walk the way the staff did either, as if their sensible shoes carried a thousand lifetimes' worth of karmic baggage. At least she hoped she didn't.

The door to room 317 was closed, which meant entering the room would be a crapshoot. Mavis's mental state tended to fall into one of two categories: frivolous amusement or furious agitation. Had the door been ajar, Hope could've read her crumpled face— invariably staring out the window and pondering that ever-spiraling air vent across the street. On good days, it resembled that of a toddler gazing at a shiny crib gadget; on bad days, a prisoner trying to watch TV through a maddening spot of sun glare.

"Hello, hello Miss Mavis?" Hope sang tentatively as she wedged the door open a crack. "Are we decent?" She hadn't even considered the possibility of what she found: her client snoring away peacefully. This fortuitous development brought a little guilty smile to her face; if she could manage not to wake her up, today's shift might be a cakewalk.

Things got even better when she noticed a small, photocopied leaflet on the nightstand, a brand-new copy of the weekly resident-produced newsletter. Despite the awkwardly morbid name, *The Weekly Heartbeat* had rescued her from countless spells of boredom.

In addition to its predictable content (updates about people's operations and a foldout calendar of bridge tournaments), *The Heartbeat* also showcased literary efforts from some of the more with-it nursing home dwellers. These ranged from sweet, corny poems about springtime to cantankerous observations about the modern world. But Hope's favorite section was an open forum in the back called *Words from the Wise*. She liked to clip out and save her favorite quotes, which the paper's editor collected from the residents during Friday night sing-a-longs. "Live fast and die young" had long held prominent placement on her fridge door—until last week's winner, "Never trust a dog to watch your food" replaced it.

She tiptoed, *Heartbeat* in hand, to the afghan-draped recliner, the tick from the grandfather clock on the dresser soothing her nerves for once. The clock usually supervised her wandering mind with an unwelcome stateliness, as though preventing her thoughts from straying too far. But now it was more like a meditation chime, announcing a new serene expansiveness with every passing second.

No sooner had she appreciated this peace than the world's loudest rotary telephone clamored her out of it. The jarring ring caused Mavis to spring upright in bed and shout, "Hello?"

Occasionally Mavis remembered to pick up the receiver, but more often than not such technicalities eluded her.

"That will be Delma," Hope reminded her with a placating smile, smoothing out her clothing as she rose to answer it. "We'll just let her know you're resting, okay?"

Mavis's daughter Delma called to check in on the two of them at least once every shift. Today's poor timing notwithstanding, the sexagenarian's quirky and tangential conversation style offered a welcome vacation from gloom.

"Oh, hi Delma . . . Mother was just having a little nap . . . no, everything's fine . . . how about you?"

Pausing and nodding along to the younger Bradley's response, she noticed Mavis monitoring her every expression with a suspicious scowl; she knew this meant she'd better cut her portion of the chat short. As part owner of the Bay Area's most popular country and western bar, Delma was a wellspring of comical stories—and many of them, like today's, involved mishaps with the mechanical bull. Too bad they'd have to skip the finer details this time.

"Wow. That musta hurt. You'd think they'd make jock straps mandatory on those things. Well . . . anyway, here's your mom." Ending their tête-à-tête early did have one advantage: there was less chance of Hope's gross unpunctuality coming up.

Mavis's side of the phone call consisted mostly of one-word responses ("Tired . . . Pain . . . No . . . What?") but the strain of talking sapped her energy so completely that she shoved the receiver back to Hope in defeat.

"Hey, does your mom like Hummel figurines? I know a lot of the ladies here collect them . . . I just got this cute book of Hummel postcards . . . she did? Cool! Oh, that long ago huh . . . well maybe seeing the pictures again will jog her memory."

As soon as Mavis heard the word Hummel, she began muttering it over and over with a look of deep concentration on her face. She chanted it obsessively throughout the phone call, and by the time Hope hung up, she'd discovered the book on the nightstand and fixed her glazed eyes on its cover. Once they began thumbing through it, every drawing—of cherubic children engaged in pastoral activities—caused Mavis to wrinkle her nose with bemused fascination. "Ha! How 'bout that! Hummel! Hummel! Hummel!" Success, Hope thought, pleased with herself. Maybe her presence here did serve a purpose after all.

This routine continued without variation as they flipped through the book a second time, and by the third or fourth round Hope had memorized every pigtail-sporting fiddler and umbrella-wielding whistler in the bunch. Somewhere around cycle seven, a hazy hypnotic trance set in and the German artist's name morphed into its own mechanized alien language. Nathan's slippery subjugation games grew brighter in her mind, waiting for her at the end like a longed-for reward.

"That was fun," Hope yawned, forcing the book closed.

"Hummel . . . Hummel . . . "

"Hey, I noticed you've got the latest copy of *The Weekly Heartbeat* here—why don't we get caught up on all the neighborhood gossip?"

Mavis's grip on the book loosened with surprising ease, though her fixation on repeating the word "Hummel" didn't waver. Hope quickly scanned the newsletter until she found something else to focus on: a picture of a sleepy but dapper gentleman posing in an amusing St Patrick's Day hat.

"Hey, look here—isn't that the guy who sat next to us at Bingo last week? My, he sure is dressed up. Look at that!"

Mavis waved her hand in a show of haughty indifference.

"Let's see what it says . . . 'Fritz Walsh, 87 years young, was discharged from St. George's on Tuesday after having four polyps removed from his colon. Get well cards for Mr. Walsh can be dropped off at the Wing B information desk.'"

Mavis tilted her head and narrowed her eyes. "Polyps?" She bit her lower lip and her eyes whizzed crazily around the room, eventually settling again on the photo. "Polyps! How 'bout that! Polyps! Ha!" A brand-new alien language emerged, even harder to break out of than the last. Mavis's tiny, crooked fingers gripped the paper with such ferocity that for Hope to try and turn the page might lead to a physical altercation, the kind those poor nurses had to deal with every morning at medication time. Fortunately, eleven o'clock arrived soon enough.

The clunky TV remote felt like a magic wand in Hope's hand as she conjured its welcome barrage of sparkly game show music. "We almost missed the beginning! Here it is! Come on down! You're the next contestant! A new car!"

"Polyps . . . "

Before meeting Mavis, Hope used to think having Alzheimer's disease would be one of the easiest ways to finish one's life. After all, so much anguish comes from having a memory. To exist purely in the present moment—eliminating the need for regret, loss, embarrassment, or guilt—sounded liberating. She imagined it would be like that feeling you get when you walk into a room and can't remember what you came in there for, but then something new quickly grabs your attention—the kind of existence her beloved animals dwelled in all day. The only way for such admirable purity of spirit to exist in human form, it seemed, would be for that form to be stripped of nearly all its human-ness. If that was all Alzheimer's did, why was everyone so down on it?

But, as she'd recently learned from her observations on the job, mortal self-awareness is never completely eradicated. Sadly, the final stubborn traces of lucidity retain their crippling power to the end.

This became apparent during Mavis's weekly visits with a plain-clothed Catholic nun they called Sister Pat. Discussions about heaven and redemption can turn an old lady—any old lady, whether she's cognizant of her own name or not—into a gripped-up wad of desperate intonation faster than anything.

Sister Pat was a master of her game, though. She knew how to keep her talks as vague as possible to avoid inadvertently stepping on ancient wounds. It was she who'd first warned Hope that Mavis was a bit touchy on the subject of sick or injured children, having lost her first born in a house fire. Hope glanced up one day to see Mavis swinging her fists at an imaginary enemy and crying, "Why do you bother me!" Remembering the friendly heads-up from Pat, she noticed the offending UNICEF commercial and quickly zapped it away. "There ya go. Problem solved."

But the "out of sight, out of mind" trick has no potency whatsoever where current physical circumstances are concerned. Mavis winced and grunted every time she had to rearrange the blankets on her bed. She creaked, moaned, and whimpered every time Hope had to help her to the bathroom. She grimaced and grouched all through *The Price is Right*, rolled her eyes in disgust at the lunch tray of lasagna and cantaloupe slices brought to her at noon, fussed and fretted with every buzz of *Family Feud* and *Wheel of Fortune*—and when the afternoon finally reached its confetti-blasting conclusion she summed it all up in one long lamenting sigh: "God, I *really* feel bad."

On that note she laid her arthritic hands neatly across her chest and plunged into a deep sleep, at last affording Hope the pleasure of snuffing out the TV. Another workday, if you could call it that, was almost over; forty minutes remained to revel in the measured vacancy of the grandfather clock, the air vent across the street still barely visible against a burnt fuchsia sky.

In slow tentative movements she unzipped her backpack and pulled out a beat-up Walkman with duct tape around it. She only listened to her tapes when Nathan wasn't around, as his tastes tended toward the aggressive side of mainstream rock, and he enjoyed dismissing everything she liked as "art faggy." "At least it's not vapid and unoriginal," she would snap back. She didn't care what he thought anyway; she would never stop loving the one album that could reach her back in her days of isolated pre-teen angst, despite his calling it "pretentious goth crap." She felt so angry as she popped in *Crystal Mint Carnival* by Wasted Grave and fast-forwarded it to the third song, "Pink Honey Meltdown," that she had to remind herself not to slam the case shut and risk waking Mavis.

Careful to keep the volume at a passable background-noise level, she again slipped her hand in her bag—she would read a little, she figured, and then bury the book in one of Mavis's seldom-used drawers. Crap writing can have surprisingly high entertainment value, she had found, given the right set of circumstances. The cageyness with which she pulled it out did strike her as somewhat ridiculous; after all, she was alone in a darkened room. Her only company was nearly blind and fully zonked. Nevertheless, she felt a noticeable reduction in shoulder tension after she'd shrouded the book in between stiff sheets of Hummel postcards to hide its title.

MANAGE, MANIPULATE, AND MANEUVER
How to Get Your Noncommittal Man Hooked in 3 Easy Steps
By Brooks Nixon

TWO

Hope had listened to her favorite song umpteen million times, but it never lost its transcendental power over her. All sorts of mental clutter always vanished in those magical three seconds after she pressed play; the center of her chest levitated, whisked away by a thousand distorted guitars into a swirling electronic landscape of sound.

> *so glowing against the air*
> *so splintering beneath the trees*
> *I'm a stranger, dying, dream-like*
> *without care*
> *it's just another pink*
> *just another pink*
> *just another pink honey meltdown*

Judging from the picture on the cover, this book couldn't have been written past 1985. Mr. Nixon sported a green polo shirt, a pastel yellow sweater knotted over his shoulders, and the dubious tight curls of a likely perm which, together with his crooked teeth and heavy arched eyebrows, created the overall impression of a man in a goofy disguise.

Before she read a whole page, Hope could already sense the arresting rhythm of prose that made these books so popular. The author started by firing off a barrage of probing questions and then went in for the kill with his outrageous promise. Hard to believe anyone would fall for such blatant marketing hocus-pocus. She plowed through the book's prologue hungrily, eager to scoff at its trite and patronizing presumptions.

Are you tired of dead-end relationships?

Do you seem to keep dating the same immature men over and over?

Do you long for a meaningful connection and fear you'll never find one?

Do you secretly suspect that all men are pigs?

If you answered "yes" to any of these questions, you are not alone.

But I have good news for you! In buying this book you have taken the first step toward finding the deep, lasting commitment you deserve. Congratulations!

The foot of the bed jiggled a little as Mavis kicked at her covers and strained her ragged vocal cords. "Delma?"

"Delma's at her house, Miss Mavis. Do you need something?"

"Toilet."

"Okay."

Mavis had worn adult diapers for over a decade now and these bathroom trips of hers usually fell into one of two categories: *too late* or *false alarm*. But she vehemently insisted on making the trips, despite what an arduous task it had become for all parties involved. Retaining this mundane habit of self-care represented her final grasp at a long-gone autonomy, one supposed. As the two of them lumbered and heaved their way into the handicapped-equipped facility, Hope made herself a silent promise: if she ever reached this stage in life, there would be no more fighting. She would graciously lie back and let the robots do all the work.

This time it was a false alarm. The trick about false alarms was not acknowledging their falseness; she sat on the edge of the tub for about fifteen minutes, hummed a few old country songs, then wasted a wad of clean toilet paper and a flush before helping the old woman back to bed.

> Through my work as a relationship coach I have heard countless stories from frustrated women like you over the years. I began to notice a common thread between these stories, and I set out to break the discouraging cycle of predictable patterns once and for all. Let me tell you, the response to my 3M system has been overwhelming! I receive hundreds of thank you letters a day from the women who've attended my seminars. And now, this valuable information is available in convenient book form. With the help of my simple strategies and concrete tools, you too will soon learn to become the top priority in any man's life with very minimal effort.

A labored sound emanated from Mavis's side of the room, followed by a long stream of whispered expletives.

"What's wrong, Miss Mavis, can't sleep?"

"Urrrrrrr . . . umph . . . God Dammit . . . "

"Well . . . okay . . . I'll take that as a yes. How about if I go get you some nice warm milk? Sound good? Hang tight, I'll be right back."

As Hope swooshed by her, Mavis lifted a mangled finger and widened her eyes as though signaling a waitress.

"Hold that thought, love," Hope shot back before slipping out (she knew it was a ridiculous thing to say to a senile woman, but she didn't want to risk having to endure another bathroom trip).

Hope couldn't tell one worker from another in the clanging steamy commotion of that huge kitchen, but they all clearly recognized her. Chaos parted like the red sea as four or five women of color in hairnets all scurried to get her whatever she needed with polite efficiency. The contrast between the drudgery of their undervalued positions and the cushiness of her own made her draw her shoulders in, seized by a sudden urge to shrink and disappear. After procuring the Styrofoam cup of microwaved milk, she revealed her ulterior motive to the women, bookending it with gratuitous apologies.

"Sorry, I hate to be a bother, but is there any way I could use the phone? I just need to make one quick call. Sorry." A very pregnant custodian led her to the noisy break room, a place far less relaxing than the one she would return to.

THE BACK OF HER NECK BECAME flush with every passing ring, and by the time Nathan's answering machine kicked on, a current of undefined resentment had reached her fingertips.

"What's up . . . this is Nate . . . leave a message . . . "

In the six months since they'd met, Hope had never once heard anyone refer to Nathan as "Nate." His roommate didn't call him that. The skate-boarding manager of the hotel where he worked as breakfast cook always clearly enunciated both syllables of his name. Perhaps certain privileged friends of his got to use the more familiar moniker? Hope wouldn't know. The only time she'd heard of his having any friends at all was when he'd needed an excuse to get out of one of their rendezvous ("I gotta help a friend move") or validation for one of his implausible claims ("my friend worked there, it's owned by Neo-Nazis.") Sometimes she wondered if they even existed at all, these chums of his. If they did exist, why couldn't she meet them? And if they didn't, why lie? In the end it didn't matter. No matter which angle she considered it from, his outgoing message still annoyed the hell out of her.

"Um . . . yeah . . . hi, *Nate*. It's Hope . . . Nate. I'm almost done work and . . . just calling to remind you about picking me up . . . so

. . . I'm off at six thirty and I'll be waiting in the circle drive out front. Okay? I'll see ya soon . . . I hope. Bye . . . Nate."

Back in the room, Mavis greeted Hope with a distrustful glare that actually made her feel a tad guilty about the length of her absence, even though she knew Mavis couldn't care less (the look plainly didn't mean *what took you so long;* rather, *who the fuck are you.)*

"Okay, Miss Mavis, I brought that warm milk you asked for. Now, sit up and use your straw so it doesn't spill. This'll put you right to sleep in no time, you'll see."

"What the . . . oh, *Christ.* Son of a . . . ."

"There ya go . . . that's good . . . one more swallow . . . perfect. That should do the trick. Now, I'm gonna turn out the light again, but I'm still right here if you need me. Okay?"

"Ahhh . . . bugger. Lordy, lordy, lordy . . . "

"Goodnight, Mavis".

"Hmmph."

> It never ceases to amaze me how a woman so smart, disciplined, and calm when facing career challenges can still exhibit such poor judgment and lack of self-control when it comes to her romantic life.
>
> Shouldn't something as important as finding a partner for life merit the same razor-sharp focus and determination as plotting one's vocational path?

The book reminded Hope of a favorite old story her grandfather used to tell. Once, at the Iowa State Fair as a kid, grandpa had seen a sign that said, "Learn to whittle, five cents to enter." He'd stood in line for forty minutes clutching a nickel begged from his mother until finally a woman had ushered him into a tent with four or five other kids. There, a curtain had whooshed open on a scene that was, well, anticlimactic to say the least; a guy with a handlebar moustache was sitting there scraping away at a twig with heaps of shavings at his feet, repeating and repeating the same eight words in stone-faced monotone. "Never cut *toward* yourself . . . always cut *from* yourself . . . "

True, Hope hadn't technically paid to learn Brooks Nixon's 3M system, but the feeling of being duped echoed her grandfather's story perfectly. She wished she could bring him back from the dead for a minute just to tell him about it.

Ten minutes remained in her shift, time enough to flip exasperatedly through the remaining pages of *Manage, Manipulate, and Maneuver* (or at least the *Manage* part.) She wanted to at least skim its bullet points, to grasp at the meat of these so-called "concrete tools" he kept mentioning. But her attempts to speed-read kept getting impeded by absurd paradoxes, sentences so puzzling in their illogicality that she had to re-read them two or three times.

"Until you fully eliminate all your need to become the center of a man's life, you will never create the kind of allure that makes him crave your company and want to stay by your side for the rest of eternity."

Hope pondered this head-scratcher as she glanced up at the grandfather clock: 6:26. She could just take off now, she knew, but a perverse curiosity made her turn the page again. It couldn't *all* read like such a blatant mockery of itself, could it? She rifled through the remaining pages and settled on a boldly highlighted sidebar titled "What to do when problems arise."

> We all have our triggers. Surely there will be times when a man says or does something that makes you feel scared, jealous, or unappreciated. Should you communicate these feelings to him? Of course! Should you do it by calling him an inconsiderate jackass? Absolutely not. Here's what to do instead.
>
> First, take a deep breath and re-focus your energy. Remember to keep your eyes on the prize; you are trying to bring this man

closer to you, not push him further away. Then, tell him how you feel. But tell him using only "I" statements. Here's an example:

I feel lonely sometimes when my phone doesn't ring.

Now, the first time you make a statement like this, it might be met with a deafening awkward silence. Do not try and fill this silence. Just breathe through it, keeping your eyes on the prize. Give him the opportunity to step in and be your hero, and you might be surprised at what happens next.

As if on cue, Mavis uttered some snarky gibberish in her sleep and burst out in giggles. Hope found it heartening to know that whatever went on in those little old lady dreams of Mavis's, a few laughs managed to creep in now and then.

6:30 came at last, and like a jewel thief in a James Bond movie, Hope zipped her Walkman into her backpack and tiptoed out. For now, Brooks Nixon's "useful information" would just have to wait. She tucked the book into a dusty, doily-draped dresser drawer that no one ever opened (and where tripe like that probably belonged).

Another day conquered, she thought with secret sarcasm as she skipped down the stairwell, her footsteps echoing like slow applause.

As far as occupations go, Hope knew she could've done a lot worse. She'd been fresh out of high school when Delma hired her, with no prior work experience other than helping out at her aunt's pumpkin farm every Halloween. So she usually remembered to feel grateful for her humble position. There were even times when she found the work rewarding, and she'd toyed with the idea of a career in the helping-ancient-people-feel-less-hopeless industry (though whether such an industry even existed she had no idea.)

But transportation to that place could be a real pain in the ass. She'd failed to research the logistics of getting to and from the job before taking it, having already been won over by the prospect of getting paid to watch TV—not to mention the flamboyant employer who hired her on the spot because she had "caring eyes." But the twenty-minute gap between her duplex in San Lazaro and the nursing home's location—a sleepy seaside enclave called Mescalero—proved harder to bridge than she'd imagined.

Surely there's some sort of public transportation, she remembered thinking. *I mean, how do people get to their doctor's appointments?* As it turned out, residents made such arrangements privately through their medical insurance. A Pale Willows staff member told her about hitching rides with a winery tour called Grape Expectations that passed through both San Lazaro and Mescalero six times a day; this option served her well, except when she missed it. Occasionally Delma could arrange for a family member in San Lazaro to pick Hope up en route to a visit, and often she could hitch a ride back into town with other residents' visitors. She tried to only use Nathan as a last resort.

"Sorry, I guess I passed out," he mumbled through the car window, pulling up half an hour past their designated meeting time. He slapped himself and shook his face vigorously, as if to portray a victim of some mysterious affliction.

"It's okay," Hope said. "I know I can always get a ride home with the janitor."

He chuckled. "I'm sure you can." He knew she meant Larry, a flush-faced man in his late fifties who'd once told Hope he preferred skinny women because "they're easier to throw around."

He exhaled audibly as he rolled up the window, and she sighed back in agreement. "I'm pretty exhausted too," she said. "Must be something in the air." She half-hoped he would pass out as soon as they got back to her place, sparing her from whatever tiresome perverted deeds he had in mind. He popped in a reggae cassette (the one genre of music they could agree on) and the dusk-colored countryside passed them by without small talk.

Before they moved to Florida, Hope's parents had given her the same two options they gave their other five children: they'd pay half her tuition at a four-year college, or two years' rent if she chose work over school. Both her older sisters had chosen the first option. Hope opted for door number two, mainly as a way of distinguishing herself from the herd. She could always apply for scholarships later, she figured, and anyway, dorm rooms didn't allow pets. She reflected on the decision with gladness each time she stood in the courtyard of her powder-blue duplex with its flaking white-trimmed windows and ragged screen door.

The first thing she heard was always Biscuit's nails hitting the wood floor as he jumped off her bed. As she fished for her keys, Peaches would commence yapping and sprinting around in circles. If she listened closely while entering, she could make out the shy rustling of Beatrix the dwarf rabbit's newspaper shavings. But the most entertaining greeting always came from Edith, her foster parakeet.

"Hey, turdwad!" the bird squawked, echoing the obnoxious catchphrase once programmed into her by some long-gone owners.

As Nathan followed Hope through the door, he gave his usual compulsory wave toward the tall, gilded cage in the corner. "What's up, fuckface."

"Don't say that anymore," Hope protested. "I'm trying to teach her some manners." She stood on her toes and leaned in as though aiming at the bird's ears. "*Hi beautiful! Hi beautiful! Hi beautiful!*"

Edith let out a confused caw. "Hey, turdwad!"

Nathan burst out laughing as Hope pushed past him and into the bathroom. "Okay, maybe we need a few more lessons."

As soon as she saw her peeved face in the mirror, Hope reached for the appropriate self-prescribed cocktail of herbal remedies: one tablespoon of kava kava tincture, one of California poppy, a dash of ashwagandha, two drops of lemon balm, and a pinch of St. John's wort from the medicine cabinet. She swirled the elixir around in a shot glass-sized mouthwash lid and downed it, following that with half a lid of passionflower for its libido boosting effects. Finally, she opened a drawer filled with lavender sachets and inhaled deeply. *That's better*, she thought. One swish of mouthwash later, the face in the mirror exuded sheer controlled confidence.

"The phone's ringing!" Nathan called out from her bed, where he'd already made himself comfortable in a nest of dirty laundry.

"Let the machine get it."

"What if it's one of your boyfriends?"

"Shut up."

She walked in the room with her tongue stuck out at him as the beep sounded.

"Oh, hi Hope, it's Delma . . . sorry to bother you dear . . . I'm just wondering if you could stay with mother an extra hour tomorrow night . . . there's an Irish dance performance on PBS that I'd really like her to watch . . . I'd pay you time-and-a-half . . . anyway you can let me know tomorrow . . . thanks dear . . . bye."

"Ooh, an Irish dance performance on PBS," Nathan said. His blood-shot eyes widened with mock excitement. "How very . . . *cultural!*"

Hope rubbed the back of her neck and bit her lip. "Dammit. How am I supposed to find a ride home at nine o'clock?"

"Well you know," Nathan said, raising his eyebrows, "I'm half Irish." He suddenly jumped to his knees, put his hands behind his head and began rotating his hips like Elvis Presley. "I can dance for you."

"Very cute," Hope offered with a bemused smile, "but that is not what Irish dancing looks like at all."

"What does it look like then?"

"I don't know . . . like, a jig or whatever. Not that."

"Well, you're the expert. Anyway, I'd love to help you out, but I'm going out with some friends tomorrow night."

"What friends?"

"Just some people from work."

"Oh? Where are you going?"

"Mystery Lounge, apparently."

She turned away from him and fixed her downcast eyes on a dusty outlet in the corner. "Oh."

He always did that—tacked on the word "apparently" like that—whenever he told her about plans that didn't include her. As if he had no choice in the matter. As if to say, "I *guess* that's what I'm doing, because that's what *they* decided, and I am nothing but a cog in *their* machine."

"Mystery Lounge . . . you mean that karaoke place?" she asked, throwing him a look that said, *the one you keep saying you'll take me to, you dickface?*

"Hmm. Do they have karaoke there? Oh yeah, I guess they do." He shrugged. "Well . . . when someone else is paying, that's all I care about."

Hope swallowed hard. "I see." She picked up the herb ency-clopedia and the vegan cookbook from earlier and began shuffling them around, rearranging items as she went, keeping her hands busy until they lost track of what they were supposed to be doing.

Nathan tilted his head and squinted as he watched her. "Are you okay?"

Instead of answering, she dropped her hands and looked toward the ceiling as if counting its tiles.

"Why are you breathing like that? Is something wrong?" He changed his tone to an exaggerated, mock-suspicious parental one. "Have you been huffing potpourri again?"

She turned toward him, the history of their entire relationship (or non-relationship, as it were) flashing before her eyes. How exactly had it happened, she tried to recall; how had she stepped into this awful poisonous quicksand?

The first fateful step had taken place on a wet park bench the previous October. That was when Nathan first sat down and introduced himself, as Biscuit and Midnight sniffed each other's butts in the background. With their contrasting colors, Nathan remarked, the two resembled a big furry yin-yang symbol. Then he said he liked animals better than most humans. "They're so simple and honest," he said.

She told him she felt the same way. Then he launched into a long story about a nudist beach he went to once. He'd loved how natural it felt, how the people were just *there*, in that basic, vulnerable state. Perhaps he was testing her, she thought, mentioning nudity like that. Perhaps she was passing the test with flying colors by showing interest.

"It was an awesome experience," Nathan said, "feeling that vulnerability, pushing through it, and realizing there was nothing to fear on the other side." He said he liked karaoke bars for the same reason. She told him she'd never done karaoke before but had always wanted to.

"Really? We should go to Mystery Lounge sometime." The idea had caused a ticklish sensation in her lower belly.

And now, her entire digestive tract was in knots. She blew out the last in a series of long, centering breaths and began wringing her knuckles together. "I feel . . . I just feel . . . "

"You feel what?" he asked, backing up and bracing himself against the blue velvet headboard.

"I feel like . . . like you don't . . . like I'm the only one who's . . . ."

"What?"

"Oh, fuck it. You're just such an *inconsiderate jackass*, that's all."

"Huh?"

She closed her eyes and cupped one hand over them; maybe if she didn't look at him, she could prevent the words from coming out wrong. Any expression of emotion from his side would weaken her stance. If he appeared hurt, she might try to soften the blow (*you're great, but . . .*) or if he looked angry, she would probably undermine herself (*I don't mean to sound like a bitch . . .*).

She would never remember most of the speech that came out, only the phrases she liked best.

"I'm not asking for a *goddamned engagement ring* here, just an acknowledgement that we're more than *just casual acquaintances.*"

Parts of her rant probably sounded a bit clingy, at least clingier than she would've sounded with her eyes open. At one point, she noted that they'd slept together exactly fifty times, and she wished she'd kept that divulgence to herself.

"You know," she said, "the other day at work someone asked me if I had a boyfriend, and I took so long to answer that they changed the subject. I mean, what was I supposed to say? *Well, I've been seeing someone for six months . . . but . . . it's not really a relationship?*" She took another deep breath, trying to ignore the fact that she had the phrase "eyes on the prize" rapidly circling through her brain like bad sitcom music.

"Just once I'd like to talk about us, about you and me, without sounding like, like . . . like some . . . *pathetic, delusional, slutty loser.*"

That last line probably saved the night from becoming a total disaster. Nathan cracked up when he heard it, forgoing his usual defensive jerk routine in favor of sweet, comical submission. She opened her eyes to find him sprawled face down across the bed, grasping at her legs as if she were a gleaming puddle in the middle of the desert.

"Please don't yell at me anymore," he whimpered, "I swear, I never meant to hurt your feelings." He rearranged himself into a crawling position. "Look, I'm on my hands and knees. Can you please forgive me? *Pleeease?*"

"What's in it for me if I do?" she asked.

"Hmm . . . I don't know . . . how about if I promise to be your slave for the rest of the night? I'll do anything you tell me to. You can humiliate and abuse me as much as you want. How about that?" He tilted his head and did his best impression of a parakeet. "Hey beautiful! Hey beautiful!"

She crossed her arms, unfazed. "How about you kiss my ass, turdwad."

"Now we're talkin'!" He lunged forward and threw her onto the bed, acting out her words literally while she giggled and squealed defenselessly.

At 3 a.m. the click of the door latch awoke her. Nathan always left before morning—he couldn't sleep outside of his own bed—and that sometimes used to bother her, but right now nothing could. Right now, all was well with the world. In his woozy post-coital state, Nathan had promised to start including her in his life more. The only reason he hadn't before, he claimed, was that he thought his old friends drank too much and she wouldn't like them.

It was a plausible enough story. Nathan did have a history of booze-related issues dating back to age 13, and he claimed to admire her for her temperance. He was "statistically fucked," he always said, belonging to just about every group known to have higher than average alcoholism rates. The father he never knew was Native American, and the trauma of that absence—plus his Irish mother's suicide—increased his own chances of developing the disease exponentially, and his employment in the restaurant industry didn't help either. "It's hard to beat odds like those," he reminded her often, his resigned tone making Hope question whether he really wanted to.

By contrast, Hope preferred to soothe herself with herbal potions and therapeutic creative acts, things like journaling and collage-making. Nathan once said she was his "only healthy addiction." Since meeting her, he said, he had given up hard liquor, only drank beer on weekends, and even smoked fewer cigarettes. He worried about tainting her innocence, he told her that night. But he needn't worry, she assured him; most alcohol made her gag. She only drank around drinkers when it seemed rude not to.

First thing that morning, Hope grabbed the notebook from her nightstand and jotted *good talk with N* on a page titled "Gratitudes." She would later rip out that entire page and set fire to it in the sink, but for now, doodling cheesy hearts on it required no effort whatsoever.

She didn't notice the antenna poking through his hair when he waved from his front porch that morning. If she had noticed it, she might have kept walking and saved herself a lot of trouble. She might have spent her morning commute gazing out the window of the Grape Expectations bus in dreamy idleness instead of rehearsing the wrathful histrionics she planned to confront him with later. But she didn't notice the phone. It didn't even occur to her that a person could be talking on a telephone outside of their house. He appeared oddly surprised when she ran over to hug him.

"Just a minute," he said, setting the brick-sized receiver down on a stucco wall next to a dirty ashtray and half-empty coffee cup. He accommodated her with a one-armed embrace, followed by a swat on the ass as she turned to leave. "Have fun at work," he called after her.

"You too."

He smacked his lips a couple of times before resuming his phone conversation. "Sorry about that," he said into the receiver, taking a few paces away and lowering his voice. "I was just talking to a friend of mine."

Just talking to a friend of mine.

The piercing words proved impossible for Hope to remove from her emotional body, though that didn't stop her from trying. She paused for a cleansing breath in the lobby of Pale Willows Retirement Village; she visualized a lush and expansive meadow while a trio of faceless workers pushed past her in the stairwell. She counted slowly to ten before turning the handle on Mavis's door. But instead of fading into the background, the phrase echoed louder with every soulless cheer from the game show masses. Instead of getting watered down by the scent of Aspercreme and baby powder, it mixed with them to form an even more vile and nauseating concoction.

She agreed to stay the extra hour (Delma hired a taxi to take her home), and in the end she had a fine time watching Irish dancing with Mavis. A better time, she reckoned, than she could ever have with Nathan and his band of drunken idiots. One of the dancers had brown skin and a wide nose like Nathan's and it pleased Hope tremendously to see this doppelgänger flouncing and frolicking about with neatly coifed hair and an argyle sweater. Sometimes the Universe finds clever ways to help you laugh off your troubles.

"That's my boyfriend," she bragged to Mavis when the camera zoomed in on his face. Whether or not her claim would be taken seriously she didn't know, but it didn't seem to matter.

"Very nice," Mavis said, nodding in approval.

A short time later the camera cruised through the audience, stopping briefly on an ancient skeleton of a man in a wheelchair; he had a cute smile and that wispy, baby-fine hair that makes all old people look like mad scientists. Mavis hauled up one of her shaky curved fingers. "My boyfriend," she said, grinning.

"Nice!"

They whiled away the entire dance program like that, pointing out their respective boyfriends. Hope loved the way Mavis never tired of the gag, in the same way Peaches never tired of chasing after her favorite squeaky toy. When the show ended, Hope made a spectacle of pleading at the TV (*Oh, noooo . . . don't leave us, fellas!*), then turning around and shrugging (*Ah, who needs 'em*) and making a gesture like she was brushing lint off her shoulder. Mavis echoed the sentiment, waving her hand with the same show of disregard she'd shown for Mr. Fritz Walsh and his over-commemorated polyp removal.

So blithe was the atmosphere in the room that moments later, when Mavis closed her arms like a vampire and creaked *Lord, take me now*, Hope burst out laughing. "Me too!" she chimed in. "I've had enough."

Mavis shot her an icy stare that made her stomach drop—it was exactly like the look her father used to give her when she giggled and fidgeted during church sermons, only this time she actually felt bad for her flippancy.

But then Mavis furrowed her brow with a sternness so over-dramatized it had to be intended as a spoof. "Me first," she croaked. With that she raised her chin and closed her eyes, grinning with self-satisfaction, and Hope relaxed into the recliner's embrace.

"Death isn't really a big deal if you think about it," Hope remembered saying to Nathan once, feeling wise and verbose after hazarding one wine cooler at his favorite fern bar. "It's really just birth in reverse, like a mirror image—and no one remembers their birth as a traumatic event. All anyone can really say about their birth is that one minute there was nothing, and the next minute they had all kinds of crap to deal with. It really is just so much crap, isn't it? This need for food, this aversion to pain, this weird longing for connection . . . You'd think folks would look forward to the end of a struggle that had been imposed on them from out of nowhere. You'd think it would feel peaceful, like the moment after your alarm goes off when you realize it's Saturday morning and you don't have to get up. I mean, we're supposed to be the smartest of all animals . . . how come we dread the return to nothingness like it's some kind of boogeyman?"

Hope listened to Mavis's breathing now, waiting for it to become deep and even before venturing any movement that might wake her. When a tentative shift in her chair didn't do it, she delicately opened the drawer and slipped her hand in. The plan was to take the 3M book out and throw it away, but not just any trash can would do; she had to find someplace far enough from both room 317 and her own blue duplex to make absolutely certain no one would ever find out she'd touched it. She had to sever its every last foul karmic thread from her own.

The dumpster behind the building had too many tied white bags in it. She briefly fantasized about handing it to that smelly lady who always paced the alley behind the grocery store wearing torn gray blankets. (*Here ya go*, she would say—*you can use this for toilet paper.*) But the old woman might have remembered her. She might have approached her later when she was out with Nathan and said, *hey, is this the jerk who won't commit to you?* Unlikely as that scenario sounded, she couldn't risk it. Better to bury the book deep in the cans behind that Italian restaurant on Fourth Street. They had sturdy lids and seemed to be emptied frequently. That would be the perfect place, she decided. And that's where it probably would have ended up.

Instead, a perfect use for the book presented itself later that night as she reached for the lamp on her bedside table. Startled by a large yellow beetle-type thing inching its way up the bedpost, she grabbed a plastic cup and trapped it then wedged Brooks Nixon's glossy face under its crusty feelers as they scanned the carved wood. The spectacular menace shuffled about frantically in its makeshift carrier while she ferried it to the door, talking to it the whole way *(hang in there, little buddy . . . soon you'll be in the grass and everything will feel normal again . . .)* It struck her that she didn't own any other book with such a crisp, flat cover; if she made this her go-to humane bug-catcher, she wouldn't have to feel guilty about the wasted paper.

Making peace with death as a concept doesn't mean you take killing lightly. In Hope's world, even nasty, creepy-crawly beings deserved compassion. Her family still talked about the fishing excursion in which she single-handedly liberated all the earthworms from their bait box. She became a vegetarian after that fateful trip, but had to wait until she left home to give up dairy and eggs; her parents deemed veganism to be as recklessly unhealthy as knife play or intravenous drug use, and to this day they forbade her to practice it under their roof.

On Nathan's first visit to Hope's apartment, he had entered through a swarm of houseflies, so on his second visit, he'd presented her with a plastic flyswatter as if it were a red rose. While she appreciated the gesture, she eventually had to admit to him that she'd never once used his gift for its intended purpose. ("Too violent," she'd said, wincing and shuddering at the thought of it.) Instead she used it to shoo the insects away, fanning the air around them while uttering long profanity-laden threats.

"Now you're gonna get outta here and leave me alone, you disgusting motherfuckers!" she would say. "We can do this the easy way or the hard way. Wanna test me, you sonsabitches?"

The dogs liked participating in this game, too, especially Biscuit. He would get all wound up and charge around barking like a maniac. She didn't mind it when he caught one. Violence between non-humans didn't bother her. At least those fights were fair.

It was during one of these household-wide frenzies that Delma's call came in the next morning. Hope would later worry about the agitation all that bug-chasing brought to her voice, but Delma didn't seem to notice. In a situation like that, social graces elude everyone. No one making a call like that ever expects poise on the other end.

It's hard to express the appropriate sentiment when a person dies long *after* her time. "I'm sorry for your loss" doesn't quite fit, as whatever was lost has already been gone for years. Fortunately, Hope had spent enough time in the nursing home to gather an arsenal of clichés for such events. "Well . . . " she offered, choking on the swollen mass of grief that she'd never thought to prepare for, " . . . at least she doesn't have to fight anymore."

The minute the call ended, Hope dialed Nathan's number without giving it a second thought. Whatever had gotten her so worked up yesterday, putting it on a brief hold wouldn't hurt anything. After all, she still had a lifetime's worth of fight left in her; there was no use burning through it all at once.

THREE

A COUPLE OF PHONE CALLS TO appropriate offices revealed there was, indeed, a helping-ancient-people-feel-less-hopeless industry, and any wingding could get qualified for it. Hope's parents even offered to pay for the 17-week course she found at the American Legion, even though doing so violated the terms of their parental cord-cutting arrangement. They liked the fact that such accreditation would guarantee her work at an agency, thereby raising their daughter's status to Legitimate Citizen. It also didn't hurt that the agency job came with health insurance, as they believed a red meat deficiency would soon wreak dire pandemonium on her immune system.

The program, offered through the California Association for Responsible Elder Support (C.A.R.E.S.), bore so many similarities to the babysitting classes she'd taken as a pre-teen that most of it felt like review. If it weren't for the childcare class having taken place across town at the San Lazaro Community Center, she could've sworn this was the same room; it had the same dirty blinds, strange plants, and faint odor of Windex. The trainings had a similar obviousness about them, but one spent more time on what to do when someone falls off the toilet while the other focused more on preventing cleanser ingestion. The ways people can fall apart may change as they age but dealing with the human psyche requires a universally rigid skill set, a certain understanding firmness. You must tell the person that while you understand *why* they don't want to brush their teeth/take their heart medicine, you're simply not going to let them out of it.

It had now been eight months since Hope earned her certificate, and her practical circumstances had improved by leaps and bounds. C.A.R.E.S. had an outreach office right around the corner from her house; it had gone unnoticed by her for two years, tucked neatly into the side door of a split-level chiropractic clinic she also never knew existed. The director of Enchanted Hands (or as Nathan called it, "Magic Fingers") turned out to be an even less intrusive employer than Delma. Picking up schedules and paychecks became a weekly chore akin to taking out the trash—something Hope just did, nothing worth lending much brain space to.

Her current client, a 68-year-old cancer patient named Jack Cohen, also resided within a comfortable distance. The ten-minute walk from her duplex—which skimmed a cemetery wall lined with sun-filtering redwoods—ranked among the most pleasant fragments of her day.

It wasn't always so pleasant, though. On the morning of her first shift, she'd suffered such crippling anxiety as to need to circle Jack's building twice before entering. *I can always just leave if I hate it,* she'd told herself, recycling a mantra originally created for middle school parties.

From the paperwork Hope had learned Jack still had most mental faculties intact, and the prospect of having to have an actual conversation with a client had given her a bit of performance anxiety. His maleness had also added a dimension of distressing unknowns. How would she react if he tried to hit on her, for example? What if a situation arose in which she had to handle his shriveled-up old man wiener? On top of all that, he had an ominous cardboard sign in his apartment window reading *Veteran—Medicated for Your Protection.*

But luckily, Jack turned out to be a harmless old coot who was easy to entertain. He liked talking about his life—a lot—and Hope didn't mind listening. She truly meant it when she complimented his storytelling skills every day before leaving. "Another great yarn," she would tell him. "I look forward to the next installment."

"Wait 'til you hear the ending," he would always reply jauntily. "You'll never see it coming."

The most fun tales were Jack's vibrant renderings of his service in World War II. He'd held the most dangerous job in the navy, according to him—front cannon loader on a tanker carrying aviation fuel across the Atlantic. Hope's sketchy memory of whatever she learned in high school history class meant she asked him loads of dense questions, but he patiently filled her in on all of it.

Every detail he described brought into sharper focus an unfathomably tension-filled existence. He'd lived on top of the constant reality of death then, German U-boats lurking beneath his ship threatening to blow him up any second. It must have been awful. But as she watched Jack gasp and wince through the stories now, his split-pea colored face tethered to an oxygen tank, she could both sense and completely understand his wistfulness about it.

As it turned out, she never saw him naked. The VA nurses handled bathing, and Jack could still make it to the bathroom by himself. On the rare instances when a flash of his stark white privates couldn't be avoided, he would diffuse the awkwardness by saying, "You'd better turn your head, Hope. I don't want to traumatize you."

Current bashfulness aside, Jack had clearly possessed an overflow of testosterone as a young man. He alluded to his promiscuous past often, his breathing getting noticeably less labored whenever he talked about it.

His heyday was Jazz-era New Orleans, the fall of 1945, just after the war ended. Recently established as a destination for the party-minded, the town was a veritable smorgasbord of skirts for all the young returning soldiers. Jack remembered gawking at the abundance of hot dames from a passing streetcar, all dolled up in their waist-cinched jackets and high heels. "In my wildest dreams, I couldn't have imagined a sweeter life," he told Hope now, his volume lowered as though revealing a secret. "I felt like the luckiest cat alive."

But the gleam never lingered more than a few seconds. His eyes would snap back to their default setting when he changed the subject to his late wife, as if shifting gears to climb a steep hill.

He'd first met Ivy when he moved to San Francisco to get in on the thriving shipbuilding industry there, and apparently her saintly virtues of womanly goodness had made quite an impression on him, so much so that his tail-chasing days had briskly ceased.

"Heck, I even gave up bourbon and curbed my sailor's tongue for her," he told Hope once, gesturing toward the dusty wedding portrait on his bookshelf. "I thought, *this is it now. This is my chance to become right with God.*"

"That's sweet," Hope said, even though it sounded pretty warped to her. It was during his conversation, about two months into her time there, when he asked her the dreaded boyfriend question. She gave him her usual fumbled answer: "Um, sort of . . . well, I've been seeing someone for almost two years, but it's not . . . I mean, we're not . . . "

He gave her a knowing look. "Ah, he's one of *those*, is he?"

She sighed. "Yes. He's one of those."

THANKFULLY JACK NEVER INQUIRED ABOUT HOPE's personal life again. But the poor guy was too wiped out from chemotherapy and radiation to talk about much of anything. His asbestos lung cancer had advanced to stage four, or as he called it, "last call before closing time." The disease's progression had been cruel and unhurried, attacking his faculties one by one, a stark contrast to the sudden onset leukemia that had stricken his wife Ivy a decade earlier. Ivy's "closing time" had come—with ruthless irony—the same day Jack won his settlement from the asbestos manufacturer.

Nathan started taking Hope out to dinner once a week, a conciliatory ritual that began after one of their fights and gave her a chance to vent some of the residual depression from her job.

"I can't figure Jack out," she told him one night over Thai food. "He's always saying how ever since his wife died he's just been killing time, that life doesn't have any meaning anymore . . . but obviously he's hanging on to something. I mean, the doctors gave him the option to stop all the treatment and go into hospice, but he chose not to. I guess it must be some sorta macho soldier complex, like he doesn't want to admit defeat. But *some victory* he's got . . . I mean, when he's not sleeping, he's so out of it he doesn't know his ass from his elbow. I barely prevented him from pissing in the laundry hamper last week!"

"That's intense," Nathan agreed, shaking his head as he wiped a dribble of peanut sauce from his chin. "If I ever get like that, just shoot me full of horse tranquilizer, okay?"

"You got it," Hope said, pausing to grin at him with her chin lowered; she loved any vision of the two of them together in old age, however morose.

Nathan took a swig from an exotic beer bottle with elephants on the label. "So . . . does buddy have any kids or anything?"

Hope winced and shook her head. "No. But there's this one niece who drops by sometimes . . . a real nerdy looking lady with frizzy gray hair. I think she's suspicious of me. She's always giving me the stink-eye."

"The stink-eye, huh," he said, throwing her a distrustful glare that made her laugh curry into her sinuses.

"Yeah, it looks exactly like that. I don't know what her problem is, but I hate it when she comes. I feel like I'm walking on eggshells the whole time, like I've done something wrong even though I know I haven't."

He peered over her shoulder at the waitress, dangling his empty beer bottle to order another. "Well, I wouldn't worry about it too much," he said. "The guy will croak when he's ready. Your job is just to keep him company, to make him tea and bring him Kleenex and stuff until check-out time. No one expects you to save his soul."

Hope stared contemplatively into her steamy coconut soup; even with all his faults, Nathan did offer good words of wisdom once in a while.

The conversation at the Thai restaurant would remain in Hope's memory for a long time as one of the best in her life. Maybe it was the ginseng in her iced tea, or maybe it was Nathan's generous mood, but things just clicked. Thoughts formed in her mind that she'd never even known she had, quickly arranging themselves into coherent sentences with the eloquence of a philosophy dissertation and the rhythm of a rap song. And for his part, Nathan not only grasped but expanded on every obscure new idea she threw out. He revealed a spiritual complexity previously unknown to her. His side was probably just the elephant beer talking, but she didn't care.

It all boiled down to the idea that death, like life, is what you make it. As sentient beings, our frame of reference is strictly limited to what we can perceive through our senses; every experience of this miniscule grain of sand we call "the world" is unique. (Or as Nathan put it, "my red might be your blue—there's really no way of knowing.") The evolved minds among us ("you and me") already know trying to find meaning and purpose from any outside source is a fruitless endeavor. We can't control the external circumstances, but we can control our inner reaction to them. To master one's own mind is to master the Universe.

About four beers in, Nathan started talking about the first time he realized he could control his own dreams. Hope tried to conceal her astonishment; what impressed her most wasn't hearing about this special gift of his but that he was willing to chat openly about the inner workings of his subconscious. It's very unlike a man to talk about his dreams. Most of the men Hope knew didn't even like admitting they had them.

" . . . I was ten, and I was dreaming that I was riding a motorcycle along the coastal highway. There were all these creepy giant-sized rodents grazing along the roadside. I was afraid of mice then, 'cause we had an infestation once and they made a nest in my bed, so it was kind of a nightmare. But then all of a sudden it was like a light went off in my brain. I went, *hey . . . I'm only ten and I'm driving a motorcycle . . . something's fishy here . . . this must be a dream.* And then, since it was a dream anyway, I figured I might as well make it good. So I took off flying. Aw, man . . . I must've circled the sun ten times on that magic crotch rocket. I had the biggest boner when I woke up. And now whenever people talk about how they wonder where we all go when we die, I'm like, 'well, I know where *I'm* gonna be.'"

"Circling the sun on a magic crotch rocket?"

"You got that straight."

"Nice."

Just then Hope had a sudden rush of uncharacteristic brashness, picked up Nathan's beer bottle and winced through a greedy swallow; he didn't appear too put out by this, just sat back grinning and made a *help yourself* gesture with his hands.

"Something like that happened to me when I was about seven," Hope said. "Only in my dream I was surfing without a surfboard. I was just sort of hovering on top of the waves in my bare feet . . . and all of a sudden I went, 'hey, wait a minute . . . I'm not Jesus . . . why aren't I sinking?' And then it hit me that if I could walk on water there was probably nothing I couldn't do. So I dove down in to see if I could breathe under there, and sure enough, I could."

Nathan nodded. "See? *You* know."

"Yeah . . . and ever since then I can explore the ocean in my dreams whenever I want. I've done the flying thing too, but, I don't know . . . there's something about exploring all those underwater caves and stuff with the light trickling in."

"Interesting. So . . . do ya ever meet any hunky mermans down there and have . . . like . . . kinky, wet 'n' wild sub-Oceana sex?"

"Hmm . . . " She looked up and pinched her chin as though trying to remember. "No mermans. But a lot of the time I'm riding around on one of those foam pool noodle things, and, well . . . that's pretty fun."

"I see." He closed his eyes, smiled with brass Buddha serenity and sighed. "Sure sounds like heaven to me."

Hope giggled and started making swooshing sounds to enhance his mental image. "Yeah, I'm gonna go down there when I die. Fuck all that white light shit."

When he opened his eyes, Nathan reached across the table to high-five her. "That's what I'm talking about! All that white light stuff is just people giving in to mass delusion. They think that's what supposed to happen to their soul or whatever, so their mind takes them on that trip."

"Totally." She had caught his contagious Buddha smile now. "I saw this documentary once where they interviewed a bunch of those near-death experience people . . . and there was this one lady on there who was an animal lover. She said during the time she flat-lined, she got sucked up into this giant Wizard-of-Oz tornado

. . . it was scary at first, but then she looked around and saw all these dogs and cats and horses swirling up with her. I thought that was pretty awesome."

Nathan nodded. "I had a fat friend in sixth grade who said he thought heaven would be an endless all-you-can-eat chicken and waffles buffet."

"Ew, gross."

"Yeah."

In the end, Hope so enjoyed their conversation that when Nathan casually mentioned, as he divvied up the leftover noodles into two paper boxes, that he wouldn't be coming back to her place that night (he had to get up early to drive a "friend" to the airport)— she didn't even react. And later as they approached the turnoff to her street, she didn't even bother to wait for unnecessary displays of affection from him.

"All right," she said, pinching his cheek as she turned to get out of the car. "Goodnight, Crotch Rocket."

He tried to reciprocate the act but missed. "Okay," he shot back. "Later, Pool Noodle."

* * *

ARE YOU IN A FAKE RELATIONSHIP?

* * *

HOPE'S TRUSTY BUG CATCHER HAD SERVED her well for many months now; so well in fact that she had forgotten all about the pointless and annoying gobbledygook printed on its pages. In fact, up until that night, its life as a book had all but ceased. When she noticed a furry caterpillar dangling helplessly from the fringe on a green velvet lampshade, she at first reached for the paperback with the mindless efficiency of a busy housekeeper. But the wayward young insect's grip on the satin strings was tight;

its five sets of legs hung on for dear life to what must have felt like the only remotely familiar object in a strange new universe. Hope's chest went soft as she patiently tried to coax the animal into a Styrofoam cup.

"C'mon, little guy . . . there's nothing for you in here. Let me take you back home, okay? Let's go back out to the *real* leaves. Then you'll be able to grow your own wings—and then you can go anywhere you want! You're just gonna have to take a quick ride with me in this weird, white spaceship first . . . I promise it won't hurt."

It took a good three minutes for the wooly creature to trust her and let go; regrettably, that was just long enough for Brooks Nixon's poisonous claptrap of idiocy to invade her previously peaceful head-space.

> We've all heard the stereotype that women value commitment more than men do, and most of us would agree that there is some truth to that. I know it seems unfair, but there are plenty of good evolutionary reasons why women tend to hit the "boyfriend and girlfriend" stage much sooner than men do. So . . . how do you know when it's safe to assume that you're in a relationship? The simple answer to that question is NEVER. As the old saying goes, "anytime you assume, you make an ass out of you and me." So if you only take away one lesson from this entire book, let it be this rule: the ONLY clear indication that you and he are in a relationship is that HE has explicitly said so.

It was the lazy semantics of his argument that bothered Hope the most. A "relationship" is simply the nature of one thing's association to another; the caterpillar's relationship to the Styrofoam cup is one of temporary dependence, its relationship to the leaves outside is one of symbiotic harmony. Is the dirt supposed to feel like a chump for assuming it has a relationship with the worm?

Once her larval guest had been safely released to its natural habitat, Hope's simmering anger began bubbling and foaming. She collapsed into the orange brocade couch in the living room, its worn piles forming a *relationship* with her pained ass. When she moved a heavy ceramic mug of chamomile tea from the floor to an end table, she crammed Brooks Nixon's smug face beneath it; here was another new *relationship* between objects. From the drawer in the end table she pulled out two sticks of Nag Champa incense and a lighter . . . her thumb had a brief combustible relationship with the ignition mechanism; the flame had an epic one with the air.

For some time, she paced around the apartment swirling figure eights of fragrance—to chase away the bad energy—trying to quell her interior rant. It could have been anywhere from two minutes to half an hour, such was her level of distraction, until the smoke alarm in the kitchen snapped her out of it. She was standing at the sink then, watching the shredded remains of Professor Dickwad's Handbook of Bullshit Artistry go up in flames. With appropriate swiftness, she opened the door and started fanning the air, offering calm assurances to Biscuit and Peaches as they charged around in frantic barky loops. "It's okay you guys," she said softly, flicking the faucet and garbage disposal on to bring a final gratifying resolution to the whole episode.

When the mechanical alarm whine finally stopped, Biscuit paced three tight circles around his bed and flopped down, looking mildly perturbed. Peaches didn't recover quite so easily from the disruption, however; the older and much more neurotic little terrier stood shivering under the table and a shy pool of urine grew around her feet.

"I'm sorry, girl," Hope lulled, kneeling down with a dishtowel to mop the warm liquid from the cool linoleum. "That was loud, wasn't it? Mommy didn't mean to scare you like that. Everything's gonna be fine."

Peaches didn't seem convinced yet, so Hope got down sideways and curled around her in a fetal position until the trembling subsided. By that point she'd had enough chamomile tea to make any hard surface feel like warm marshmallows, so when the phone rang it caught her off-guard in a state of sleepy disorientation.

"Hello?"

"Whatcha doin'?"

Nathan's voice sounded breathy and distant, as if he too had just emerged from a semi-hypnotic trance.

"Oh, just spooning with the dog under the kitchen table."

"I see . . . " He paused as if waiting for the rest of the story, then laughed when it became clear that no further explanation would be forthcoming. "Well, are you the big spoon or the little spoon?"

"I'm the big spoon. Peaches is the little spoon."

"Hmm. I like being the little spoon myself. That's why I have a big dog."

Hope laughed a little, then took a deep breath and let it out with a long, dilapidated groan.

"Sorry," Nathan added, "I didn't mean to make you jealous."

"Ha . . . *you wish*." She laughed again, her amusement at the image of Nathan curled up in Midnight's brawny Doberman arms morphing into a fit of punch-drunk giggles over Brooks Idiot Nixon, his ridiculous premises, the idea that anyone would buy into them, and the fact that she'd given them one iota of her attention.

"Why'd you call, anyway?" she asked, putting on a tone of sharp impatience.

"*Why'd I call?*" he repeated, confused by the question. Normally she only demanded explanations when he *didn't* call.

"I missed you, that's all," he said. "Is that okay? I just missed you."

"Whatever," Hope said, letting a few silent seconds pass before adding, "Crotch Rocket." She cradled the phone on her shoulder while she opened a bag of dog treats and Peaches slowly rose and yawned, looking restored.

"I also wanted to tell you that you looked really hot in that jean skirt you were wearing today."

"Thanks . . . is that all?"

"That's all. You have yourself a good night, and sweet dreams. Okay?"

"'Kay. Sweet dreams."

On her walk to work the next day, Hope forgot all about glancing into Nathan's driveway. She had the volume on her headphones set to max and was so swept up in the ecstatic vortex of pummeling bass and guitar strums running through them that avoiding the traffic required hypervigilance.

Critics were always pronouncing the title track of *Crystal Mint Carnival* to be its weakest song, so Hope took a certain fanatical pride in her enjoyment of it. You have to really love a band to wade through their occasional fails—in this case, a foray into glossy production over what she had to admit were relatively generic instrumentals to begin with. With patience, though, she had acquired a taste for the least beloved of all Wasted Grave's offerings. These days she even kind of adored it, like a blotchy birthmark on the delicate neck of a lover.

> . . . *It's coming soon, soon, soon*
> *The Crystal Mint Carnival*
> *Rising through the dark electric sky*
> *Chased by the moon, moon, moon*
> *We run like wounded rabbits*
> *Be luminous, your fear is gonna die*

Today was one of those days when the sun warmed her shoulders to an ideal temperature. A day when a gentle breeze shook the yellow leaves around her, making everything glisten. A day when she wished she could hit the pause button on her life—at least for a few seconds—long enough to savor the alignment of every atom in her body with the Universe's intentions. She was entirely centered in the here and now, focused on the journey and not the destination . . . until she stumbled over the edge of a curb and her Walkman flew into the gutter.

"Dammit!" Senseless accidents always occurred anytime she drifted into peaceful reverie. It was as if she were being punished for her gratitude, bitch-slapped by the hand she was trying to kiss. This resentment deepened when she knelt to gather her scuffed player and saw a blue station wagon parked in front of Jack's building. That leery niece of his was there, waiting for her like a swarm of hungry mosquitoes.

Dread filled her stomach as she climbed the steps to Jack's second floor apartment. As was customary, she knocked three times in slow succession before entering using her key.

"Good morning, Hope," Jack yelled. The uptight niece nodded at her over a pile of cardboard boxes off the front hall, where she stood studying some papers in a manila folder. She followed Hope with her beady eyes while the rest of her remained in a business-like posture.

Crossword puzzles were an activity Jack enjoyed on his good days, so the sight of a book titled *510 Large Print Word Games* came as a welcome one. Jack squinted at her over the top of it from his bed, where he sat with several pillows propping him up.

"Can you think of a five-letter word for 'antipasto morsel?'" he asked, his voice several decibels louder than usual. "It starts with O."

Hope got the answer right away but crinkled her forehead and pinched her chin for a few seconds before offering it. "Um . . . olive?"

He struck the palm of his hand to his forehead. "Dagnabbit! I could see that thing in my head clear as day, I just couldn't think of what it was called. Olive. That's it."

As soon as his shaky hand finished fitting the letters into the grid, he held the book to the side of his face as though he needed to tell her a secret, so Hope leaned forward. "The vultures are circling," he uttered in a hushed voice, indicating the front room with his eyes.

When Hope tilted her head inquisitively he coughed, shook his pen in the air, and declared, "That takes care of three across," with blatant showiness. He widened his eyes on her—not the puzzle—as he continued. "Okay, now that means seven down is 'covered,' not 'smeared.'" The whole display sent a clear message that he couldn't elaborate until their company was out of earshot, so Hope nodded to show she understood.

"Wait," she added, continuing the ruse, "Isn't that more letters? C-O-V-E-R-E-D. Oh, no, it *is* seven. You're right."

Jack scrunched his nose and pointed at her with a pleased "you got it" smirk on his face, and Hope sat back in her chair with relief. Whatever paranoid theory he had going on would probably fizzle out by the end of the day.

About an hour later, with every box now housing its appropriate letter (finally), Hope began reading to Jack from the ever-growing stack of unread *Studz* magazines on his dining room table.

"I've tried to cancel the damn subscription a dozen times," he said. He made this claim constantly, but Hope knew he would sooner die than officially relinquish his identity as a member of the magazine's target demographic. "Keep it for me," she urged him, following the script. "I like those celebrity interviews."

Every article ignited something in his dusty eyes, but the fashion pieces got him the most animated. One writer, profiling an up-and-coming men's sleepwear designer, had the gall to suggest that the brand's pajama tops could transition seamlessly from the bedroom to the boardroom. "That's fantastic," Jack remarked. "You can wear the same thing all the time. Just like in prison."

"Well, that's basically what those office jobs are anyway," Hope said.

The same page had a sidebar called "Lessons in Peacocking," about how and when it's okay to sport bright colors and gaudy jewelry. Jack confessed to having done his share of peacocking back in the day, but said, "by a certain age I started to feel like I was putting a for-rent sign on a burning building." Hope laughed, but insisted he was handsome enough to wear whatever he wanted. It's all in the attitude, she assured him. That's when that frizzy-haired lady poked her head around the corner and made a startling throat noise.

"Sorry to *interrupt*," she rasped, her emphasis on the word "interrupt" making the sorry part sound a bit insincere. She addressed Jack directly, avoiding any eye contact with Hope even though the two had only an end table's length between them. "I'm going by Mac's Deli for lunch. Do you want anything?"

Jack bowed and shook his head. "My doctor would fire me if I ate anything like that," he said. "Anyway, I got Meals on Wheels coming in twenty minutes."

"Anything else you need before I leave?"

"That'll be fine, Alice."

When the door clicked shut behind her, Jack let all the air out of his lungs as if he'd been holding it in for hours.

"I don't think your niece likes me very much," Hope said. Her matter-of-fact tone made Jack laugh a little and caused him to have a minor coughing fit.

"She's not my niece," Jack said. "She's my wife's sister's daughter-in-law . . . all *my* family are out east, and Alice used to be an ultrasound tech, so they all think she's some kind of medical expert . . . honestly I think they just send her here to spy on me."

Hope vaguely recalled the C.A.R.E.S. handbook mentioning something about situations like this—potential disputes with family members—but she must've skipped over the part that detailed what to do when they arose. Someone official was supposed to be consulted, but she couldn't remember exactly who. She would have to look it up when she got home. For now, the best course of action she could think of was to change the subject.

"That sucks," she said. "Well, let her spy. I mean, it's not like you're running a speakeasy in here . . . I wouldn't worry about it too much. Hey, check out this article; it's called 'The Timeless Elegance of the Gabardine Trench Coat.' You have one of those in your closet, right? "

Jack hung his head and shielded his eyes with a marbled hand. Hope's gut clenched; was he about to cry or something? His shoulders bobbed up and down as he stopped the emotional current from brimming over. *Oh, shit,* Hope heard herself think. *What have I done now?*

"Guess I never told you the story about that coat," he said, composing himself.

Hope shook her head. "I'm sorry. I didn't know it was . . . you don't have to . . . I'm sorry."

"No, it's my fault. I should have told you about it."

The coat had been a birthday gift from his late wife, Ivy. She'd ordered it from the Brooks Brothers' catalog after years of listening to him reminisce about the time he'd spotted Frank Sinatra wearing one in a Los Angeles night club. But she'd passed away a week before his birthday, missing the chance to present it to him. It wasn't until months later, when Jack finally gained the strength to go through her things, that he'd found the wrapped box in the back of one of her drawers. Since then he'd kept it neatly pressed and hung in his coat closet. He was saving it, he said—along with a suit and tie she'd bought him—to wear to the only special occasion he reckoned he had left: his own funeral.

When sad things happen in movies, you see them coming and have time to prepare. You knew the drill going in, you tell yourself;

it's only fiction, and you'd better recover quickly because no one wants to see your face with those ugly rivers of black on it. But real-life tear jerkers don't give you any warning, nor do they provide you a nice, darkened room to cry in. When watching true grief and heartache unfold, all you can do is try to change the channel in your brain. And when it's really devastating, any old thought will do . . . like how you once had a parakeet who called out "Hey, turdwad!" to anybody who came in the room.

Jack seemed to change the channel in his brain, too. But not to a comedy. He sat up in bed suddenly and, like a broken-down witness in a police interrogation, started blurting out a series of no-nonsense confessions.

" . . . I wasn't a good husband . . . I didn't deserve a woman like that . . . I was never faithful . . . I broke my vows over twenty times . . . I was a total sonofabitch . . . "

He kept the same rhythm as he chronicled his extramarital exploits, one unholy admission per exhale. "The first one was a cocktail waitress . . . it grew like an addiction . . . I started going to massage parlors . . . "

At first, he sounded kind of relieved to get it off his chest. But with each new revelation, the tension and speed of his voice increased. Ten minutes into the rant, he'd acquired the frantic air of a man begging for his life.

When he finally paused for a breath, Hope panicked. Was it her turn to talk now? Should she intervene? Was there a section in the C.A.R.E.S. handbook about *this*?

Thankfully he resumed his usual speaking voice, adding a carefulness that made it clear the climax of his story had finally arrived. *This is the important part,* his tone conveyed. *Pay attention. This is the part I want chiseled on that stone tablet they're gonna lay above me.*

"But you see, Hope—those other women were all just chips and salsa."

The oxygen tank continued gently humming in the background, serenading the silence until Hope stopped nodding and tilted her head sideways.

"Wait, what?" she asked, making a face she thought must have resembled the one Biscuit made whenever Peaches farted.

Jack's face looked a little blue, so Hope told him to hold that thought while she fetched him a glass of water, then dawdled in the kitchen in order to give him plenty of recovery time.

"Do you like Mexican food, Hope?" he asked when she returned.

"Sure."

"You know when you go to a Mexican restaurant and the first thing they do is bring you a basket of chips and a little bowl of salsa?"

"Yeah."

"So . . . you're starving and your order's gonna take a while, so you start eating the chips. They're not very satisfying. But when you're hungry they taste pretty good, right?"

"Yes." She handed him the water and he took a sip.

"I used to love to go to that little place off of Fourth Street," he resumed. "The Hacienda De . . . Guacamole . . . or something."

"Guadalupe?"

"That's the one. I always ordered the steak fajitas. That was back when I could eat steak fajitas. Anyway, I'd be eating a big plate of steak fajitas, drinking a cold cerveza, just as happy as a pig in shit . . . then along would come the waitress and fill up that damn chip basket again. I mean . . . who needs chips when you've got a full meal in front of you? You know what I'm saying? But I ate 'em anyway. Not only that—I asked for more. And do you know why?"

"Because they were free?"

"Exactly."

Jack leaned back into his pillows, and for a second Hope thought he'd finished this exhausting business of unburdening himself on her. She sat down and crossed her legs, hoping her posture conveyed a clear "well then, that's that" message.

"I used to order the chips and salsa as a main course," she smiled. "It was the only vegetarian thing they had . . . even their beans were full of lard. So I'd get the chips and salsa with a side salad, and I'd have them cut up some avocados to make it feel like more of a meal . . . "

But then she noticed a wad of sheets gripped so tightly at Jack's side his knuckles had turned white and she knew she had to revise her response. Jiggling her head to imply a retake, she called on those emergency reserves of empathy in her brain. How must it feel, she wondered, to have so much left unsaid while death is in the pipeline?

"I . . . I know exactly what you mean," she stammered. "Your wife was the only woman who ever really meant anything to you, and you feel guilty for . . . for giving in to your . . . your manly impulses. I get it."

Jack loosened his clutched hands and let the sheets drop.

"Most married men cheat," she assured him. "I read a statistic . . . it's like 80 percent." This assertion was a complete fabrication of course, but it didn't sound too far-fetched in the context of her (mostly TV-based) world view.

"I'm sure your wife loved you just as much as you loved her. I mean, she bought you that trench coat, didn't she? No need to torture yourself over a few slip-ups, Jack . . . nobody's perfect."

He closed his eyes, nodded, and sighed. After a pause, he said, "I just wanted you to understand that, Ivy." Whether the slip was a simple Freudian one or a troubling sign of dementia didn't matter. The following stillness contained none of the weighty angst of the previous minutes, and the room became filled with air and light again.

She waited until she thought he'd fallen asleep and started to reach for the rolled up *Studz* on his nightstand. But then she heard him slurp back his tongue, a noise she'd come to recognize as a signal of impending speech. Without opening his eyes, Jack grinned furtively and emitted a muffled giggle as if he were remembering some ancient dirty joke from the forties.

"Last call for righteousness," he said.

She laughed quietly. "Yeah," she concurred, keeping her voice nice and low. "You don't have to go home, but you can't stay here . . . "

Appraising his level of consciousness, she decided to keep babbling . . . maybe her voice would keep him pacified.

"Why do they always say that in bars, anyway?" she murmured, leaning in. "I mean, isn't home the safest place for a bunch of drunk people to go?"

Jack wormed down further beneath the covers, rolling onto his side as much as he could without the oxygen tubes forming a noose. Outside a summer rain started, but Hope opted against closing the window. The expansive gray hum provided a fitting backdrop for her monologue.

She kept talking more out of guilt than anything else; her entire vocation suddenly felt like such a scam. She recalled Enchanted Hands' mission statement, engraved on a plaque near the desk where she picked up her checks, "To enhance the lives of elderly Californians and their families, bringing optimism to the aging process." As Jack shifted in bed, several blood-encrusted Kleenexes tumbled out of his pillowcase. Hope rubbed her eyes and shuddered as a wave of doubt came over her.

"That's a nice way of looking at it," she pondered aloud but discreetly, referring to his "last call" comment. "Life is like a night at the bar. One day closing time comes, and you have to leave . . . but it's up to you to decide where you're gonna go next."

The rain got louder for a minute and then faded again, punctuated by some hoots and splashes from a giddy young couple running for cover. Jack's siesta continued uninterrupted.

" . . . there are always those people who need to go raise hell and get into fights and stuff when the bar closes, right? I don't understand those people. I'm always so exhausted after a night out I just want to go home and shut it all out. That's partly because I'm never as wasted as everyone else . . . but it's also because it's so draining being in crowds. You know what I mean? I hate that thing where there are like ten different conversations going on at once, and you can't even keep up with one of them."

There were still no signs of alertness coming from Jack's side of the room, a good thing as this wasn't the most life-enriching tangent she'd gone off on. But at least she was trying. Her eyes drifted past him and into the kitchen, where a long-neglected coffee maker sat wrapped in its cord. She considered tiptoeing in and brewing herself a pot—she could sure use a pick-me-up right now—but then she glimpsed the dusty digital clock above the stove, caught herself calculating the amount of time left in her shift, and the guilt returned. *Renewed optimism*, she repeated internally. She would earn her paycheck, if only with her attitude.

"It's like with dreams," she said, half to give this whole life-enrichment thing her best shot, half to unburden herself. "You can have terrible nightmares, or you can have great dreams where you're flying and stuff—it's all just in your mind. The way I see it, heaven is like a big, giant dream your mind has when it shuts off. So you might as well make it good, right?"

A gentle rolling thunder sounded in the distance, like nature nodding patiently to her meandering thoughts. Jack shuddered in his sleep, his lungs expelling some kind of toxic fume powerful enough to wilt distant crops and kill off migrating birds.

"Anyone can go to heaven," Hope said. "And it doesn't have to be some boring, sterile cloud with marble arches and crap either. Heaven can be anything. When I die, I think I'll go to a giant thrift store where the clothes are all super cheap and cute. Every knickknack in there will have sentimental value only to me. And they'll let my dogs in. They'll be super dog friendly. No, wait—dogs will run the place! Yeah! And instead of Muzak, they'll only play Wasted Grave songs."

If he could hear her, that last bit might have confused him, so she clarified by explaining that Wasted Grave was her favorite band. Then she went on to describe another sort of hypothetical heaven, one more suited to his tastes. This paradise would be a 24-hour Bourbon Street Jazz club, a place where all the girls are beautiful, and all the drinks are strong.

This time it seemed he'd heard her; a smile sprouted from beneath that winding headgear of plastic tubes. And when she got to the part about how you can smoke as much as you want there ("because it's the 40s and smoking isn't bad for you yet!") all bets were off. He weakly lifted the blanket from one side of the bed with a wry grin while his free arm whirled through the air, beckoning her to join him on a magic carpet ride.

She pulled a kitchen chair up to his bedside, placing another chair across from it to rest her feet on.

"Now, Jack . . . you're supposed to be resting right now. Bourbon Street can wait." She settled into the chair and allowed her own eyelids to droop, pleased when the passage of several silent minutes indicated the effectiveness of her bedtime stories. Taking care not to disturb the delicate peace she'd achieved, she lifted the *Studz* magazine and peeked in at a random page. But the first headline she landed on threatened to undo her good mood in one fell swoop.

* * *

Ten Reasons Your Girlfriend
Wants to Sleep with Brooks Nixon

* * *

Oh, for fuck's sake! The words inside her head rang so clear and loud, they must have been audible throughout the entire apartment building. But Jack didn't stir.

Hope let the magazine fall to her lap and rolled her eyes heavenward—Brooks Nixon couldn't possibly have any allure whatsoever to a woman with half a brain!—as the thunderstorm intensified, then dissipated, leaving only the puddle sprays of passing cars in its wake. It wasn't until she heard the latch on the apartment door some time later that she realized, with much surprise, that this elixir of annoyance and boredom had somehow put her to sleep.

"Oh, I'm sorry to *disturb* you," the frizzy haired lady barked, clearly meaning to sound as disturbing as possible. "You can go home now. I'm back. That'll be fine."

Hope squinted at Jack's clock radio and tried to wipe the blur from her eyes. "But I still have another . . . "

"You're done," snapped the daughter's brother's sister's wife or whatever, giving her the kind of wide-eyed look people usually give while they're miming slitting their own throats.

"Um, well, okay," Hope stammered, rising to gather her things as Nurse Bitchface hastily signed her time sheet and placed it on the ledge above the coatrack. She also gave her the *Studz*, which had fallen on the floor open to the most unfortunate page possible; a raunchy pictorial of game show spokesmodels.

"Here. Don't forget your *Playboy*."

Hope rolled the magazine under her arm and left, too nauseated by the smell of dead animal sandwiches to stop and explain the mistake.

FOUR

"What do you mean, *deselected?*"

The next morning, when the supervisor called to fire Hope using the most maddening series of euphemisms ever, it was one of only three times in her life when she'd hung up on a phone call prematurely.

She remembered the other two calls with clarity in the heated moments afterward. One was from a boy in eighth grade who stole her purse and then called to mock its contents (*"mmm, peach lip gloss, maxi-thin panty liners . . ."*); the other from a wise-ass telemarketer (*"so I guess saving money isn't something you care about . . ."*). But in those past instances, a soft yet abrupt click had been all it took to calm her inflamed nerves. She hadn't found it necessary to slam a receiver down so hard it emitted a pained echo of a ring. In fact, before then, she wouldn't have thought herself capable of hurling a phone across a room and watching its wires spill out like tangled fish guts when it hit the wall.

Desperation for any distraction whatsoever was what led to her grabbing the *Studz* magazine from the coffee table in that moment. But turning to the most annoying article in it—the one about why women were supposedly lining up to sleep with Brooks Nixon—was a move that defied all logic.

She read the first reason on the list: "He knows how to use the 'Mama's Boy' thing to his advantage" and found herself, rather infuriatingly, compelled to read further.

Was she trying to experience the foulest mood possible here? Perhaps she was; perhaps she had masochistic tendencies. Or maybe her anger at people's general fakeness had become an addiction. Maybe she was some kind of rage-aholic.

> . . . In his popular 3M videos, Nixon often waxes nostalgic about the way his single mother raised him. "We lived below the poverty line," he says in one, "but even when we had to sleep in cars, I never thought we were poor."
>
> While mom-love like that can signal weakness to some women, on others it works as an effective aphrodisiac. As "Cathy," a 24-year-old flight attendant from Missouri, says, "A man who has a good relationship with his mother tends to treat women with more empathy and respect." Watch and learn, dear readers.

A fly buzzed past Hope's ear and landed on the edge of the table; she hit it with the magazine, killing it instantly and smearing its black guts allover Brooks Nixon's face. She felt not a trace of remorse.

Though she hadn't worked in the caregiving industry for very long, Hope had thought she could take certain principles about it for granted. She'd thought, for example, that the most important function of her job was to genuinely *care*. She'd thought that as long as she showed up with real concern for her clients' welfare in her heart then she couldn't get canned for no reason. But evidently, she had overestimated the value of compassion in the caregiving field. Evidently, the prejudiced opinions of uptight relatives were what really mattered. She would have been much better off had she just faked it.

She was being "relieved of her duties," the supervisor had explained, because "the family decided to take a different direction with the client's care." Hope's attempts to obtain more information ("What *family*? What *direction*?") had only yielded endless mazes of crapspackle—the kind of empty rhetoric politicians use when trying to deflect specific policy questions.

"I just know the annoying twat-face niece was behind it," she told Nathan on the phone later, her voice as raw as if she'd spent the whole the day screaming even though she'd barely spoken a word in hours.

"Annoying twat-face niece?"

"Or brother's sister's daughter-in-law or whoever the fuck she was. The one who always gave me the stink-eye. Remember?"

"Oh, right . . . Well, look on the bright side. At least you don't have to deal with her anymore. You'll get reassigned to someone with different annoying relatives."

It was the exact same patronizing tone her father always used when she complained about anything. "Welcome to the real world, kid," she could almost hear him saying.

But then, what did she expect? Nathan didn't care about the nuances of her emotional life. She could vividly picture his expressionless face through the phone line as she relayed every cursed detail of her morning.

"Well, uh . . . hmm," he stammered, "I'm sorry to hear you're having such a rotten day. That sounds very," he hesitated for a minute as he searched for the right word, then borrowed one of hers, "*frustrating*. Yes, I can see how that would be extremely frustrating. I would be frustrated too if that happened to me."

At first, she thought he was mocking her tale of woe. But then she realized he simply hadn't been paying very close attention. He'd been nodding along, offering tired murmurs of acknowledgement, and waiting for his own chance to speak. And when his opportunity did come, he managed to make her feel exponentially worse with a few short sentences.

"I'm about to go through a bit of a vocational change myself," he said, making background noises she recognized as opening the patio door and going outside for a smoke.

"Oh?"

"Yeah. I told you about how my boss got promoted to Hospitality Director at the Seattle location, right? Well, it turns out there's an opening for a bar manager there . . . it comes with great benefits . . . the pay is pretty decent and . . . apparently, I'm moving next month."

"Wow," Hope said, noticing the shakiness in her voice as the future she'd foolishly let herself envision rapidly evaporated.

"Yep. In two weeks, to be exact."

Hope swallowed hard. She couldn't believe she'd set herself up for disappointment yet again. She was supposed to have learned her lesson years ago, when she was six years old and found out you can't make a treehouse by planting rusty nails in the backyard.

The memory of that day still haunted her with strange frequency. She'd wrangled her younger brother Asher into the treehouse idea by telling him it would include video games and a snow cone machine—but their father had noticed the nails missing, found them digging in the dirt with soup ladles and had a good laugh at their expense. He'd then put them to work in his garden picking green beans as punishment. "That was pretty dumb of us," Asher had said, generously shouldering half the blame as he tossed a fuzzy green bean in his mouth and crunched it.

Come to think of it, her brother's behavior had gotten progressively weirder after that day; his entire downfall could probably be blamed on her stupidity. First her brother had been taken from her, now Nathan. Better to never love anyone again.

" . . . and I had another interesting thing happen today, too." Nathan went on.

"What's that?"

"After I got out of my meeting, there was this little pink note on my car. At first I thought it was a parking ticket and I was like, *aw, fuck*. But then I read it, and . . . apparently, I have a secret admirer."

"Really?"

He laughed. "Crazy, right? It says, 'I always see you out walking with your pretty black dog and I think you have the sexiest hair ever. I work at Blake's Coffee Shop, I'll be there tonight from six to close.'"

"Interesting. You gonna go?"

"Might as well. Probably get a free coffee out of it at least."

Hope curled into a ball on the couch, burying her face in her knees. She would gladly look on the bright side in all this, she thought, if she could find one. But right now she felt as though something had killed the part of her that could imagine a path to happiness. She was reminded of a creepy nature documentary she'd seen once about a wasp that goes around paralyzing random spiders and laying its eggs in the carcasses. She wanted to tell Nathan exactly how she felt, but what would she say? *My soul has been paralyzed like a blistery spider corpse?* That might have made great material for a Wasted Grave song, but some thoughts are best left unspoken.

Peaches began tugging impatiently at the phone cord, displaying what Hope liked to believe an interspecies intuitive connection ("*This guy's a major tool,*" she imagined the little fur-ball saying. "*Let's go for a walk.*")

"All right," she sighed, relaxing her tight grip on the receiver. "You have fun. I gotta go now. I'll talk to you later."

A gentle click of her thumb on the hook switch did the trick this time; she didn't need to throw anything.

* * *

SAN LAZARO, CALIFORNIA HAD AN IMPRESSIVE ratio of health food stores to people. Hope's favorite place to buy groceries was a cute little mom-and-pop operation called Fern & Feather—not as cheap as the various co-ops scattered around town but a lot less cult-like and pretentious. She could find just about every-thing she needed there, so she rarely had to set foot in a price-gouging corporate chain like Full Circle Foods (which Nathan liked to call "Empty Wallet Foods") or Health Max ("Credit Card Max").

But procuring necessities isn't always the primary objective of grocery shopping. There are times when the urge to blow seven dollars on a three-ounce artichoke salad from the deli comes on like sudden gravity. And this was one of those times. She dug out the biggest backpack she owned while formulating the indulgent self-soothing list in her mind: a two-liter box of mango coconut water, some high concentrated rose oil, a colorful box of exotic tea, a CD with a name like "Totally Stress Free" or "Zen Focus."

She chose Health Max instead of Full Circle Foods, mainly because the Birch Avenue bus happened to come by first. At the double automatic door, a blast of cleansed air welcomed her in like an old friend. *Come in my child,* it said. *Listen to my coffeehouse jazz and sample my zucchini and hummus sticks.*

Hope meandered toward the Inspired Living book section. She enjoyed perusing the titles, though she would never pay full price for any book. The mellow rhumba beats in the background but-tered her up like gospel hymns.

Her eyes landed on the spine of a book called *Open for Joy.* She recognized the title, having found a dog-eared copy of the same book at a bus stop once and then skimming it impatiently before abandoning it three miles later.

The author of *Open for Joy* recommended ignoring all your cravings in order to make room for unforeseen miracles. If you want something life-changing to come along, you've got to make room for it.

Well, duh, she remembered thinking on the bus that day. But right now, *Open for Joy*'s obvious message struck her like a blunt palm to the forehead; these "wellness" benders at Credit Card Max had become a desperate, pathetic crutch. To buy all the crap on her list today would accomplish nothing except to drain her resources and leave her sunken with guilt. All she really needed were a few soup packets, a carton of soy milk, some bananas . . . not even enough to fill a handbasket.

And anyway, the real purpose of this afternoon's outing was to avoid awareness of time. Nathan's date with his secret admirer slut was set for some time between six and eleven, and Hope needed for her mind to be as far away from Blake's Coffee Shop as possible during those five hours. Fortunately, she never paid much attention to clocks anyway. She would probably be fine. That is, as long as she didn't watch TV, listen to the radio, hear the church bells, or look out the window.

"Did you find everything you were looking for?" asked a cherub-faced checkout girl with bobbed purple hair. Hope's standard response to this bit of perfunctory banter would be to smile and say, "Yes. And a few things I wasn't looking for, too." It usually elicited a small but genuine chuckle from the cashier.

She paused in the middle of counting out her change. "Actually, I discovered that I needed much less than I thought I did."

The checker smiled. "I love it when that happens."

With her light backpack in tow, she breezed past a massive incoming trolley of watermelons and stopped to browse the free newsletters by the door. That's where she spotted the familiar but out-of-context combination of teased copper hair, turquoise windbreaker, and bedazzled cowboy boots.

"Miss Delma?"

In the year and a half since Mavis Bradley died, her daughter Delma had allowed a bold white streak to infiltrate her bangs. She'd also had some tightening done around her jaw line, and Hope decided both of these changes looked good on her. She was posting a large flier to the cluttered bulletin board, and when she stopped to give Hope a hug she slipped the stapler back into her handbag as if concealing something illegal.

"Oh, Hope! Wonderful to see you, dear. How have you been? Did you get that homecare agency job? I was so delighted when they called to ask me for a reference . . . "

They'd already had this conversation, of course. Hope had already sent Delma a corny thank-you card relaying the news—a card featuring Snoopy, Woodstock and a bouquet of flowers—and Delma had already responded with a handwritten note on monogrammed gold foil stationary.

"Yes, I did, thanks," Hope said, letting the memory lapse slide. "They put me with this really sweet, old World War II veteran with lung cancer. I was with him for a few months, but . . . well . . . " She lowered her eyes and dropped the backpack to the floor as it became unbearably heavy all of a sudden.

Delma gave a solemn nod and lightly stroked Hope's forearm. "I'm sorry, dear . . . "

"Oh no, he's not dead," Hope corrected, a little too brightly. "It's just that some of his relatives decided they didn't like me so they let me go. I just found out today."

Delma kept her pitying expression but tilted her head to one side. "Are you all right?"

"Well, I'm disappointed," Hope said, hoisting the backpack over her shoulders, "but I'll be okay. We had a good run, Jack and me. I think I helped him make peace with a few things in his life, and he taught me some stuff too. But everything ends I suppose . . . and I'm grateful for the experience."

The calm in her own voice astonished her; either she'd achieved a massive feat of perspective-gaining in the past hour, or she'd suddenly become awesome at lying.

Delma nodded. "Well it's too bad, dear. They'll be hard pressed to find someone as nice as you. What happens next? Do they find you a new client?"

"I guess so." Hope sighed, casting her eyes downward as the truth that she had no freaking clue what happens next set in for the first time.

"Well," Delma offered, pointing with sudden spokesmodel enthusiasm at the bulletin board. "If you're looking for a career change, today may be your lucky day." The poster behind her read, TELEPHONE PSYCHICS WANTED; NO EXPERIENCE NECESSARY.

Regrettably, the two-second pause that followed gave Hope enough time to burst out laughing and insist she wasn't quite that desperate yet, but not enough time to realize Delma had meant the suggestion seriously and was referring to the flier she'd just tacked up. She caught herself and rearranged her face to adopt a phony contemplative air.

"Hmm. Do you really think so?"

Delma pulled another flier from her purse and placed it squarely in Hope's hand, coiling her fingers around it and squeezing them tight to make her intention clear. She really did think so.

To answer the obvious questions, Delma—always the hungry venture capitalist—explained how she had recently become a stakeholder in an outfit called Mystic Partners. The bar she co-owned had gone belly-up after a Hooters opened across the street from it, but according to her, this latest enterprise was a "freakin' goldmine." The company managed at least three dozen independently contracted spiritual advisors, and Delma herself had played the role a couple of times.

"I was just supposed to direct call flow," she said. "But we got so busy I had to start taking on a few clients—and it turned out they loved me!"

Hope took a literal step back. "Really? I mean . . . I had no idea you were a . . . what did you tell them?"

Delma leaned in closer and lowered her voice. "Whatever they wanted to hear, hon. It's really not that different from tending bar."

The main thing Hope would always remember about that fateful meeting was hearing herself think *this lady must be high.* The whole venture sounded like something conceived at 4 a.m. and charted out with squiggly arrows on a cocktail napkin. It was most likely a classic con game dressed in lace and perfumed with incense. She nodded and tried to look as serious as possible while she took the paper from Delma's hand, playing along as one does with senile people.

"I don't know, Delma . . . "

"Hope, do you ever look at your horoscope in the paper?"

"Well, sure, sometimes, for entertainment . . . I mean I don't really . . . "

Delma swatted her on the arm with her remaining roll of fliers. "Well there ya go, darlin'! That's exactly what a psychic hotline is, entertainment. You don't really think you're gonna solve all your problems when you read that horoscope section. You just figure, 'What the hell. It can't hurt.' Then you find some nugget of wisdom in there and it makes you feel a little better, like you're on the right track. That's all there is to it. And what we do at Mystic Partners is just as harmless."

A kid of about twelve with long wavy hair walked by, slinking behind his mother in an impractical polar fleece vest and reminding Hope very much of Nathan. Nathan was a Taurus. Hope was a Sagittarius, and this was a pair ill-suited for romance, according to him. She still remembered verbatim the passage he had read to her once from a book he owned despite claiming he didn't believe in astrology. "These two would be well-advised to avoid any form of romantic entanglement."

"We just help our callers confirm what they already know," Delma continued. "It doesn't matter what we say as long as we keep it vague and let them read whatever they want into it. That's what I do, anyway. And folks thank me. Boy, do they thank me."

Hope's meditative gaze on the sulky teenager didn't break until he reached the parking lot. She watched him help his mother load groceries into a hatchback, and she didn't snap back to attention until an invasive beeper in Delma's handbag signaled the end of their conversation.

"That's me—gotta run! Where does a person find a pay phone in a place like this?"

Hope raised her head and gestured toward the café. "I think there's one over there," she said, stopping short of making a dumb joke about telepathic communication.

"Ah, there it is. Well, it was lovely seeing you, dear, and I hope you'll think seriously about this opportunity. Don't be a stranger now!"

"I won't."

Leaving the store, Hope caught a snippet of the newest Wasted Grave single ringing from someone's car window and her heart sank. "Fantastic Dream" was the band's first (and it would turn out, only) top forty hit; it was far too corny for a die-hard fan like her to take seriously, and hearing it filled her with depression over the inevitability of artists selling out. It was also infuriatingly catchy. She got so wrapped up in trying to stop singing along to it that when a stranger at the bus stop asked her for the time, she instinctively glanced down the street to a bank sign, forgetting all about her clock boycott.

7:47. Damn. Nathan was probably at the coffee shop now. He'd probably already busted out a whole arsenal of his signature charms on that poor, unsuspecting barista.

In the best-case scenario, she (the coffeehouse slut) would see right through Nathan's veneer of sweet vulnerability to the thick, macho asshole layer underneath. If things were unfolding perfectly, she might have already realized she deserved better and tossed Nathan's punk ass into the alley along with a bucket full of used coffee grounds.

> *Living like a fairy*
> *I like to fly on Sundays*
> *But when I start to daydream*
> *My mind just turns to flowers*
> *Oh! Oh! Oh!*
> *Take me there, Fantastic Dream*
> *Oh! Oh! Oh! Take me there*
> *Fantastic Dream*

When Hope got off the bus and saw a figure pacing in front of her walkway, she thought it was the mailman and felt hopeful for a second. With the mail, there always came some possibility of change, however remote. Maybe she'd won a raffle she didn't remember entering.

She recognized Nathan only when he waved at her. She waved back, and he started walking toward her blowing cigarette smoke off to the side and tossing the butt. She tried to stifle her inquiring mind as long as possible, but her desire to get the conversation out of the way took over.

"How was your date?"

He pretended not to know what she meant, but then quickly shook off the confused expression as if realizing such posturing wouldn't fool anyone.

"Oh, that. I didn't go."

"Why not?"

"I couldn't be bothered. It was probably a guy anyway."

"I see." Hope said, nodding like a psychoanalyst. "So basically, you totally chickened out. Hmm . . . "

"What? No, I just didn't—"

She interrupted him, jabbing at his chest with her finger and grinning. "You were scared she'd be too streetwise to fall for all your bull-fuckery. Yeah, I can see why you'd be worried about that."

He looked a little frightened now. She grabbed both his shoulders and stared hypnotically into his eyes. "*You* didn't want to risk getting dissed in front of all those coffee shop nerds, so *you* stayed home and jerked off instead. See, I know this stuff. *I* have psychic powers. Betcha didn't know that, did you?"

"Um, no," he said, cautiously peeling her hands off as though fearing he might get choked. "I didn't. What's going on? Are you all right? I think you'd better stop sucking on that crazy juice."

"Crazy juice?"

"Yeah, the stuff in your pantry that looks like lawn trimmings soaking in formaldehyde."

In truth Hope *had* swallowed an extra dropper full of her home-brewed passionflower tincture on the bus, but Nathan didn't deserve to know that. Come to think of it, he didn't deserve to know she'd given one moment's thought to his secret admirer situation either. A radical conversation shift was in order.

"Where's Midnight?"

"At home. Why?"

She lifted his wrist and squinted at his watch without reading it. "It's dog walking time, isn't it? I mean, isn't that why you're here?"

"Uh . . . "

"Well, I've gotta walk *my* nincompoops anyway, and you might as well come. I have an outrageous story to tell you. You'll never guess who I ran in to at the Credit Card Max today."

Implying a truce on the whole coffee shop subject appeared to relax Nathan. Or maybe Hope just felt better having the threat extinguished. But by the time they reached the dog park—and the part of the Delma story where the psychic flier changed hands—his icy aura had turned warm, sparkly, and fluid.

"You should totally do it!" he beamed without the slightest hint of sarcasm. "That shit is hilarious. It's all cold reading. I read a book about it in high school . . . me and a buddy thought it would be a good way to pick up girls."

"Was it?"

"Yeah, but it only worked on the dumb ones. I think I still have that book, actually. You can borrow it! It covers all the basic techniques."

"Techniques?"

It turned out Nathan knew a rather impressive number of psychic "techniques" and the technical names they went by. He rattled them off in the same showy way he liked to rattle off computer and car-related terms.

"You know . . . half-and-half statements. One-way verifiables. Diverted questions. Jargon blast. There's a real art to it."

Hope steered the dogs toward an out-of-the-way park exit—a wordless suggestion that they take the long way home—and Nathan removed a tiny flashlight from his pocket as an indication of his agreement. As they entered the grounds of a brightly muraled elementary school, she asked him to please explain to her what a jargon blast was.

"Jargon blast," he repeated, relishing this new role as teacher. "That's when you use a lot of esoteric terminology from whatever divining method you're using. Like . . . if you're doing a tarot card reading, you start talking about *conjoined archetypes* and *synthesized implications* and stuff like that. Or if you're doing astrology, you go off on a tangent about *degrees of planetary declination*. Basically, you just baffle them with bullshit."

Hope swiped the flashlight from his hand and playfully pointed it at his face. "You mean like you're doing right now?"

Nathan closed his eyes and grinned. "Exactly."

As they traced the school's stucco wall with its quaint mural of spiky-haired children, Hope began to sense an unpleasant tickly nervousness setting in. It reminded her of puberty, of becoming the unwilling participant in a naughty game of Truth or Dare. If she didn't speak up about her reservations soon, things could get out of control fast. She did not want this crazy talk of her becoming a phone psychic to continue but feared saying so might make her a buzzkill. As they passed beneath the yellow glare of a streetlight, she stopped walking, pointed at the wall and squealed, "Oh my *god*!" in an effort to end the discussion.

Nathan stopped short, startled. "What?"

"I just figured out what's happening in this mural. Check it out. See those vultures playing tug-o'-war with the big apple pie over there next to the sun? I think the words 'We can be peaceful' across the top are supposed to be sarcastic. Man, kids these days have dark minds."

Nathan nodded and made a drawn out *hmm* sound. "It's the teachers. I know, I went to this school . . . I started out as a pretty optimistic kid, but they poisoned me with all their cynical rhetoric about war and pollution and stuff. Stupid hippies."

"Really? Cynical hippies? That's weird. My hippie teachers were all about sunshine, folk songs, and good vibes."

The distraction worked for a while, but as soon as they reached the broken chain link fence surrounding the cemetery, Nathan started going on about the power of suggestion in fake séances.

Hope swiped the flashlight from his hand and took a sharp turn off the paved path. "My favorite grave is over here," she said, beckoning him with her free hand. "Have I ever shown it to you?"

Nathan followed behind obediently but didn't answer.

"This part of the cemetery is sad because it's where all the young corpses are. A lot of the headstones around here have cool original quotes on them and stuff . . . anyway, here it is." She aimed the beam at a small, unassuming slab of granite.

BILLY "BJ" ABERNATHY
JUNE 1. 1964–NOVEMBER 11, 1987
HIS LIGHT MADE RAINBOWS DANCE IN ROOMS
HIS MUSIC MADE US BRAVE

Nathan emitted a low-pitched laugh much like the one he used in his Beavis and Butthead impression. "BJ was a flaming gay DJ who died of AIDS," he concluded. "He did tons of ecstasy and he had a great collection of disco balls."

Hope groaned with annoyance. "God, you're such an asshole," she snapped. "Would it kill you to show a little respect?"

Nathan cleared his throat. "Sorry. Rest in peace, dude."

They returned to the path, and Nathan's aggressive selling of the whole ludicrous psychic idea continued. "I just don't see what you have against it," he pressed. "I mean it would be such easy money."

"What I have *against it*," Hope retorted, in that slow, explanatory tone she loathed being forced to use, "is that I'm a *human being* and I have these things called *feelings* and *integrity*. Taking advantage of people when they're at their most vulnerable just isn't my thing. Okay?"

But Nathan wasn't satisfied. "Nah, you're looking at it all wrong," he said, making a politician-like gesture with his hands. "You gotta look at it like you're *helping* people. Just like when you told that old guy his dead wife forgave him for cheating or whatever you said. Ya know? You'd be making people *feel* better, that's all."

The whole crew paused as Biscuit, their leader, noticed a four-foot angel statue and took an aggressive stance against it. When Hope saw this, she smiled and nudged Nathan; they both stood breathlessly watching him, trying not to laugh and interrupt his standoff. A couple of tense seconds passed before Biscuit tentatively stepped forward, waited, and stepped forward again—but then he began sniffing around the base of the figure, realized there was no threat and dropped his fierce demeanor. He raised one leg for a perfunctory territory-marking dribble, turned around, and jauntily resumed the business of walking.

"Good boy!" Hope gushed. "Thanks for protecting us from that big scary bird!"

The comic interlude came at just the right time, giving Hope a buoyancy that stayed with her for the duration of the night. Animals are great jesters, and their goofy antics can sometimes have an uncanny way of coinciding with your overly serious moods. Biscuit possessed particularly well-honed skills in this regard. *Oh you humans,* he seemed to be saying. *Always overanalyzing things that aren't even problems. Look at me! I'm pissing on a grave right now!*

And besides, maybe Nathan did have a point. People seek advice in all kinds of sketchy ways. They talk to their low-life friends, they buy corny self-help books, they shake Magic 8 Balls . . . and any one of these things has the power to royally screw a person up. But in the end, we're all just products of our own hopes and fears. We follow the advice that most closely resembles what we were going to do anyway, no matter where it comes from. A psychic hotline is just one more thing to hold on to during times of uncertainty. When Hope really thought about it, there were probably far worse occupations she could fall into.

"Look at it this way," Nathan said in conclusion, clearly scrambling to toss out as many convincing points as he could before they reached her street. "Working from home will mean spending more time with your pets. Just think of how happy little Turdy-Bird and Bunny Fufu will be! And hey, if you end up hating it, at least you'll have another interesting life experience under your belt. Hell, I'd do it just for that."

He looked at her with expectation as she began jingling the keys from her pocket at the gate.

"Hmm," she said, facing up to the stars and coercing a contemplative air. "A divergence along the sacred path . . . I guess I'd better go and meditate on this for a while."

"See?" Nathan smiled, poking her on the shoulder and winking. "You sound clairvoyant already."

*   *   *

THE INTERVIEW WITH DELMA THE NEXT day turned out to be as much of a joke as Hope expected. Delma greeted her in the parking lot of the Mystic Partners complex with an unnatural ebullience usually indicative of medications not sold over the counter. The longer Hope spent in the office itself, a tight beige space rimmed with disorganized bookshelves, the less she felt like a job applicant. Instead, her defensive mannerisms resembled those of an innocent passerby receiving a manic and unrelenting sales pitch.

The most Hope had ever asked for in a vocation was for it to fund her modest thrift-store existence without messing up her mental health too direly. Helping old people enrich their lives by bringing optimism or whatever had fulfilled those conditions at first, until it didn't. She told Delma the truth: that she was hesitating about the psychic position because she was a sensitive soul. She worried she might get too emotionally involved with anonymous clients. What would she do, for example, if one of them called and said they were suicidal?

Delma responded to this objection like a pro, whipping out a list of hotline numbers all operators kept on hand for redirecting the seriously distressed callers. She added that the company also had a strict rule about never answering any legal or medical questions. "We don't get tangled up in anything too serious. Most of it's just the usual *loves me, loves me not* stuff."

By the time Hope left the office, she had begun to feel a little upbeat about her strange new calling. She already knew Delma to be about as blasé an employer as one could hope for. That was a pretty good start.

Years earlier, upon first entering the job market, Hope had bought herself a coffee mug that said ASK ME IF I GIVE A SHIT. The mug served as a kind of symbolic armor as she took those first tentative steps into adulthood, guarding her heart against ghastly phrases like "self-starter" and "team-player." One dark day, she'd knocked the mug over while roughhousing with the dogs, and the event had threatened to destroy her delicate emotional balance.

But she'd patched the cup back together with super glue and kept it on her dresser to this day, using it to hold dried-out pens and the occasional lip gloss. She thought about it now, on the walk back from Mystic Partners, as the sun warmed her shoulders and an invigorating breeze cleared her lungs. She couldn't wait to get home. She could hold that mug up in the mirror, smile, and toast herself. If intuition served, this new gig of hers was going to take not giving a shit to a whole new level.

The main goal of Mystic Partners, a goal which Delma had wasted no time sugar-coating, was to keep people on the phone for as many minutes as possible. She'd even given Hope a small demonstration in a favorite trick of hers, repeating and rephrasing the client's questions. "Sounds like personality mirroring," Hope had offered enthusiastically, remembering a term from Nathan's tiresome lesson.

"Bingo," Delma had said, winking. "I knew you'd be a natural at this."

For the fortune telling itself, the product the company was technically selling, operators could choose from a boundless variety of methods. Resources were stored in a closet they cheekily referred to as the "Channeling Room," a panic-inducing labyrinth of bookshelves sectioned off by a kitschy beaded curtain. Hope liked the curtain. She wasn't lying when she told Delma she would love to redecorate her bedroom using only that color, a sort of fizzy Listerine blue.

The Channeling Room's selection extended far beyond the usual tarot and astrology tomes. It went beyond numerology and I Ching, too—it even went farther than past life regression. A person could appropriate from any combination of sacred traditions they wanted to in this well-stocked Spirituality Warehouse, mix up their own little shamanic cocktail, and give themselves a jazzy new guru name. For "homework," Delma invited Hope to pick out the books she felt most connected to, go home, and study them, then return having filled out a form labeled "Associate Mystic Profile."

It didn't take long to find the winners. Hope's eyes widened at the stunning cover art on *Your Ultimate Guide to Totem Animals*: a turquoise-draped wolf flanked by a sage-burning antelope on one side of him and an uber-muscular mountain lion on the other. Her second pick, *Unlock your Future through Dream Interpretation*, was also a no-brainer. She couldn't wait to tell Nathan.

Nathan. In all the drama of the past couple of days, she'd forgotten all about his impending departure. Few nights remained to elevate herself to a plane high above the hordes of Seattle coffee house sluts. He'd said he might drop by when he got off work today and added that he'd probably be pretty busy packing for the next week and a half. She glanced at the clock frantically; she had exactly four hours to prepare.

A cleaning frenzy of hurricane proportions overtook her. She grabbed stuff off counters, carried out trash bags, washed sheets, and swept under the bed. When he came by to see her later, she envisioned, Nathan would be visibly taken aback by the sight of her freshly sponged surfaces. He would inhale her purified air deeply, and a rapt grin would appear on his face. Or maybe not, but at least the place would no longer smell like a barnyard in which an incense factory had recently exploded.

The plan was to be reclining comfortably with a book in her hand when he arrived. That way she would betray no evidence of having exerted any energy to impress him. But too many thoughts were whirring around her brain to read anything she actually wanted to absorb. She reached, once again, for the July 1994 issue of *Studz* magazine.

It opened easily to its last read page:

Reason number two: She wants revenge.

If you're like most men, you resent Brooks Nixon a bit for turning your girlfriend into a slippery, scheming little robot. You may have found yourself making comments like, "Hey, if this love guru of yours is such a friggin' genius, why isn't he married?" Now imagine you two have a fight, and she goes off to one of these 3M seminars. Who do you think she's going to be fantasizing about having sex with in order to get back at you? That's right, Mr. Love Guru himself. If you think about it, the guy probably is a genius.

Hope laughed a little, dripped blueberry juice on her cranberry brocade couch, then used the hem of her skirt to rub the spot until it became camouflaged in the pattern.

"Wow, what happened in here?" Nathan remarked from the threshold when he finally showed up. An hour earlier she had finished reading every word of every god-forsakenly cheesy article, review, exposé, letter to the editor, and advice column in *Studz* magazine, thrown the whole thing in the trash, and fallen asleep. "You moving or something?"

"Spring cleaning," she answered casually.

"I see." He took a scrutinizing stroll through the kitchen, nodding with his arms folded while Peaches yipped and nibbled at his heels. "Very impressive." To emphasize the comfort he felt in these improved surroundings, he reclined on the sofa and crossed his work boots on the coffee table. "So, how'd your interview go?"

She could have told him the truth, that the experience she'd gone through earlier had been more of an indoctrination than an interview. She could have told him about the depression she now felt at having proven herself the perfect candidate for such a recruitment, just desperate enough to set aside her integrity for a fast buck. But why put a damper on the mood?

"I nailed it," she beamed, arching her back and extending her arms like a winged Venus. "They were blown away by my divining skills. I even used that personality mirroring thing of yours." She intentionally used the word "they," hoping he would picture her auditioning before a panel of experts. Without giving him a chance to press her for more details, she pulled out her borrowed books from the Channeling Room.

"Check this out. I'm supposed to come up with a schtick for myself, right? So I decided I'm gonna be an Animal Spirit Dream Guide. What do you think?"

She handed him one of the books and he started flipping through it, scanning the pages quickly and looking studious.

"Sounds hot."

Then he reached over and caressed the back of her leg with his free hand. "Hey, maybe I can help you practice."

Even though he didn't leave for Seattle for another thirteen days, this would remain the night Hope preferred to think of as their last together. Not yet burdened with the heavy expectation of a goodbye, it hung suspended in some sort of timeless light-plane of fun. The two books offered such an abundance of sexual innuendo it was hard to believe they hadn't been created for use in fantasy role playing.

Nathan: "I keep dreaming about eating lots of warm bread with sticky apricot preserves."

Hope: "To channel snake medicine, find rhythm while you glide through the bush of consciousness."

He stayed the whole night for the first time ever, rasping her a sweet, bleary-eyed "hi" in the morning.

If she had any girlfriends with whom she could discuss such matters, Hope probably would have complained to them about the timing of Nathan's sudden transformation. *So I guess he's decided to start behaving like a real boyfriend now,* she would say in a sarcastic monotone, *now that he's moving a thousand miles away. Yeah, that makes a whole lot of sense.* Not until years later would she see the real wisdom in his actions. By leaving at the precise moment when things reached their height but before they could descend into a deadening staleness, he would stay in that sweet spot forever.

* * *

IN THE BACK OF THE BLUE duplex was a rarely visited addition whose intended purpose Hope could never quite figure out. An adobe box with sandstone flooring, it was too stuffy for a room and too big for a closet, and over time it had become the default catch-all for a mishmash of similarly purposeless items. But its strangeness made "The Void," as she privately called it, her favorite spot in the house. Its single narrow window now held an array of undomesticated plants in whimsically painted coffee tins and glass jars. The muddy smell back there gave it an ancient ambiance, like the tomb of some sultan, and being in it seemed to grant her the humble wisdom of a thousand old souls. It had no furniture, just a stack of orange milk crates that somehow became softer than her bed on the nights when she couldn't sleep. Thunder sounded louder in The Void; troubles looked smaller. On the night of Nathan's first phone call from Seattle—he'd promised he would call her exactly one week after he left—she untangled the phone cord, carried the phone into The Void with her, and waited restlessly.

The jitters were needless when she thought about it. The conversation would probably flow without effort, like it always did—but instead of covering their usual subjects, Nathan would fill her in on all the details of his new circumstances. Of course, she would have to tease him relentlessly about Seattle "grunge" stereotypes ("do the dogs there wear flannel too?") and by the time they got around to discussing life back in San Lazaro, the fact that she'd already quit her gig as a phone psychic would have completely shrunken in significance. It would be a humorous piece of obsolete history by then.

All she would need to explain when they reached that comfortable stage of banter was how she'd gotten "debunked" by some wise-ass teenagers on her third night. Of course, it shouldn't have mattered. It wasn't like she'd had a large chunk of self-worth riding on her ability to read fortunes anyway. Nevertheless, the pranksters had shamed her back into reality. Bailing on her new career had proven equal in easiness to starting it, a tidy windup she hoped Nathan would appreciate.

But when they did reach that stage in the conversation, her attempt to breeze past the subject went over like a bad nightclub joke.

"Wait a minute," he interrupted. "Back to the hotline. Why did you let one bad experience get to you? I mean, it's showbusiness, right? So you bombed once. What's the big deal? Everyone knows it's an act."

Hope grabbed the back of her neck and massaged her tense muscles, and right then the giant mirror in the hall flashed her a ghastly reflection in which her facial contortions resembled those of old Miss Mavis. This must be what it feels like to have Alzheimer's, she thought. Your brain is crammed with spiraling, crisscrossing thoughts, thoughts no arrangement of words can possibly set free. What a nightmare.

"Yes, everyone knows it's an act," she repeated, clenching her teeth to prevent herself from shouting at him, "but no one ever *says* so. That's what makes it such a head fuck."

Nathan made a long, drawn out "uhhh" sound, the one he usually made with a comical headshake when ideas didn't register with him.

She backed up a little, telling him about her first trainee workshop. She had expected to meet like-minded vocational explorers there, normal eccentric types who'd answered one of Delma's ads on a lark. She'd thought it would be fun, all of them practicing their just-learned cold reading techniques on each other. To her disappointment, though, the group had turned out to be nothing but a bunch of self-important crackpots. Instead of swapping tricks, they swapped lists of which oracles spoke to them, quotes from ancient texts, and data from all their previous incarnations.

By this point in the story, she was rubbing her face with one hand and pacing tight circles around The Void. "It was like hanging out with conspiracy theorists," she said.

"When have you hung out with conspiracy theorists?" he asked.

"We had a family of them on my block when I was a kid . . . any time something didn't go their way, they blamed the Illuminati. It's weird because you're sitting there thinking, *this is pretty fucked up*, but you can't say anything because you don't want to be rude. Then, after a while, you get used to the fucked-up-ery and you sort of forget there's anything wrong with it, you know? When everyone around you is telling the same lie, it stops feeling like a lie. It becomes another harmless mass delusion, like Santa Claus and the tooth fairy."

Nathan chuckled breathily. "And God."

Hope sat down on one of the orange crates, relieved to have finally been heard. "And weddings."

Nathan liked that example. He let out a surprised cackle, making Hope blush and seeming to vindicate her unrehearsed rant.

"I like to think I'm the type of person who doesn't blindly go along with stuff," she said. "So when those teenagers called me on my BS, it felt awful."

"Yeah," Nathan said, his voice now sweet and understanding.

When Hope stood up, she caught another glimpse of herself in the mirror. Only this time, she was smiling. The transformation seemed almost magical; she bookmarked the feeling, vowing to summon it the next time she had her picture taken. If she could keep a recording of his saying "yeah" in that precise manner, if she could play it on a loop in the background of her everyday life forever, she might always look this good.

"Then again," Nathan said, "Everyone has to act fake for their job. I know I do. I mean that's why they call it work, right?"

"Anyway," Hope continued, the magic of the moment already fading. "I went in to pick up my first paycheck and I kept thinking, *what if everyone here feels the same way I do?* I mean, what if I made a rude joke about what a bunch of scammers we all are, and everyone just started laughing and high fiving each other?"

"That would be awesome," Nathan chuckled.

"Yeah, but it wouldn't happen," Hope said. She'd moved to the floor now and started drumming her restless fingers on one of the crates. "They would look at me like we were one big Mormon family and I'd just gotten pregnant out of wedlock while on a caffeine binge or something. So I knew I had to quit."

"I see," Nathan said, allowing a pause while the entire scope of the story sank in. "So what's next then? Back to the Lonely Old Fart's Club?"

Hope sat up and pulled her unwashed hair into a topknot. "I don't know," she sighed. "Enchanted Hands doesn't have any work right now. But Delma moved me to an office where I'm just directing calls and tracking minutes and stuff . . . it's not too bad. At least I don't have to lie to people directly."

She could tell from the background noise that he'd moved outside, and soon she heard the unmistakable flick of his cigarette lighter followed by a deeply relished puff. "Well," he said on exhalation, "congratulations on your promotion."

She laughed. "Thanks."

Distance really does make the heart grow fonder, Hope decided. At least in the case of confused hearts like the one she seemed to be stuck with. This 400-mile buffer would make daily life a lot less stressful for her. She could buy clothes without giving a rat's ass what Nathan might think of them. She could sprawl on the couch in supreme ragamuffin mode, safe from the anxious anticipation of a possible booty call. The life she shared with him now was a tightly edited and polished one. And even when the editing wasn't so tight, it didn't matter. Nothing was at stake anymore.

She bid him goodnight with a series of corny well-wishes, and he promised to call her again in two weeks. And when she laid the phone down in its cradle, she did so gently—kissing its plastic back as if it were a baby's soft forehead.

FIVE

"If I see one more picture of Monica Lewinski's chubby-ass face, I'm gonna puke."

A greasy-haired woman in scrubs was holding up the supermarket line as she flipped through tabloid after tabloid, popping her gum in a manner which made her far more nauseating than any of the magazines' subjects.

"She makes me miss O.J., ya know?"

"Seriously," the turquoise-clawed cashier concurred, spraying Windex on the conveyer belt. "Get over it, people." The two clearly knew each other and neither of them seemed interested in carrying out acts of commerce, so Hope picked up her 50-pound bag of dog food and heaved it to the next line over with dramatized effort.

"Looks like Pee-wee Herman's in the news again," the scrubs woman giggled. "Oh, and here's an interview with old what's-his-nuts."

The cashier put the spray bottle down, leaned forward and asked, "Who?" But upon seeing the picture, she winced and resumed her robotic price-scanning. "No, thanks."

Nurse Greasy looked confused. "But I thought you liked him. Didn't you used to watch all his tapes?"

The cashier made a talk-to-the hand gesture. "Yeah, but his new book made me so mad I burned it."

Hope smiled a little inside, glad to know she wasn't the only one on earth crazy enough to burn books that pissed her off. Then, at the front of the checkout line, she spotted the headline the two had been discussing:

BROOKS NIXON ON THE CHANGE OF HEART
THAT TURNED HIS FANS AGAINST HIM

Her smile turned into a muffled laugh that made everyone ahead of her turn and look. Once again, she was the craziest one in the room. She covered her mouth. "Sorry, it's just, I . . . never mind."

The book in question—Brooks Nixon's first in nearly ten years—had hit the shelves a month earlier, apparently igniting quite the media shit-storm. Come to think of it, Hope had seen ads for *Better Off Alone*, but she'd been too focused on the author's laughably conspicuous weight gain and hair loss to notice the book's glaringly cynical title. With morbid curiosity, she grabbed the unavoidable copy of *Notoriety* magazine to see what this so-called "exclusive interview" was all about. What grave personal catastrophe could've befallen poor old Brooks? Something laugh-out-loud ridiculous, she hoped.

The interviewer, Steve Bowen, got straight to the point.

SB: Mr. Nixon. Your new book, *Better Off Alone*, promotes a deeply pessimistic view of long-term romantic partnerships. On page one, you write, "Any attempt to search for happiness in another's arms is nothing but a futile waste of energy." Many have speculated that this book must be a bitter reaction to a bad breakup. Are these people mistaken?

BN: My heart was broken two years ago, yes. Broken beyond repair, in fact. But it wasn't broken by a lover. I simply realized everything I'd once believed in was wrong. It happened after my mother died.

SB: You were very close to your mother?

BN: Oh, yes. She was a huge influence on my early writing. She raised me by herself, and I grew up listening to her and her girlfriends complain about the noncommittal men in their lives. I thought I could help women like her by offering advice from a uniquely male perspective. Mom led an exceptionally rich life; she travelled the world, loved painting and fashion, and exceled at appreciating the simple things. Well, in 1997 she died in a motorcycle accident at the age of 74, never having married once or even lived with a man. Not counting me, that is.

SB: Wow. So despite all your hard work, you'd failed at helping the person you cared about most. That must have been very disappointing for you.

BN: That's just the thing, though. When I was cleaning out her apartment, I came across a small stash of souvenirs from her various romantic escapades. You know, a faded Polaroid here, a turquoise ring there. I was struck by the profound insignificance of these trinkets compared to the greatness of her life. It confirmed what I had suspected all along; that Mom had been fine by herself—more than fine, actually, amazing! Her life had never been missing anything at all. And I felt deeply ashamed for ever having presumed that it was.

SB: Your mother sounds like a fascinating lady.

BN: Yes. As extraordinary as she was, though, I think there are many more women out there like her.

SB: But why did she complain about all those non-committal men in her life if she didn't want them to commit?

BN: That's an excellent question, and it's one I explore at great length in my book. I think my mother was just acting according to society's expectations. You see, relationship culture oppresses truly independent-minded women, making them constantly feel as though they have to explain why they aren't paired up. This leads many to pursue doomed partnerships and then swap war stories over cheap chardonnay. Peer pressure has a lot to do with it.

SB: You write at length about peer pressure and so-called "relationship culture." But your critics argue that, as human beings, we are all biologically driven to seek mating partners. What about that?

BN: *[chuckling]* Hey, I didn't say I had anything against mating. Of course, sex is a vital and important part of life. And a sense of emotional attachment increases its allure exponentially. That feel-good brain cocktail we call "being in love" is a grand thing, to be sure. But it is, by nature, an ephemeral thing. When society pressures us to arrest it and secure it—locking it into a domestic partnership, for example—we only end up disappointing ourselves.

SB: Does it bother you that some commentators have started calling you "the man who murdered love?"

BN: I don't worry too much about public opinion, but that label is inaccurate. My attitude gives love a chance to reach its greatest potential.

SB: They've also nicknamed you, "Narcissus Nixon."

BN: *[laughs]* That one I don't mind so much.

SB: Why not?

BN: Well, in the original myth, Narcissus wasn't such a bad guy. He wasn't hurting anybody; he just preferred his own company to anyone else's. I mean, it wasn't his fault he was so attractive and he had all those suitors who wouldn't leave him alone. Those heartbroken nymphs wouldn't have been so heartbroken if they didn't falsely believe that they were incomplete.

SB: Interesting perspective.

"Miss?"

The conveyor belt was whirring ahead emptily through the intermittent beeping of code readers. "Will you be needing any help carrying that out, Miss? Miss?"

Hope's attempt to skim the final paragraph as she slipped the magazine back into its slot caused her to knee someone's unleashed child in the forehead. "No, that's okay, thanks."

*　*　*

SIX YEARS. WAS THAT REALLY ENOUGH *time,* Hope wondered, *for someone's entire reality to do a complete 180?* Hard to believe, but she found herself taking strange comfort in the possibility. She pondered the relative stagnation of her own past six years on the drive home. The hum of her 1982 Honda Civic reminded her that at least one circumstance had improved—she no longer had to rely on flaky dudes and kitschy tour busses for transportation. It was better than nothing, and she kissed her finger and patted the car's dusty dashboard as a gesture of gratitude.

She'd always known what she *didn't* want to do with her life. She didn't want to go to college because she didn't want to sit through years of boring lectures only to end up in debt with nothing but a lousy piece of paper to show for it. She didn't want to have children because she didn't want to undergo a disgusting carnal mutation just to end up stuck with some whiney mini-me. Greedy humans had already fucked up the planet enough, thank you.

But this defiance of social expectations hadn't exactly rocketed her into a realm of perfect self-actualization. What the hell *did* she want to do with her life, anyway?

During periods of mental inventory-taking, her thoughts often turned to Nathan. He'd remained a constant—though far away—presence in her life, and there had been no other men since him. None that counted anyway. She managed to make one or two errors in judgement a year: brief flings with bodies she barely considered human, dry runs with man-shaped practice dummies.

"Maybe you can be my housewife when I grow up," she'd said to him at the end of their last phone call.

"I'd make a damn good housewife," he'd said back, his tone comforting and even. His sincerity made it all the sadder; in truth, she could imagine nothing more irritating than to have him following her around all day dusting and serving tea.

At the next stoplight, she turned to admire the car next to her. It was the same model as hers, about five years newer. She could tell because it had smooth curves along the hood, roof, and trunk instead of looking like a series of interconnected boxes. That's the car she would trade up to when her circumstances improved.

Something moved near the front right tire; a field mouse was sitting in the shade of the wheel, having stopped midway through a dash across the road. He stood looking around for a minute and then scratched himself with one hind leg like a dog, innocent to the danger of his resting place. Poor little guy probably thought it a safe spot, sheltered from the sun's harsh rays.

Hope winced and looked away, exhaled through her teeth and murmured "no, no, no!" She thought about honking to get the driver's attention, but what would she do after that? Before she could decide, it was too late; the light changed, and she glanced back over to see a small gray stain where the mouse had been.

She felt that bone-crushing extinguishment with distant but heavy sorrow, like the death of a relative she didn't know very well. It made her want to crawl back to the place she came from and hide there. Why must she experience these things so intensely? Other people didn't; if they did, then mousetraps wouldn't exist. She pulled forward, blew a kiss in the direction of the gray stain, and whispered a silent tribute to the sky. "Your life mattered," she said.

Maybe she just hadn't found her niche yet. She must have more to offer the world than providing administrative assistance to a bunch of phony clairvoyants, the job she'd fallen into and gotten stuck in like a tar pit.

She still had some involvement with the homecare agency, but only as a relief worker, which meant she picked up a few shifts a year and the clients were always different—an arrangement that ensured she would never get too attached to any of them. Every assignment offered a fresh new adventure; even if it was horrible, it would be over in a few hours, and at the very least she'd have a funny story to tell.

She had no shortage of funny stories about elderly Enchanted Hands clients, and Nathan proved a patient and appreciative audience for all of it. There was the lady with smudged red lipstick who forced her to play Gin Rummy for six hours straight, for example. The five-hundred-pound semi-literate dude who called it "Martha Ruby King Day." And the "Karaoke Nazi," a former Cabaret singer who had her own top-of-the-line system and forced Hope to listen to her belt out old Sinatra numbers but would never let her have a turn.

"What would you have sung?" Nathan asked her cheekily. "'New York, New York?'"

"Anything but Sinatra," she said. "That machine had a surprising amount of decent stuff on it. It even had a Wasted Grave song!"

"Which one?"

"The only bad one, 'Fantastic Dream.'"

"Don't you mean the only *good* one?"

"You *would* say that."

She never told Nathan her dating stories, though—not because she feared it would make him jealous, but because she knew it wouldn't.

Her heart grew heavier with each burdened step to her third-floor walkup, the apartment she'd moved to last year because it was across the street from Mystic Partners. She could now run home on her frequent coffee breaks, and she guessed that also represented an incremental change for the better.

Things weren't perfect in her life now, but they weren't awful either. This benign thought kept cycling through her brain as she dropped the cadaver-like dog food bag at her door. Repeating the words hardened their certainty, and she committed the affirmation to memory as if it were information she'd be needing soon; an important phone number, a bank machine code, notes on the final exam. Things aren't perfect, but they aren't awful either. She sat down on the crunchy bag and began rubbing her forehead in her palms, hoping against hope that she would make it inside the door before her new impromptu mantra lost all its power.

"Howdy, neighbor."

A sunburned guy in khaki shorts slowed his downstairs jog to a stroll as he passed her, lifting his wrap-around sunglasses in acknowledgement. She nodded back and the jogger continued on his way, but then he paused and turned to face her with a look of concern. "Everything okay?"

"Taking a little rest," she smiled, trying to act as though he'd caught her in a perfectly normal state of affairs. She noticed the class ring cutting off his swollen finger's circulation as he fiddled with a gigantic pager on his belt; these details instantly voided out the faint level of attraction she always felt toward caring strangers.

He squinted over her shoulder as though studying the lion's head knocker on her door. "Oh, is this your apartment?" he probed. "Are you that balcony with the painted purple railing?"

She nodded, warming to him now, as if they'd just discovered they went to the same high school. In all reality, they could have gone to the same high school and she never would have noticed him. The simple fact that he had enjoyed high school enough to buy a class ring ensured this. And she was certain that he, too, would have looked right past her and her cluster of misfit friends in the lunchroom, rolling their eyes as they mimed an endless array of creative suicide methods.

"I always notice your balcony when I walk by," he said with a coy grin. "I mean, it's hard not to notice it."

Hope was pleased. She took great pride in her collection of quirky lawn ornaments—the brass squirrel, the marble Buddha statue, the googly-eyed owl made from mismatched seashells—perhaps if he also appreciated such things, the two of them might have something in common after all.

But it took the jogger all of five seconds to snuff out this prospect. "You sure do have a lot of crap out there," he remarked, keeping his eyes on her as he bent down to tie his shoelace. "Maybe you ought to think about doing some de-cluttering. Put a nice little table and chairs out there instead, you know? It could be a decent spot. And it would look better from the street, too. That is, if you care about curb appeal."

Having said his piece, he ducked down to finish his shoe-tying and Hope noticed an oddly placed bald spot in the back right corner of his head—a strange flesh-colored lump had sprouted there, wiping out all the hair follicles in its path.

Maybe you should start wearing hats, she snarked back, but only in her head ten minutes after their conversation had ended and she'd gone inside. *Cover up that putrid-looking bald spot of yours. You might actually have a tiny little smidgeon of sex appeal then, you know? And you'd be sparing people from having to look at your disgusting head warts, too. I mean, that is, if you care about not grossing people out.*

In the actual moment all she could manage was a stunned stare, a blank look which she held for a second or two before shaking it off like a sudden chill. "Well," she offered weakly as she rose to fish her keys out of an embroidered knapsack, "thanks for the advice, I guess." When she turned her back to him she made sure to exhale as loudly as possible, reasoning that a passive-aggressive response would be better than none.

When she turned to drag the kibble bag in, he had his hands held up in a defensive pose as if to say, "What? I was just trying to be helpful!" And that's no doubt what he would have said if she hadn't stifled him. She repeated the *thank you* in a noticeably more emphatic tone, softened it with a neutral "all right, nice to meet you then," and then slammed the hollow wooden door.

Biscuit lifted his lazy head from the linoleum when she came in. He was her last remaining animal companion; his wolf genes having outlasted those of poor little puppy-mill-reject Peaches. They'd been a family of two for the past year, and it had been almost that long since Biscuit had greeted her at the door with sniffing, wagging enthusiasm. Thankfully he was in the kitchen when she arrived home this time; if not, she'd have had to wander around the house with an escalating sense of dread until she spotted him asleep in some corner and he made a life-affirming movement like an ear twitch.

She dragged the dog food to the pantry, where a broom promptly fell out and bounced against her head, causing her to mutter "fuck" to herself. This habit—cursing at every minor annoyance—had become such a prevalent personality quirk that several of her past friends and lovers had commented on it. Remarkable, as she had so few past friends and lovers.

A series of murmured fucks followed; one when a housefly buzzed in her ear, one when she stepped on a broken hair barrette, one when she couldn't get the industrially-sealed dog food bag open, and one when she did get it open—by using an ice pickand stabbed herself in the process. By then she was riding an adrenaline wave so powerful it made her slice the bag open violently and send an avalanche of dusty brown pebbles across the floor.

Just months earlier Biscuit would have wasted no time pouncing on such an opportunity, vacuuming up as much of the mess as he could while Hope lovingly shooed him away. But presently his graying muzzle didn't even twitch at the tantalizing scent. Hope rolled onto one side and covered her face with her trembling and bleeding hand. There was nothing to do now but give in to the tears she'd held in ever since the neighbor told her her balcony looked like crap. Or maybe she'd been holding them in since the drive home from the grocery store, or maybe since months earlier, when her best friend first failed to greet her with slobbery dog kisses at the door.

* * *

NOSTALGIA ISN'T SUPPOSED TO FEEL GOOD. Hope had learned this surprising fact recently from her chatty coworker Lisa, a frightfully underweight Reiki Master who got off on flaunting her underused bookishness. The word *nostalgia* first appeared in the 1700s as a military diagnosis for the severe homesickness that overcomes soldiers fighting abroad, sometimes leading to death. But Hope loved experiencing nostalgia, she told Lisa. Enjoyed it more than most other feelings, in fact. Didn't everyone?

"Not everyone," Lisa teased. "Only psychos and misfits."

The first Wasted Grave song to rock Hope's thirteen-year-old world had been "Stagnation Room," from the 1985 album *Gutted*. A neighbor for whom she sometimes babysat had both MTV *and* a big screen TV—two indulgences scorned by her parents—and ever since then, both held special significance as symbols of her transition into womanhood. The video featured the four band members—"pale fairy monsters" as her dad would come to call them—squirming and writhing inside a small wooden shed which gradually wobbled toward the edge of a cliff and fell off. The intense despair it conveyed was far more interesting to Hope than anything in her young life so far. Perhaps listening to the album now, with its deep reverberating chords, reminded her of once having longed to suffer from powerful, overriding emotions. It unburdened her to return to that juvenile perspective, to remember having welcomed the onset of grown-up pain. It almost made her depression feel glamorous.

> In this prison we are fighting, with nails and teeth and pillows
> In this dungeon we are crying, the devil's child and me
> Stagnation Room, a dingy house of doom
> Stagnation Room, where flowers never bloom

Hope knew her life looked lonely from the outside. She knew from the pitying looks her coworkers gave her each time they inquired about her weekend plans and she didn't have any. In the past, she'd made the mistake of accepting these coworkers' charitable Christmas and Thanksgiving invitations—disasters where she'd sat sullen like a hostage in their noisy homes. But she only felt isolated when forced into such gong show scenarios. As long as people left her alone, the loneliness ceased to exist.

During long periods of hibernation, particularly those in which Wasted Grave music provided the dominant backdrop, Hope loathed the harsh sound of a telephone ring more than anything. She dreaded it even more lately, as her new digital phone's electronic ring echoed those incessant blinking monstrosities at the office. Her old princess phone had finally bit the dust (maybe she'd thrown it against the wall too many times) and she'd failed to find a suitable replacement at the thrift store, so she'd made a grudging trip to K-Mart for a new one. Now every ear-splitting intrusion represented the pain of having to drop twenty bucks on something she hated.

The new phone did come with one handy new feature though: caller ID, a fantastic innovation as it made screening calls possible without having to wait for a message. She answered about half the calls from work—just enough to give the impression she gave a shit—and applied the same rule of thumb when her parents' number appeared. But if anyone else wanted to talk to her, they'd be out of luck.

A local number showed up one Tuesday at 11 p.m., interrupting a messy but relaxing homemade facial treatment and leaving her hesitant and skittish. She knew that number; she knew it acutely. In fact, it was probably the first sequence of digits she'd ever memorized. Seeing it now turned on floodlights in the ancient, well-worn pathways of her brain.

With sudden aplomb, she pressed the cold receiver up to her ear, forgetting about her lavender-infused oatmeal mask until its sticky fragrant granules smeared the plastic.

"Hello?"

The Diaz family lived next door to the Townsends for most of Hope's childhood. Their split-level home punctuated a sperm-shaped cul-de-sac in Redwood Heights, a fringe subdivision anchored by pasta buffets and video stores with a public pool as its hub. The ages of the five Diaz children aligned with those of the Townsends' six in such a way as to provide same-gender counterparts for everyone in both families—except Hope. Her already awkward middle school years were made even less fun by the constant exclusion from teenage gossip circles; her two older sisters and the two older Diaz girls lowering their voices to a hush whenever she came around. One of them would invariably snap at her to "Go read a book or something." Not until years later did the additional insult of their branding her a nerd even register.

Maybe one of those girls was calling to apologize now, Hope considered. Maybe Jordana was in AA now and regretted having been such a bitch all those years ago. Or maybe Raquel was experiencing a similar change of heart after taking up reading.

Or maybe it was Jesse Diaz on the phone. A less probable but more intriguing mental picture emerged; a grown-up Jesse Diaz, mature enough to have developed a tolerable personality but not mature enough to have let adulthood dull his edge.

Jesse was four years younger than Hope, he was her brother Asher's partner in skateboarding and other crimes, and from the time he hit puberty he'd had a raging and very poorly disguised crush on her. He'd expressed his admiration with the use of vulgar taunts, calling her "Scoop" in reference to her sunken chest and then illustrating the moniker by making two swift scooping gestures in front of his scrawny torso. He never tired of that gag. If he spotted her at the pool, he would squint at her from across the crowded deep end and signal her with a broadly dramatized double-dip. His other witticism involved taking anything she said out of context and repeating it while pointing to his crotch, like the memorable time she was working on a school project and asked him if he'd seen her staple gun.

"Have *you* seen *my* staple gun?" he asked.

Asher would always roll his eyes and say "Give it a rest, dude. She's not your type." And Hope would grow flustered in his presence despite herself, trying to quell the itchy feeling in her gut as she coolly applied her lip gloss.

But it wasn't Jesse on the phone. It wasn't Jordana or Raquel, either. An even less expected voice greeted her on the other end of the line, and she knelt on the carpet to steady herself from the surprise.

"Asher?" she squealed, wiping her face with the terrycloth sleeve of her robe. "Dude! What are you doing out? I thought you had two more years!" She lowered her voice, suddenly seized by the irrational thought of her parents somehow listening in. "You didn't escape, did you?"

He laughed. "Good behavior," he explained. It was a calm laugh, not the maniacal kind she'd gotten used to in the troubling year before he went away.

They hadn't seen each other in five years, the exact amount of time it had taken her to stop feeling responsible for his poor life choices.

If anyone else deserved to share blame, other than Asher himself, it would be Jesse Diaz. He was the one who'd gotten Asher into graffiti and initiated that dumb tagging competition, thereby getting him expelled from school. Had the expulsion never happened, Asher wouldn't have gotten sent off to Stonewall Secondary Academy (motto: STRUCTURE, TEAMWORK, SELF-DISCIPLINE) and his innate hell-raising nature wouldn't have become aggravated to the umpteenth degree by vain attempts to corral it.

But the real trouble started in his final year at Stonewall Secondary, when he got mixed up with that Russian kid. Of course, she'd only ever heard Asher's version of events, but she had no reason to doubt it; Asher had many flaws, but dishonesty was never one of them. They only broke into that media room because of the Russian kid's idea to record an obscene freestyle rap and leave it there as a prank; Asher didn't know the Russian kid planned to steal two video cameras. Knowing Asher's temper, it made perfect sense to her that he'd proceeded to beat the shit out of that Russian kid in the hallway of juvenile court. And now, reflecting on how the assault had earned her brother a three-year prison sentence, Hope kind of wanted to beat the shit out of that Russian kid herself.

Then again, long before these shenanigans began, their mother used to describe Asher as someone who "could start a brawl in an empty house." The only thing Hope found more worrisome than the incurable nature of his curse was the secret knowledge that she probably shared it. She'd managed to keep her own brawls contained to this point, and she didn't need reminding how quickly they could spill into the street.

"Where are you?" she asked, even though she already knew the answer.

"Here in town, at the Diaz's house."

"What are you doing there?"

"Getting ready for Jesse's wedding! Well, technically, planning the bachelor party . . . I'm the best man."

She made an audible gasp—"Someone's marrying Jesse?"—and then laughed nervously, trying to hide her disappointment. "Wow. What a world."

In the background, a startlingly deep male voice shouted, "Hi, Scoop!" and then grunted as if reacting to a firm slug in the arm. After Hope heard the voice, very little of what Asher said concerning the details of his visit registered. She emerged from her trance only when the call was ending, as she and Asher made plans to meet up the next day. She sighed when she hung up the phone, having covered an entire notebook page with dreamy spiraling cubes.

* * *

HOPE HADN'T VISITED THE OLD CUL-DE-SAC in the near decade since her parents' move to Florida. She felt almost no nostalgia about the place, nothing at all like what she felt for Wasted Grave songs. The songs were her escape from the cul-de-sac, after all. Why would she want to revisit a place she'd so craved escape from?

As she entered the cul-de-sac, a sense of suffocation threatened to overcome her; it was late September, and the tacky front door adornments were in full bloom. Wreaths made from red corn, old rakes with fake leaves stuck on them, baskets of painted gourds. She imagined entering through the Diaz's mudroom and could almost smell the store-bought air freshener already. *Please let it be the apple cider*, she heard herself think. *I can't stomach the pumpkin pie spice.*

But maybe she could skip the entryway altogether. She might run into her brother in the driveway; due to an overflow of guests, the family had put him up in the Winnebago out front. "Beats the hell out of solitary confinement," he'd told her graciously over the phone.

She parked a block away and tentatively approached the camper. On her way, she spotted an unscratched lottery ticket in the gutter and picked it up, thinking it might make a nice ice-breaker. She would offer to split the money with Asher if they won. They could start things off on a positive note, talking about what they'd do with their hypothetical riches.

From 10 feet away, she could see the vehicle rocking vigorously, figured Asher must be reuniting with an old girlfriend and retreated sheepishly to her car. "If it's rocking, don't come knocking," as the saying goes. Then she made a second attempt, pulling into the driveway and tapping on the horn with an innocent little "beepity beep beep" rhythm.

Asher emerged from the miniature tin door with surprising promptness, alone and fully dressed. He looked like hell. Whatever life on the inside consisted of, she could tell what it didn't consist of: working out or getting haircuts. He gave her a forced smile and a nod, then held up two fingers as if to say *be right back* and disappeared again. Hope shut off the engine, and not long into the silence she heard a startling metallic thud followed by a stream of unconventional curse words.

"Dick-knob! Fuckerhead! Assbadger!"

He came out a second time, palming his eyes as if he'd just been pepper-sprayed, locked the door and waved again, this time with a goofy theatrical smile. Hope made a show of opening the passenger door for him and he slumped into the bucket seat, exhaling loudly.

"Hey," he mumbled. "Sorry about that."

"Everything okay?"

He shook his head. "Just blowing off steam."

Backing out of the driveway, Hope felt relieved to have gotten their initial greeting over with. For years she had pictured herself running up and hugging Asher on the day he got out of prison; realistically, though, she'd never known him to be much of a hugger. Also, if she'd had to face the adult versions of all those Diaz children, the situation's awkwardness would have only multiplied. All things considered, phase one of this visit had gone remarkably well.

She rolled down the window, cleansing her thoughts in the damp, leafy air. "You sound just like me," she offered cheerily, "every time I lose my keys." She then let fly with her own comical string of swears, as if to prove it. "Asswad! Fuckbag! Cockwaffle!"

Asher chuckled and shook his head. "I actually did lose my keys just then," he confessed. "Maybe it runs in families."

Hope considered the idea as she turned up the radio. "Yeah, it probably does . . . Key Displacement Syndrome. Profanity Incontinence. I'll bet there have been studies done."

The setting for this visit, at Asher's request, would be Chapterhouse Records on East Cedar Street. A fittingly nostalgic choice; he and Hope spent many a Saturday afternoon there as teenagers, blowing a week's worth of deferred lunch money expanding their tormented music collections. To this day, Asher credited Hope for his having become a Wasted Grave fan, and straightaway he used their reunion to thank her again for the long-ago introduction.

"Man," he sighed. "I musta listened to 'Gutted' five times a day during my time inside. It was the only CD I wouldn't let anyone borrow."

"They let you have CDs in there?" Hope asked, affecting an air of innocence. She already knew the answer—she'd sought out an extensive education about prison life as soon as her brother went in—but she figured feigning ignorance would calm his nerves and give him something to talk about.

He flicked his head forward as though determined to make his messy hair even messier. "Yeah, you can listen to 'em on a Walkman. I guess they figure it keeps dudes from going all crazy and shit."

"Makes perfect sense to me," Hope said.

Chapterhouse Records was now just called Chapterhouse. After some major remodeling, it now included a café and a huge book section. Hope pulled open the jingly door and watched cautiously for Asher's reaction to the changes. But to her relief, he started sashaying around with a goofy wide-eyed grin on his face, waving his arms as if he'd just entered a zero-gravity zone.

"Whoa, I feel like Rip Van Winkle."

They wandered around a bit and eventually settled at a high black table, where she filled him in on the possible future extinction of record stores over hot Styrofoam cups of elaborately named beverages.

"It has something to do with more people getting their music from the internet."

"How do you get music from the internet?"

"I don't know."

To steer the conversation away from her own embarrassing lack of technical savvy, she asked him if he'd heard from any other members of their now very scattered nuclear family lately.

"Just Mom," he said, blowing steam off his quadruple-shot, thrice-blended macchiato. "Dad's still not talking to me."

He chugged the macchiato as if it were malt liquor. "I got a letter from Beth a couple months ago . . . she wrote a whole page about their new hot tub but then dropped in like eight pictures of the rug rats and none of the hot tub. I woulda rather just heard about the kids and seen pictures of the hot tub."

Hope smiled. She had gotten the same letter two months ago and thought the same thing when she saw the pictures.

He wiped a drop of coffee off his tee shirt, which Hope suddenly noticed had a picture of a ball-cap-and-chains-wearing Tasmanian Devil making an unfamiliar hand gesture. She wondered if the hand gesture was gang related.

"I haven't called anyone else," he continued. "Jesse's family are the only ones who seem happy I'm out. No one else gives a shit."

Hope threw him a dramatized look of righteous indignation. "*I* give a shit!"

"Besides you I mean," he clarified in an offhand tone, as if to say he took her caring about him as a given. "I mean, Jesse's dad's gonna get me a job in his landscaping company. Mom wants me to move to Florida, but . . . "

"Don't!" In Hope's frantic rush to nip this idea in the bud, she swallowed her Roasted Elderberry Spiced Chai too fast and choked.

"You do *not* want to go there," she coughed. "It's full of trashy and ignorant alcoholics and con artists." She'd only been to her parents' adopted hometown of Darbydale, Florida twice, but she felt confident in the accuracy of her assessment of the whole state. And anyway, she needed Asher here.

Being the last remaining family member in San Lazaro made Hope feel like an orphan at times. True, she didn't miss the tedious family get-togethers—everyone repeating the same old polite lines as if rehearsing for a play they can't get right. But passing time alone on Christmas Day—with no stores open and nothing but corny holiday movies on TV—didn't exactly fill her with joy, either. Nor did it provide her any comfort to list Delma as her emergency contact on all those doctor forms over the years.

"Besides," she told him, "you won't know anyone in Florida. Here in San Lazaro you've got Jesse, and . . . "

Asher raised an eyebrow as though challenging her to name one more friend he could count on.

"You know . . . everyone else. All your other homeboys."

He laughed and shook his head. "Jesse's pretty much the last homeboy standing," he said. "And, well, he's . . . " He smiled as if remembering a joke she wasn't in on. "That dude is *terminally whipped.*"

Hope laughed with him, in advance of whatever he was about to say next. She'd been waiting for the right moment to press him for details about Jesse's new fiancée. Now she wouldn't have to.

Asher pulled a small piece of soapstone from his pocket and began vigorously rubbing it with his thumb—the trinket was a prescription, he explained, from his court-ordered anger management counselor.

"Dude's new lady is about the most god-fucking awfully annoying chick I have ever met," he said.

"Oh really?" Hope said, trying not to smile. "Interesting. So what's her deal?"

He winced when he answered her. "Her name's Jillian. She'll tell you 'Jilly' is her nickname, but no one ever calls her that shit. Except Jesse sometimes . . . when they're talking baby talk to each other. And that's just one of about a hundred things I can't stand about her."

He started itemizing his other grievances but Hope stopped listening after the first couple of minutes. She became transfixed by the almost hallucinatory vision before her: her spastic, dinosaur-obsessed seven-year-old brother trapped in a gruff and tarnished twenty-something guy's body. No matter how big he got, Asher would always remain seven years old and dinosaur-obsessed in her mind. Somehow it was this version of him that served as his eternal avatar; it might have just as easily been the three-year-old carrying a half-used roll of duct tape around like a teddy bear, or the brooding 15-year-old crushing Coke bottles against his head for shock value.

Jesse Diaz had shared Asher's dinosaur fetish in that memorable year, both boys' seventh. Hope remembered a constant stream of shelf-knocking and lamp-breaking incidents as the two of them charged around in prehistoric battle mode. Her father tried to solve the problem by instituting a "no dinosaurs in the house" rule, and he even made a sign on a leftover piece of faux wood paneling, a roughly drawn Brontosaurus with a diagonal red line through it. It probably still existed in a dusty box of memorabilia somewhere.

" . . . man, if a chick ever tried pullin' somethin' like that on me," Asher was saying now, gritting his teeth, "I'd give her a swift combat boot to the cunt."

Hope gave no visible reaction (she'd spaced out and missed the first part of the story) and Asher interpreted her lapse in attention as an expression of disapproval.

"Sorry," he said, cocking his head to one side. "Feel free to tell me if I'm being an asshole."

Hope smiled and shook her head. "You're fine," she said honestly. "I don't really care what you say. As long as you're not talking about me."

"Cool."

She squinted over his shoulder, scanning the merchandise behind him for a distraction. "Hey," she said, widening her eyes with excitement. "You wanna go check out those ten-dollar music magazines?"

"Sure." He stood up and shoved his cup in the trash, along with the five or six wadded-up napkins he'd been fiddling with, but he didn't head toward the magazine rack as she'd suggested. A pyramid of shiny pink hardbacks stopped him mid-stride, causing him to point, roll his eyes, and chuckle.

"Ooh, they've got the *banned* cover," he said.

Hope shook her head in befuddlement.

He picked up one of the books and waved it emphatically at her like a preacher spouting Bible verses. "I should get this for Jesse," he said. "Jillian hates this guy."

She moved in closer to try and read the fast-moving title. "What are you talking about?"

"Narcissus Nixon!"

"Oh, right." The *Notoriety* interview's final paragraph started coming back to her. Several retailers refused to stock *Better Off Alone* after its initial release because of a controversial cover image, and now most chain stores only carried a generic black-and-gray version. Hope couldn't help but mirror Asher's eye roll when she saw the source of all the ruckus: a chalky, heart-shaped Valentine's candy with a rough middle-finger illustration stamped in red.

Asher looked at the cover and laughed again as though for the first time. "It's kind of awesome, though. I mean, you have to respect the guy."

Hope picked up a copy and turned it over, flicking her hand at the price tag on the back. "$18.99? Yeah, I guess I *do* have to respect him. Christ." She fanned through the pages and stopped somewhere in the middle, confident any quote she landed on would be good for a laugh.

But Asher had lost interest by then, burying his nose in a giant glossy hardcover called *Tattooing on the Fringe*. His short attention span had always driven her crazy, but now she forgave him for it.

Deciding which shiny object to focus on in a brand-new technicolor world would test anyone's concentration, she imagined.

"I like looking at all the fucked-up stuff people do to themselves," he said, almost to himself. He held up the book to show her a bald guy with the word "animal" in bubbly cursive letters across his forehead. "It makes me feel better about my own shit, ya know? At least mine's not permanent . . . I hope not, anyway."

Hope's first reaction was to declare half-ironic appreciation for the tattoo ("Hey, nothing wrong with that. We're all animals.") But then she noticed Asher's serious expression and changed her tone.

"Nothing's permanent," she said with a sigh. "Not even tattoos are permanent these days. You can get them removed now."

Asher said goodbye to Hope not much later, making what she would eventually come to know as one of his signature exits: he abandoned her to chase after some chick. The siren who lured him away didn't seem like his usual type—she wore cat-eye glasses and bright floral leggings—but then Asher didn't always have a type. When the right mood struck him, they were all his type. This was something she envied him for immensely. While the planets ruling her own love life crept around in perpetual retrograde, his galaxy expanded in all directions like a spectacular meteor shower.

"Smell ya later, sis," he said as he scuttled out the door, echoing a phrase from the last time she'd seen him all those years earlier. He claimed he recognized the girl from one of his therapy groups; this turned out to be a lie, but even if true it wouldn't have lessened the insult of his sudden departure. It was bad enough he left her standing there with an open copy of *Better Off Alone* in her hand—he'd also saddled her with the giant encyclopedia of freaky tattoo enthusiasts on top of it.

But overall, she decided, returning the merchandise to its proper places, she'd enjoyed her visit with her brother. She was glad she'd never gotten around to detailing the cluttered dullness of her own life to him; to do so would have been a huge buzzkill. Better he didn't have to hear about her recent clumsy one-night stand with the Star Wars fan who'd worn stained sweatpants on their only date. Or that she'd recently found herself fantasizing about the slightly arrogant and not-so-slightly married maintenance guy at work. He would learn soon enough how she spent her days at Mystic Partners, surrounded by people who all claimed to have exceptional access to the Divine Mind yet all failed to recognize her contempt for them. And really, who was she to complain about any of it? *Beats the hell out of solitary confinement*, he might have rightly said.

If only to have an icebreaker for their next visit, she glanced inside the Brooks Nixon book before setting it back atop its pyramid. She still hoped to find one juicy nugget of supreme uselessness in there, something the two of them could discuss, make mincemeat of, and then proceed to mock ruthlessly. She found a doozy of a quote on the first page—of course—but, as with all of his musings, it left her burdened with a maddening craving for more.

"If people didn't fail to see how intimately connected we all are in life, they wouldn't be so afraid of facing death alone."

She would never recall exactly how many minutes she passed in that red vinyl armchair by the window. But by the time she left Chapterhouse, the gondola-style streetlamps of East Cedar Street were glowing yellow against a cherry-orange sky.

Walking to her car, she realized with some surprise that she didn't want to go back into the store and set that whole paperback tower ablaze. Something had changed. But it couldn't have had anything to do with *Better Off Alone*. No words on a page could affect someone's entire vibrational alignment, especially not words from such highly questionable sources. She began taking a mental tally of the week's events, trying to pin down the exact origin of the shift.

On Monday, she'd replaced the rose oil in the tiny flask she wore around her neck with an amber resin. But aromatherapy could only cause the subtlest of mood tweaks.

On Tuesday, she had gotten her brother back. She now had a male counterpart as close as her own blood, his naturally rebellious mind ready to help her through all of life's tangles. A significant development, but hardly a cosmic turnaround by itself.

On Wednesday, she had passed Jack Cohen's old building and noticed—for the first time in years—the window open. The "Medicated Veteran" sign was gone, and the room looked vacant. Old Jack must have finally boarded the trolley in his gabardine trench coat, she guessed. One more turn in the wheel of life. She'd been more than prepared for it, though.

Then there was that other event she'd been trying to forget—the one involving her work crush, Rush Holbrook. She'd liked Rush ever since he introduced himself and said, "I'm your maintenance man." There was just something about hearing the words "I'm your" and "man" in the same sentence that really did it for her. Every time he saw her he would wink and say, "let me know if you need me," and she'd found herself wishing for hardware-related mishaps—anything that required use of tools—any reason to summon him.

Thursday, Rush had come to her rescue after she unintentionally caused a power surge. He'd given her a showy lecture about the effects of dirty electricity on noise-sensitive appliances, smiling at her as he ran his finger along the flesh-colored plastic of the outlet's smooth slit. As he did this, she'd felt every quivering sensation the little piece of plastic must have felt.

He'd most likely noticed her stupid spellbound grin, as he'd chosen that moment to casually mention his connection to the building's owners. "Oh, yeah, I'm Phillip and Janice's son-in-law. My wife manages the restaurant on the corner. Anyway, let me know if you need me."

Wife? He didn't wear a wedding ring, not that she'd looked for one. Bastard.

Much had happened in the week, she realized, and all of it put together created a cocktail of entertaining new sensations. Things were about to get interesting. Brooks Nixon's book had simply caught her in a state of openness to infinite possibility.

Reaching for her car keys, she found the unused lottery ticket she had retrieved from the gutter earlier. She would still save it for Asher, she decided, but if scratching it resulted in the two of them being buried in an avalanche of money, she'd let him have all the winnings. "Just buy me a coffee," she imagined herself telling him. "You need this more than I do."

SIX

TRAINING NEW PSYCHICS WAS ONE OF the easiest of Hope's varied work responsibilities. Giving her practiced spiel to the fresh recruits felt like performing a song she knew by heart. In fact, parts of the orientation address often got stuck in her head like the jingle from a shampoo commercial.

A refrain about problem calls—calls the company allowed its representatives to terminate early—played in her mind with particular infectiousness lately.

"Problem calls fall into three categories," she would catch herself chanting while she did the dishes. "Pervs, debunkers, and bible-thumpers." She would repeat this line three times, then finish it off with a final satisfying refrain; "You've got the wrong number, buddy. Click."

The only snag in training days came when a newbie got testy with her. People who fancy themselves gifted in areas like intuition can get offended easily, she'd come to discover, and sometimes one of them would object to her blunt, business-like manner. But fortunately, most genuine seers have enough common sense to steer clear of shady hotlines in the first place.

It probably wasn't Shawna's fault that her first meeting with Hope failed so spectacularly. That day began its fiery descent as soon as it started.

Mystic Partners' freshly upgraded reception hall now boasted migraine-inducing commercial light fixtures, and the minute Hope adapted to their crude glare she was hit with a smell she could only describe as "syrupy blistering death."

"Hungry?" the hiring manager Lana beamed, carrying over a silver tray of vile little turd-colored coils. "Now, I dare you to try one of these and tell me it's not the most heavenly thing you've ever tasted."

"What—"

"They're chocolate-covered bacon roses!"

"I'm good," Hope said, waving the tray away and making an exaggerated gagging noise with her throat. Everyone in the office knew she was vegan, but they all seemed to think a single whiff of sweet flesh would tempt her out if it.

"Your loss."

She'd forgotten about Delma's 70th birthday party. Too bad, as she could have steeled herself for the event with an extra dose of the skullcap and lemon balm tincture she kept in her pantry labeled "dealing with obnoxious people." A dozen or so coworkers she barely knew milled around in the birthday girl's cluttered office making cheap champagne tributes to her above the bouncy chatter of the daytime talk shows. Delma always kept those talk shows on in there, even during important meetings.

HOPE NOTICED TWO NEW EMPLOYEES IN fold-up chairs glued to the TV set as if waiting for a severe weather update. On screen, the hosts of a driveling hour-long gabfest called *The Grapevine,* usually concerned with little more than Hollywood gossip and suburbia-friendly lifestyle tips, both wore serious expressions and their audience seemed locked in a trance.

You couldn't escape the guy's face lately—his picture popped up regularly alongside movie stars and public figures on the periodicals circuit—but Hope hadn't seen Brooks Nixon animated since those 80s Oprah and Donahue appearances. Back then, he'd doled out his glib nuggets of wisdom with a commanding self-possession. But now something about him was receding, something besides his hairline, something behind his eyes—his buoyant, salesman-like zeal. He'd become the poor man's version of his former self. The fat above his cheekbones sagged like baggage he no longer cared to lift.

"There's always been something off-putting about weddings to me," the glassy-eyed Brooks related, "even when I was a kid. It's sort of like watching a hot-dog eating contest. I mean, I can't figure out why anyone would want to do this thing in the first place, but even more baffling is why all these people are gathered with wide-eyed enthusiasm to watch it. It's like, *why isn't everyone here gagging simultaneously right now?*"

Hope laughed at this, as did Delma and the only man in the office—a 19-year-old tech support guy named Fred, who Hope had only recently learned was also Delma's grandson. Fred took advantage of the moment's buoyancy to try and sneak a ladle of sangria, but Delma slapped his hand away. ("Nice try, kiddo. No underage drinking on my watch.")

"Can't you see *any* value in it though?" the *Grapevine* hostess asked, affecting a tone of righteous bewilderment. "I mean, having the assurance that someone you adore will be yours forever, and that they'll adore you right back, flaws and all?"

"Feelings like that can't be pledged," Brooks insisted, "no matter how undying they might seem. Their permanence can't be promised or assumed. Trying to do so is like taking another shot of tequila when you're already drunk; you won't prolong the high, and you'll likely make yourself sick. Better to let the feeling alone and enjoy it while it lasts. It probably won't stay, but it won't disappear forever either. You can have it again one day, or something like it anyway."

The chorus of confounded murmurs from her coworkers gave Hope the panicked consciousness of being trapped in a stale, airless room. She made her way to a window to open it. When she saw a bottle of champagne and two plastic cups on a ledge beneath the windowsill, she poured herself one and drank it quickly.

"If you've always felt this way," the hostess asked, squinting as she leaned back and re-crossed her legs, "why did you make a name for yourself by offering people the promise of lasting love?"

At this, Lisa the skinny reiki master stood up, pointed at the TV and snorted, "'Cause I'm a pretentious old blowhard who gets off on the sound of my own voice!" The remark elicited chuckles from a trio of temp workers to whom Lisa often gave discounted sessions during off hours. Though Lisa's reiki practice had taken off lately, she resembled one of those former child stars found sleeping in a van after their life goes off the rails. The four of them together reminded Hope a little too much of a gaggle of stuck-up cheerleaders. She wanted Brooks' response to put them in their place, a clever comeback from the nerdy, tousle-haired underdog.

Mr. Nixon didn't disappoint her. "Like any entrepreneur," he explained, "I saw an unmet need and set out to fill it. Advice is an easy sell, you see. People are pretty transparent. It's just a matter of figuring out what they want to hear and then saying it to them with authority."

Hope laughed a little louder than she expected to, owing to the second cup of champagne she'd begun nursing. "Sounds familiar," she said.

Delma laughed too, but the rest of their associates only groaned.

He got in another zinger a few minutes later when the interviewer asked him to respond to the public's characterization of him as a narcissist.

"People are free to have opinions," he said with renewed poise. "I would argue, however, that individuals who never feel comfortable unless they're somebody's 'one and only' are the real narcissists. Such people are obsessed with their own reflections . . . in the eyes of another."

Hope turned to the open window for air, just as a couple in the parking lot—dressed in matching powder blue tracksuits—initiated a nauseating make-out session. She moved to an empty chair near the door, comfortably far from her coworkers. When one of them turned and beckoned for her to join their circle, she waved them off as if they were a tray of bacon roses.

"Like my friends in the LGBT community," Brooks Nixon was saying now, "I've learned that society doesn't take kindly to having its traditional coupling constructs messed with. But the bravery of so many LGBT folks also demonstrates to me that living your own truth is much more important than maintaining other people's comfort."

To everyone's surprise, young Fred, who'd so far come across as meek and virginal, blurted out, "Ha, tell that to my boyfriend!"

Delma bluntly shushed him. "People here don't need to—" she started to say, then stopped herself short. The awkward revelation poisoned the room with a cringe-inducing sense of paralysis.

Delma's covert homophobia was well-known around the office, taking the form of slow-dripping microaggressions made worse by her pathetic attempts to correct them. ("Don't get me wrong; I *adore* fairies.") Mystic Partners had recently lost one of their top-performing psychics, a pansexual woman, after months of Delma's nagging her to "pick a team already." Now, one by one, the staff turned to face Fred, offering him a series of half-shrugs and weak sympathetic smiles.

As soon as Delma had distracted herself, opening a bronze compact mirror to smooth out one of her unruly eyebrows, Hope carried a full champagne cup over to Fred and slowly set it on the table in front of him. She whistled and cast her eyes around the ceiling as she did this, drawing attention to the act while trying to make it appear accidental. Fred flashed her a zit-speckled grin as he picked it up, and Hope winked before slipping out to the bathroom to splash water on her face. She dropped the worry about how Brooks Nixon would fare against the tediously wholesome talk show hosts in an instant; things had a way of balancing out, she decided. Old Brooks would probably have the last word in the end, no matter how or when the end came.

When she emerged from the bathroom, still dripping, Hope saw an unfamiliar forty-something woman waiting in the hall; with a jolt of embarrassment, she snapped back into the dull reality of her work routine.

The woman's fashion sense immediately compelled Hope to do a double-take. She possessed a style one might describe as "business provocative"; a low-cut white tee shirt tucked neatly into a tight tweed skirt with a chunky gold belt and high-heeled boots. None of the fabrics on her body moved when she did, not even the tee. She sat on a bench clutching a small black rock reminiscent of Asher's worry stone, and her posture dared you to do something drastic—like hug her or kick her in the head—just to see how she would react.

She raised her eyes expectantly. "Oh hi. I'm here for training?"

"Sorry, I'll be right with you," Hope said, darting off to her office cubicle to gather the orientation materials. Having forgotten all about this appointment, she now experienced a perplexing case of nerves reminiscent of her school days. Knowing the material by heart doesn't always make a pop quiz any less daunting.

Tyrannized by the harsh new lights, she stopped at her desk and decided to try a little creative visualization to compose herself. As her detached hands opened desk drawers and rifled through papers, her mind focused on the vaguely oceanic hum of the air conditioner. She imagined her bare toes in warm sand and began mentally packing for a weekend beach getaway with Biscuit. A swim would do wonders for his arthritis, she thought. Mystery Bay would make a fine destination; she'd heard about a new juice bar right off the coastal highway.

Midway through mentally savoring a cold mango smoothie, she realized the handbooks she'd come into the room for did not exist anywhere in her desk. Nor could she find them in the nearby filing cabinet. Now she was almost twenty minutes late and it became painfully clear she'd have to improvise her entire presentation. Maybe now wasn't the best time to get lost in a daydream after all.

She pulled the trainee's resume—which she hadn't looked at—from a drawer and committed the name Shawna Van Belle to memory as she dragged herself back out to the hall. "Right this way, Miss Van Belle," she said to the woman in a flimsy attempt at formality. The Dixie cup-and-a-half of champagne she'd downed was making everything she said sound like a mockery of itself.

A more professional setting might have improved her confidence. But for some reason, the room allocated for training remained uniquely untouched by the company's restoration budget. Ancient motivational posters tried feebly to disguise spots of crumbling drywall, turning the place into a museum for tacky inappropriate sayings. A bright yellow one reading "Results, not excuses!" had curled at the edge, prompting Hope to discretely re-pin it at the corner upon entering.

They took seats opposite each other at the end of a large table. What first appeared to be paisleys on Shawna's tee shirt gradually came into focus as spiraling abstract birds. The image reminded Hope of the cover of *Velvet Echoes*, one of the lesser known Wasted

Grave albums but definitely one of the band's finest. This serendipitous association felt like encouragement from the Universe to cut the crap and get straight to the point.

"Since we're getting a late start, I'll just give you the basics," she began. Something behind her was distracting Shawna's gaze, so Hope turned around to see an image of a rock climber with the words, *Attitude makes the difference.* She gave Shawna a shrug, turned back around and continued.

"This is basically a telemarketing job," she said, as though surely someone as hip as Shawna would've already grasped something so obvious. The posters alone conveyed as much.

Shawna pressed her lips into a fine line and began fidgeting with a dark crystal at the end of one of her long necklaces.

"See, advice is an easy thing to sell," Hope went on, pressing her fingertips together and forming a steeple. "People are pretty transparent. It's just a matter of figuring out what they want to hear and then saying it to them with authority."

The improvised speech didn't stray too far from what the Psychic Envoy handbook said, or what Delma had told Hope herself when she first started. Beginners usually responded with studious, comprehending nods, and Hope expected Shawna to fall into line with the rest of them.

But Shawna didn't nod. Instead she glanced around at the other posters in the room, then at the school gym-like clock on the wall, then at a stack of cardboard boxes with different dates on them and the words "projected revenue" in black marker. At each new panic-inducing sight, Shawna's face rearranged itself with the fantastic drama of a mime in a pretend glass box which was slowly filling with imaginary water.

Hope straightened in her seat and offered an awkward smile. "Sorry if that sounded a bit harsh. Really all you have to do is listen to people's life story and offer them broad and general reassurances. It's super easy when you get the hang of it, like talking on the phone with your grandma. The only rules are not to give specific predictions with a specific timeline. I mean, you can give a generic prediction with a specific timeline or a specific prediction with a vague timeline, but not both. Does that make sense? Oh, yeah, and never offer legal or medical advice. I'm sure you'll do fine."

Shawna's eyes settled into a fevered stare and her fingers slowly turned claw-like, as if she were transforming into a character from some weird, office-based horror movie. Suddenly Hope regretted every word of her unrehearsed initiation spiel. To make things worse, the lonely tick of the school gym clock got interrupted by an eruption of raucous laughter from the party in Delma's office. Something about the noise pushed Shawna's indignation over the edge; she stood up and pushed in her chair with a teeth-clenching squeak, shaking her head as if trying to rid herself of unbearable demons.

"I'm sorry," she said, pushing out her chest in defiance, "but I'm not interested in degrading my intuitive gifts to become a cog in your soulless commercial enterprise." She walked briskly for the door but paused to add a sarcasm-laced "thank you for your time" before going through it.

Hope sat shell-shocked in the stark florescence of the room, seized by a sudden overdue curiosity about the thick, ivory-colored pages on her lap: Shawna's lavish resume. A cursory glance at is contents revealed numerous red flags that would have warned of this epic misunderstanding. Among the credentials listed: seven years as an "intuition instructor" at the Travelling Light Institute, a five-star rating on oraclefinder.com (whatever that was), and personal references from cold case detectives in three counties. From now on, Hope promised herself, she would give any paperwork she received at work a preliminary once-over wherever person-to-person interaction was expected.

The peculiar responsibility one feels after igniting undue rage in another was a burden entirely new to Hope. Part of her wanted to run after the sensitive stranger to try and make amends, but she quickly suppressed the urge; this office couldn't afford to nurture the delicate sensibilities of some crackpot with special "intuitive gifts." Better Shawna found this out now than waste time waiting for the inevitable clashes down the road.

* * *

"PRETTY BRUTAL BUT ALSO KIND OF hilarious," Hope later summed up her day in a phone conversation with her brother. She'd called Asher to hear about Jesse's wedding, having failed to get the time off for it herself (having *said* she couldn't get the time off for it, anyway—in truth she hadn't tried) and she spared him the play-by-play of her own day so they could skip to the juicy details of his.

"So how'd it go with the nuptials?" she asked him breezily.

"Hmm . . . *How did it go with the nuptials?*" He repeated, stretching out the question as if searching for the exact right set of words to answer it with. "Well, the nuptials were . . . *pretty brutal but also kind of hilarious.*"

Hope laughed. "Did you wear a tux?" she asked. "And more importantly, are there pictures of you in a tux?"

Such pictures would've made their parents' year, as to this day Asher's steadfast aversion to any kind of formal attire caused them almost as much anguish as Hope's unconventional dietary habits.

"No, I did not," he said, raising the pitch of his voice and affecting a bad European accent of some sort. "You see, it was a Medieval themed wedding. My costume was a super gay toga with chainmail armor on it."

Hope laughed again, harder this time. "What?"

He dropped the accent as the music behind his voice changed from gangster rap to thrash metal. "I shit you not," he said. "But I also got to carry a big club with metal spikes in it, which was kinda cool."

"What was *that* for?" Hope asked, cradling the phone's receiver on her shoulder while she poured steaming water into a mug of loose tea leaves. "To hit yourself over the head with?"

"All part of my Best Man duties," Asher explained, his tone not nearly as sarcastic as Hope thought it should be. "Back in the day, I guess, those Medieval dudes used to kidnap the chicks they wanted to marry from their families and the best man's job was to fight off anyone who tried to stop them."

"Whoa. That's pretty fucked up."

"Word."

"Well, it sounds entertaining at least. I mean, they tried something different, right? You gotta give them some points for inventiveness."

"I actually thought the idea was pretty cool at first, Jesse's woman riding in on this white horse with all this crazy harp music playing and shit. It was like all of the sudden everyone was on acid or something. But then they had a bunch of people get up and read poetry and stuff. After about twenty minutes or so, I was like, *okay, guys, we get it.*"

"I hate it when they drag out the ceremony," Hope concurred, blowing the fragrant steam away from her teacup. "And I hate it when people write their own vows, too. It's like, *come on.* No one needs to hear you list the million varying ways you promise to be perfect doormats for the rest of your lives."

"Don't even get me started on the vows," Asher said. "When the priest, or whatever she was—this old lady with long gray dread-locks—said something about rings, I was like, *finally.* And then she starts in with the *do you Jesse take blah blah blah*, and they both said 'I do,' so I'm like, *Cool. We're done.* But then she turns to *me*—like *I'm* supposed to say something—and I'm like, *Oh, shit, what's my line?* She makes me repeat this long spiel about how I'll keep Jesse on the straight and narrow."

"Oh, barf."

"Yeah. Then she made everyone in the audience stand up and vow to support their union and shit. It was insane."

"Oh, God. Well, how was the reception? Did they feed you well at least?"

A jumble of muffled voices started greeting each other in the background. Hope guessed someone in the Diaz family must have just walked in and the rest of the harrowing wedding tale would have to wait for now. A few seconds of chaos passed before Asher returned sounding stifled and the background music abruptly ceased.

"Uh, Hope? Can I call you back in a bit?"

"Sure."

He called back minutes later from a noisy payphone and began to fill her in on "the most pathetic damn reception in wedding history."

"So, what kind of food did they serve?"

"You wouldn't believe it. Chips and motherfucking salsa."

"That's all?"

"Basically."

"No guacamole?"

"There was one bowl of guacamole. And one bowl of bean dip. And a couple plates of crackers. And, what else . . . oh, yeah, pickles. Lots and lots of pickles."

"Sounds kind of good, actually," Hope chuckled. "What else did they do?"

"Hmm, what else," he said, pausing before startling her with a loud "Oh!" when he remembered the story's crowning touch.

"So you know that thing where everyone lines up and congratulates the couple? Well, I go up there and I'm shaking Jesse's hand, and he's holding it longer than normal which is kinda weird. Then his eyes get all serious and he goes, 'Thank you for bearing witness.' I was like, *What the fuck happened to you, bro?*"

"You *said* that to him?"

"No, I just thought it. But right when I was about to give up on homey, he leans in my ear and goes, 'Dude, I've never needed a beer so bad in my life.' So as soon as the line ended we went back to the camper and got really shitfaced."

"Uh-oh. What did the bride think of that?"

"She was not impressed. She's quite pissed at me right now, in fact. But I think it's more 'cause me and Jesse decided we're gonna start a band together."

"Sounds fun," Hope said, remembering how Jesse and Asher—who possessed not an ounce of musical background between them—used to constantly declare this same intention back in high school. "What kind of a band?"

"Um, a punk band," Asher said, his sarcastic tone implying she should have known the answer.

"Cool. Do you have a name yet?" She thought the name should have something to do with dinosaurs.

"Yeah."

"What is it?"

"Apeshit."

"Ooh, nice. I like it."

* * *

LATER IN HER LIFE, WHEN HOPE would reflect on the giant cinematic scope of it all, some scenes would always seem like they didn't quite belong there. They'd seem like they'd been cut from a film in a totally different genre—something she would never even watch—and pasted in. She almost didn't recognize herself in those scenes. It was as if the real Hope had just taken the day off, played hooky, and the producers had brought in an understudy.

But as disorienting as it felt to replay those reels, she would always treasure their existence. Every time she pulled them out to admire them, she would polish them like trophies and brag about them to her imaginary friends. The truth of her having no idea how they'd gotten there would remain unmentioned, of course. As unsettling as she found these weird existential shake-ups, she would never dream of giving them back. In fact, she shuddered to imagine the blank and barren gaps they would leave in their absence.

The last Friday of every month, Hope was tasked with the tedious, draining, and downright painful assignment of writing performance reviews.

Each review consisted of two parts: averaging each operator's call times and giving personalized feedback to help them improve. Did the psychic in question speak in a calm and soothing voice, for example? Pick up on the callers' dropped signals? Show they were listening with sufficient verbal cues?

The skill set required for the first part—organization, attention to detail, and basic competency in math—was simply a skill set Hope lacked. The problem with the second part was it required listening to recordings of actual calls, something every cell in her body violently rebelled against.

She would've preferred to never think about the customer base of the company she worked for. To regard those sad individuals with the same degree of detachment with which most people considered the animals they ate would've been markedly preferable. But despite years of trying, she'd never figured out how to do this.

As a result, Mystic Partners' representatives all thought the openings of their calls needed more work than the other parts. If anyone ever asked Hope why she never reviewed the middles or endings of calls, as Delma did occasionally, she kept a ready answer on hand: "Research shows most people have already formed their opinion of someone three seconds into any conversation. It's all about first impressions."

On the day after Jesse's wedding, she found her enthusiasm for the call-reviewing task especially scarce. In all honesty, Hope harbored nowhere near the emotional fortitude needed to do the work of the underlings she criticized. Whether this made her more of a compassionate person than them or less of one didn't matter. Either way, she didn't need reminding of her failure.

In an impressive act of efficient laziness, she typed out one short form letter and printed it 23 times:

Dear partner,

By slowing down your speaking voice, our evaluation shows you have achieved significant growth in call time length. This, as you know, is the most important function of your role here, besides helping people of course. Keep up the good work.

As independent contractors, the psychics all worked from home and rarely saw each other, if ever; Delma went over these reviews once about every three years, so her bluff would likely never be caught. She addressed each letter by hand and proudly carried them to the outgoing mail slot, never in her life having felt so acutely aware of how little her existence on the planet mattered.

On the way back to her desk, she noticed a small velvet bag sitting on the bench outside the training room. Reckoning it must have been left there by Shawna Van Belle, she picked it up with the intention of calling the poor delusional twat and getting it back to her. Returning someone's possessions seemed a fitting way to make amends for having accidentally insulted them. But when she brought the bag near her face, she was overcome with a deadly odor—some kind of menthol, garlic, cod liver oil, and pond scum mélange—and she set it back down, resigned to letting the Universe sort out her karma for her.

Half an hour remained before the warm amber glow of the weekend. To get through it, Hope pulled out an old deck of spirit animal cards from her desk drawer. She'd bought the cards at the beginning of her Mystic Partners journey. Each beautifully rendered image—coyote, eagle, horse, lizard, dragonfly—had a message on the back about how to channel the specific animal's characteristics, embodying their natural wisdom as medicine. She'd long lost the printed directions for how best to access this wisdom—how many times to shuffle the cards before drawing one, etc.—but she remembered it had said an openness to receiving guidance was the most important thing. A person must seek to connect to the Great Oneness of All Life in her own unique way.

She shuffled three times and, by sheer luck, drew her favorite card: the skunk.

"Humans and other animals always give the skunk plenty of room," read the back. "Its unique reputation and playful irreverence demand this. Assert what you are with dignity, and favor naturally follows. Skunk medicine people are experts at managing their energy flows to attract sexual partners while repelling possible threats. Be careful with this power; it can be dangerous if you are not currently seeking a mate."

4:40 seemed close enough to 5:00 to mentally check out for the day, so Hope gathered a few newspaper clippings and Styrofoam cups and headed out the back door to the dumpster behind the craft supplies store. Sometimes the manager of Just Craftin' Around threw out nearly-full paint tubes, and she needed a few more colors to complete a mural she'd been working on above her bed. It depicted an elaborate underwater scene, and she needed the tube of glitter-infused teal she saw in the far corner atop several tied plastic bags for the sparkling rocks near the water's edge.

Normally, fishing something out of the trash would be the kind of thing Hope would've glanced around before doing, just to make sure no one was watching her. But not today, she decided, channeling skunk medicine. This was her natural behavior and she was going to assert it without ego or shame. She forged a ladder out of two overturned plastic milk crates and stretched her upper body as far as it would go, reaching for the prize, the hot metal edge of the dumpster cutting into her exposed belly like a sword of fire.

She heard a startling male voice erupt in laughter about ten feet behind her.

" . . . and she's goin' in for the deep dive!" the voice was saying, mocking a sportscaster's fevered commentary. In her clumsy effort to swivel around, she lost her balance and the milk crates toppled beneath her. She pushed herself off a rusty broken shelf and jumped to the ground, landing ungracefully on her butt.

"Oh-whoa!" the voice exclaimed. Glancing up, Hope winced when she saw its source: her surfer boy maintenance man, Rush.

" . . . looks like she's gonna lose points on that dismount."

Waiting for a reaction, Rush's face turned from amused to concerned as Hope cursed and brushed the dirt off her calves. "Sorry," he said. "I didn't mean to scare you. Are you all right?"

"Yeah," she mumbled, squinting at him straight into the setting sun. The low, heavy rays jutting out from behind his head of tousled blonde hair would've made a great cover drawing on a bad 80s romance novel. She could easily picture him with his shirt off right now, and the image gave her a chilling sense of déjà vu.

"So," he said, altering his pose to assume the air of a cocky patrol officer, "do you always dumpster dive during work hours?"

"Only on Fridays," she said, and then added, as if deliberately trying to make the situation even more cringe-worthy, "My spirit animal is skunk."

For her to say something weird in the presence of someone she found intimidating was an all-too-familiar scenario. But for said intimidating individual to respond by widening his eyes with interest, smiling broadly, and nodding at her was not. This came as a delicious, invigorating surprise.

"I see," Rush said. "Sounds very . . . *animalistic.*" As he spoke, his eyes drifted down the entire length of her, pausing where the gap in her wrap skirt left one leg exposed to the thigh. When he met her gaze again, he punctuated the not-so-subtle ogle with one of his signature winks.

Panic set in as Hope wondered what to do next. The ball was in her court now. His tone of voice conveyed the exact same energy she'd spent years training her psychics to project, an energy of complete rapt attentiveness. If he were one of her trainees, she'd have given him a rave review on vocal performance alone.

Having him absorbed in this way oxygenated her blood like a sudden aerobic workout. Whatever happened next, she needed to hold on to this new dramatic state of aliveness. Prolonging this moment seemed imperative, more imperative than keeping her job, her health, and all her self-respect combined.

That's when the everyday Hope, the one who normally controlled things, decided to duck out and become a spectator, and something else—something she could only describe as pure instinct—took the wheel.

"I'm glad I ran into you," she said.

"Why?" he asked, tilting his head like a retriever.

"Yeah, um, there's something I need your help with in one of the training rooms."

"I'm at your service," he said, smiling sweetly. "What seems to be the problem?"

She licked her lips and adjusted her bra in a manner she supposed an expert seductress would. "There's a sticky drawer in there. It's really getting on my nerves. I think someone tried to jam an oversized training log into my personnel file."

He laughed. "I hope they bought you dinner first," he said.

"What?"

"Nothing. I'll see what I can do."

As she stood, he made a gentlemanly bowing gesture and placed his hand near the small of her back without touching it, directing her to lead the way. All her mental resources frantically converged on the twin tasks of making coy small talk while planning which drawer she would pretend to struggle with once they reached their destination.

"Yeah," she said, feeling her cheeks redden. "There's been friction building in there for a while, but now it's like, something's got to give, you know? It's a tight little space, not meant to have something so thick shoved in it."

"I'm sure I can help you with your tight little space," he said.

At first Hope wondered if it was merely her own dirty mind making every word out of Rush's mouth sound like a sexual metaphor. But the way he laughed and shook his head right then, as if in disbelief, told her he saw her words the same way. And with minimal effort she soon found herself a fluent speaker of this new language. The more she explained the problem to him ("It's really *hard* to make that thing *slide in and out* at the right angle"), detailing various ways she'd tried to correct it ("I couldn't get at it with my hand, so I tried using a broomstick"), the faster she lost sight of whatever boundaries she'd ever feared crossing.

"It probably just needs some lube," he said.

"Have we had this conversation before?" she asked. "I mean, I feel like we have. Or maybe I just dreamed it."

He smiled. "Or maybe *this* is the dream."

"No," she said. "This can't be the dream because I'm not naked."

At that point, right before the training room, he stopped walking, glanced around to make sure they were alone, and asked, "Hey, uh . . . are you trying to give me a boner?"

The stand-in Hope felt no embarrassment whatsoever at this accusation. Without an ounce of shame, she responded, "That depends. Is it working?"

He swallowed. "Yes, it is."

They entered the training room and the first thing Hope noticed was an obtrusive poster reading, *Never lose sight of your objective.* The slogan suited this office moment just as fittingly as any other, she told herself.

"Well, here we are," Rush said, contemplating her and hesitating awkwardly. But when he kissed her, all the awkwardness melted away. His mouth tasted of crystal clarity, an answer to a question she'd been asking in her head for months. And when he took a couple of steps back and, maintaining eye contact, methodically went about the business of releasing his belt buckle, she sat on a table and lifted her nylon skirt like it wasn't an odd thing to do at all.

She inhaled deeply as he came nearer, bracing herself for a moment of satiating turbulence. But the only struggle occurring as he glided into her was the one of her mind batting away all the obvious warnings; her body didn't resist at all.

"That was fun," Rush said after approximately three minutes, stepping away and pulling his pants up.

"One for the memoirs," Hope agreed, immediately wishing she could take back her words. The familiar voices of doubt and angst were returning in full force now, just as quickly as they'd vanished.

Before Hope could worry about how this development would play out, a mechanical ring sounded outside the door indicating a visitor in the lobby. Rush peered through the little plate-glass window and said, with deadpan seriousness, "The Avon lady's here."

Hope checked the window and laughed. "Oh, that's the new trainee from yesterday. She didn't work out because she's a *real* psychic. We only let frauds and hucksters work here."

Rush cut his laughter short when Hope opened the door.

"Oh, sorry," Shawna said, appearing startled as she picked up the velvet pouch of smelly God-knows-what from the bench and kissed it. "I just came back for my medicine bag. I'm lost without it."

Remarkably, she didn't seem to detect anything unusual having occurred in the balmy room, even though Rush's belt was still hanging open and Hope was still barefoot.

"Must be some powerful stuff you got in there," Hope said, reaching over to tap the velvet bag gently with her forefinger.

"Yes," she said. "Also, I was hoping I could talk to you again."

Rush retreated into the background and initiated a careful round of pretend work, opening and closing every filing cabinet in the room repeatedly.

"I had a vision this morning," Shawna said. "I realized I can serve my higher vocation here after all. You see, your clouded energy challenged my psychic balance. But now I've recognized the call and determined how I can help your organization."

"Help us . . . ?"

"Overcome your negativity and limitations. I mean, if you're willing to give me another chance?"

Around the office, lights and computers flicked off and staffers began chatting about their plans for the weekend.

"Sure," Hope said, as though by making another bad decision she could dilute the previous one's adversity. "Come back on Monday. We'll start over."

"Great."

As they shook hands, Rush slipped stealthily out of the training room and ambled toward the office's back exit.

"See you later, Hope," he said. "Let me know when you're gonna need me again."

SEVEN

There was no question Hope preferred the company of dogs over people. Simply put, dogs were better. Their patient, loving, forgiving honesty made her own frail humanness feel shamefully inferior by comparison. They possessed every quality organized religion ascribes to its invented deities, and she worshipped them accordingly.

At the outset, she'd never expected Biscuit to make it past his twelfth birthday. But now, with sweet sixteen right around the corner, she thought it would be cool if he stuck around long enough to break the world record for canine longevity; she even daydreamed about the two of them touring the talk show circuit to brag about the accomplishment. And she fed him a carefully researched hodge-podge of health supplements in service of this far-fetched goal. But as the patch of gray hairs around his nose spread to the gap between his eyes, it gave him a permanent worried expression, mirroring the dull ache she felt every time she looked at him. And his breathing became more labored every day, the sound of it almost meditative, calling to mind the transcendent whir of the ocean's eternal cycles.

She felt guilty leaving Biscuit alone whenever she went to work, and the guilt increased tenfold when her main reason for going to work was to see Rush. Her paramour didn't work in the building every day, only when issues requiring his handiness came up—the rest of the time he did contract work as a roofer. But yesterday Delma had mentioned something about the air conditioning ducts needing cleaning. So as a matter of course, Hope spent the hour before work waxing off all her body hair and slathering herself in amber-scented lotion.

Most people have things in their life they're not proud of. Most also have things in their life they're very proud of but would never think of bragging about out loud—not to anyone, not ever. For Hope, Rush Holbrook represented just this sort of highly classified accomplishment.

Her first surreal romp with him in the training room had sparked a dirty and incurable habit, continuing on a semi-monthly basis for the next four years. Their depraved high jinks eventually branched out to include the break room, the stock room, the conference room, and the tool shed—and, occasionally, Hope's apartment on lunch breaks. The meetings at her place were rare, but they were her favorite; Rush acted genuinely unperturbed by the piles of artful clutter everywhere, and he always talked sweetly to Biscuit when the old dog faithfully tried to follow them into the bedroom. ("Sorry, fella, I gotta borrow your mom for a minute. I promise I'll take good care of her.")

Most of the time Rush stubbornly insisted they meet in the same uncomfortable office spaces, claiming the inherent risk of getting caught was something he found "way hot." But Hope suspected an ulterior motive; the necessity of maintaining a "business as usual" facade at work left no room for conversation before or after the deed.

Not that there would be anything to talk about. The possibility of Rush leaving his wife never even came up anymore, though the reasons he stayed married remained a source of exponential bewilderment to Hope.

He'd met his wife Angie ten years earlier at the height of his short-lived pro skateboarding career. She'd been a fresh-faced high schooler then, a skate park groupie, and all-around party girl. Hard to believe it now, Hope thought, having only ever seen her in her work uniform. Her family owned the popular pancake restaurant/ unapologetic obesity exacerbator known as Butter House, a place where apparently not even the top levels of command escaped the indignity of strutting around in vaguely Dutch-inspired get-ups topped with pointy yellow bonnets.

According to Rush, he'd kept his eye on Angie for two long years while he waited for her to turn eighteen and, owing to the extraordinary buildup (perhaps also to the ecstasy he took a lot of in those days), experienced unparalleled sensual heights when he finally got to deflower her. He'd proposed shortly afterward, calculating (wrongly, it would turn out) that the fortunes of her flesh would easily keep him supplied for a lifetime.

Not surprisingly, things didn't go as he expected. As Rush so eloquently put it in one of his rare confessional moods early on, "I haven't buttered that bonnet in almost two years. I've finally just given up trying."

"If you're so unhappy, why stay married?" she'd asked him then, from across a conference table after one of their "dates," as she rolled her messed-up hair into a bun and secured it with a pencil. The question made him squirm in his seat and pinch the bridge of his nose.

"I didn't say I wasn't happy," he said, making tight parallel lines with his hands like a corporate lawyer laying out contract stipulations. "Look. Ninety percent of my relationship with Angie is great. For me, ninety percent is enough."

"But if it's so great, then why are you—" she'd started to say, the first and last time she broached the subject, but he'd stood up and pushed in his chair with a forcefulness that made it screech against the floor.

"I'm not leaving my wife, okay?" he snapped. "I gotta go. I'll see you later."

Since then she'd tried to obtain answers using less confrontational methods, but it never brought her one iota closer to the explanations the situation begged for. She finally determined that, like many people, Rush probably just placed too much importance on the outward appearance of stability.

When socializing around the office, Hope would watch Rush's strained smile as he described his and Angie's weekend activities, which to her sounded dreadfully spiritless—golf at his in-laws' country club, patio refinishing, the occasional blockbuster film at the Multiplex—and sneering little comments like "woo-hoo, party time" would escape her before she had a chance to censor them. She couldn't help it; whenever she tried to picture him engaged in any of these pastimes, the scene always ended in him clubbing himself over the head with a skateboard.

"You're just jealous," he would tease back, sticking out his tongue at her when the bystanders turned away, then groping her ass as soon as they left the room.

The cruelest of the Universe's many jokes, Hope thought, was the way biology drives us to forge sexual connections while society says we must become half of a couple first. As a result, you can bet that at any given time, at least half the population is devoting their entire day to doing something they have absolutely no interest in doing.

A young lacrosse player named Kurt Harris first taught her this lesson in tenth grade.

Jocks had never appealed to her before, but Kurt stood out from the herd. His art class renderings of fire-eyed trolls and psychedelic swan-women reflected her twisted insides in the same way her beloved music did. He often lazed alone under trees during off periods, scribbling in his notebook with an air of silent ferocity about him. She knew this because she engaged in similar behavior patterns. One day he showed her a charcoal sketch he'd made of her from across the lawn—it had unrealistically peach-shaped breasts and tight, sculpted arms—and with impossible quickness and ease, the two fell into coupledom.

Exactly what coupledom entailed, she soon found out, was having to learn all about the sport of lacrosse. It meant getting dragged to tedious pizza parties in which fast-breaks and body checks were the main topics of conversation. If Kurt enjoyed the game so much, she reckoned she should at least try to appreciate its value. She guessed lacrosse's having originated with Native Americans hundreds of years ago made it kind of cool, but it still seemed like a bunch of guys running around trying to prove their manhood in an ultimately silly way. At least the players didn't all think they were going to become millionaires like those football douchebags did.

The following year when her first love went off to college and they settled on an amicable breakup, Hope resumed her ferocious daydreaming as naturally as a rubber band going slack again.

Now, 15 years later with Rush, she thought she'd found an ideal solution to love's eternal catch-22; she kept the sex part of her life separate from the life part of it, thereby ensuring neither one could tarnish or dilute the other. She didn't have time to notice Rush's flaws, and he didn't have time to chisel away at her sense of self. It almost felt like she'd discovered some mythical philosopher's stone—except for the deception part. If she could exist as an open and aboveboard mistress like she imagined women all over Europe did, the dilemma would become irrelevant.

The morning Rush came to fix the air conditioner started off on a dodgy track. Instead of raising his eyebrows and smiling when he saw her, he met her gaze with a concentrated squint, then distractedly lowered his head and averted his eyes.

"Hey . . . I gotta get to work. See ya later."

"Um . . . okay?" Hope said, turning her head inquisitively.

Normally he would make any excuse to visit her cubicle on days he was around. But today he made himself so scarce she began racking her brain for reasons he might be avoiding her. Might she have done something wrong? Impossible, she concluded, unless she'd somehow sleepwalked and left his wife a threatening voicemail without remembering the event. She went out of her way to use the bathroom near the main air conditioning vent instead of the closer one in the lobby, but he always needed to go get something from his truck the minute she came around. At the end of the day, she pulled out the cellphone she'd recently purchased and did what she'd managed to avoid doing up to this point—sent him a needy text message.

Hey, Mr. Fix-it. What does a girl have to do to get some maintenance around here?

She hoped for a reply but prepared for silence. Something must have happened at home, she reasoned. Maybe he'd gotten caught watching one of those orgiastic porn videos he was always telling her about. There were countless ways for the rebellious personality he kept hidden to leak out and wreak havoc in his world of fake complacency. Whatever it was, it was all on him. She'd just have to wait to find out.

Five o'clock arrived and the florescent lights started dimming, and Hope made one last unnecessary trip to the out-of-the-way bathroom. This time, she didn't look at Rush at all when she passed him, but she did feel him looking at her and her stomach tightened in response.

She stood at the mirror, wondering if she should say anything to him on the way out. But then again, did it matter? It wasn't like she needed the sex, really. It wasn't as if she yearned for his touch or hungered to let his surging manly passions engulf her. She simply didn't want to break the streak. In four years, she'd never coexisted in the same building with Rush for an entire day without their giving in to carnal urges at some point, and she rather prized this covert statistic.

But the day was over now, the streak already broken. Her evenings belonged only to her—this remained one of the best perks of the whole arrangement—and she didn't want to mess with tonight's lineup. She been looking forward to grabbing takeout from the Indian buffet on the corner and watching true crime dramas while rearranging the curled pictures and quotations on her inspiration board. Rush's lack of concern for the four-year streak wouldn't matter to her if she could manage to not care about it either. She reapplied her charcoal eyeliner and walked out, not looking at him as she passed.

When she reached the front hall, he called her name in an urgent-sounding voice and three other people reflexively turned their heads along with her.

"What do you want," she groaned, realizing only afterword how strange her perturbed tone must have sounded to the bystanders.

"If you wanna wait just a minute," he said, jumping down off the ladder and brushing the dust off his jeans, "I can . . . I mean, we can talk about . . . that drain you needed snaked."

She smiled, forgetting her irritation. "I'll be outside," she said. The parking lot might technically be considered part of the building, she thought, and this would reverse the issue of the broken streak.

The phrase "be careful what you wish for" never seemed as appropriate as it did minutes later, when she opened the passenger door of Rush's antiquated pickup and climbed up onto the ripped vinyl seat. Car sex presents a slew of unique challenges and is hardly worth the trouble.

But then, without saying anything, he started the truck and began rolling forward.

"Where are you going?" she asked.

"I'm taking you on a little adventure," he said, patting her on the thigh as though to assure her.

"I have to get home to Biscuit," she protested. "If I don't give him his pain meds every four hours, his hip will start hurting him again."

"Biscuit's probably just sleeping right now," Rush said. "This won't take long. I have to be home by six anyway."

"Okay," she sighed. "Twist my arm."

"I'll twist yours if you'll twist mine," he chuckled.

HE STILL WOULDN'T TELL HER WHERE they were going, and every house he passed was more ostentatious than the one before.

"Hmm," she said absently, "It doesn't look like you're taking me to the woods to kill me."

"Don't press your luck," he said.

At last, the truck parked in a long tree-lined driveway. She thought she recognized the contemporary style concrete mansion at the end of it from videos he'd proudly shown her—videos of zany skateboarding stunts involving rooftops, videos he'd made instead of doing the roofing work he was paid to do, apparently. He'd told her often about how many of these giant palaces sit uninhabited much of the time, their owners having bought them as vacation homes or to use for sketchy tax reasons. She guessed his ability to trespass like this was some kind of unofficial employment benefit.

He led her through a wrought iron gate to a backyard straight off the home renovation channel; a polished mosaic pathway wound through hedges, gazebos and fountains, ending up at a cauldron-like fire pit. He raised one eyebrow comically at her as he flicked on the flames with a remote-control switch, then gently sat her down on the stone bench next to it, moving her knees apart with one hand and sweeping her hair from her face with the other.

The fire pit messed with her head a little. As its heat tickled her calf, she kept picturing a smug devil nudging her closer to the flames with his blazing pitchfork. As much as she knew she would relish replaying this scene in her mind later, in the moment she couldn't wait to get out of there.

"Thanks for that," Rush said on the drive home, breaking a long silence. "I really needed it."

"My pleasure," she mumbled. She started to ask him if he knew for certain they didn't just leave a porn video on someone's security camera but decided to leave it alone. Let him worry about the potential consequences of his crazy danger fetish.

He scrunched up his face and rubbed the back of his neck. "So anyway," he said, squirming as if suffering from a stomachache, " . . . that was my in-law's house."

Hope braced herself against the dashboard with both her fore-arms. "What? Oh, for fuck's sake."

He laughed breezily. "Relax, jumpy. They're in Hawaii right now. Nice place though, huh?"

She rolled down her window, suddenly carsick. "It's all right I guess . . . a bit sterile for my taste. I mean, what's the point of having a big yard if you can't get it dirty?"

He pursed his lips and nodded. "Fair point." Then he sighed and said, "Anyway, that's where the big party's gonna be."

"What big party?"

He looked stunned. "Um . . . Saturday? The anniversary party? Didn't you get an invitation? Angie said she gave them to everyone in the office yesterday."

Hope genuinely had no idea what he was talking about, but suspected she should clench her teeth when she asked the next question, "Whose anniversary is it? Yours?"

Rush blared the horn at an offending driver and turned to give them the finger. "Yep, ten years," he said. "It's a . . . a whaddya-call-it thingy. Vow renewal ceremony. Sorry, I thought you knew."

"Well, I did not," Hope said. She allowed a couple minutes' more of dead air to pass between them. This explained why he'd been acting so strange today, but it only deepened the mystery of what made him so strange in general.

"Hmm," she finally said, having decided to distance herself by treating the news with the absurdity it deserved. "Well, my advice would be to renegotiate the contract."

"What do you mean?"

"I don't know. Adjust the fine print a little. Put in a porn allowance, a blow job clause . . . *something.* Make sure all your interests are protected before you write your name on that dotted line. That's all I'm saying."

He laughed at her remark—a gentle, easy laugh like warm flowing water—and she felt the tension in her spine dissolve.

"So," she asked as he pulled up in front of her apartment building, putting on her best deadpan expression. "Saturday, huh? What time? Should I bring anything?"

All the color drained from Rush's face. "Uh . . . I didn't think you would—"

She punched him hard on the arm. "I'm kidding. Jesus. I wouldn't be caught dead at a shit-show like that."

He affected an exaggeratedly pouty look and rubbed the spot where she'd landed the blow. "Ow," he said. "You're mean."

"Thought you liked it rough," she teased, climbing out of the car without looking back.

"On second thought," he said, "can you do that again? Harder this time?"

She slammed the door.

Somewhere along the stairwell to her apartment, Hope began mentally reciting the same internal rant she'd been trying to shake for longer than she cared to remember:

It's not like I want to own him or anything hell I wouldn't even care if he had other women I just hate how he insists on living this ridiculous lie and then makes me support the whole ridiculous lie as though it's a perfectly natural thing but it's not natural at all it's so not natural I mean who confines themself to a sexless domestic partnership as if they have no choice in the matter even though they do have a choice and then he acts all woe is me like he's a victim of circumstance I mean seriously who does that I can't stand that how can I respect someone who would do that

The thoughts' repetitiveness got so irritating she found it necessary to pinch her own cheek when she heard herself say "sexless domestic partnership" for about the fourth time. At that point, the narrative took a turn:

But I do enjoy it I mean I actually enjoy it in the moment while it's happening I'm not just getting through it because I think there's some huge reward awaiting me at the end of it the way most people are doing all the time with most of the stuff they do in their daily lives and it's not really hurting anyone except me so I guess I'll keep doing it until it gets too annoying

Rush resisted maturity so fiercely it was hard to imagine anyone could look forward to growing old with him. She'd never actively imagined herself growing old with anyone, except, on rare occasions, Nathan. But not so much lately; the frequency of her talks with Nathan was dwindling, from two heart-to-hearts a month to a fact-based conference four times a year. They often argued whose version of reality bore more similarities to the true one—just like, it warmed her to consider, an old married couple. On their last gab session, they'd devoted two hours to which kind of cell phone she should get; Nathan loved any exchange in which he could act like an expert. She kept asking him questions long after she'd made her decision because she could feel him luxuriating in his role as teacher.

Between these two men, Hope recounted to herself as she reached the top of the stairs, she almost had herself one whole boyfriend. And the only dirty socks she ever had to touch were her own.

She opened the door to find Biscuit looking up at her from a nest of coats in the front closet. His hip dysplasia gave him more obvious trouble these days than ever. She hated herself for living on the second floor and often considered moving to a house—she even picked up rental guides when she saw them. She'd also gotten him a heated bed and started taking him to aqua therapy and acupuncture, remedies which the vet said would help for a while. When the pain won out over those therapies, she would spring for the three-thousand-dollar hip replacement surgery without hesitation.

She hurried to get his pain pill into a ball of peanut butter and fed it to him, then scratched behind his ears and buried her face in the fluff around his neck while he smacked away the stickiness.

"What do you think," she asked him, "do you want to go to the doctor and get a new robot leg?" He licked her nose with his peanut-buttery breath and then moved to her cheek as a thick, salty tear ran down it. "You do? Okay. Cool. We'll get you a new robot leg then and you'll be good as new. Yes, you will. You're such a good boy."

She made the appointment for the following Tuesday and spent the weekend trying not to make herself crazy. *Just a routine procedure,* she kept assuring herself. No need to memorize the wispy patterns in his speckled brown fur just yet, or to make mental records of the happy little grunting noises he made when he got his belly rubbed or chased cats in his sleep. Doing so would turn her into a sniveling bucket of tears and crying around him would stress him out. Dogs mirror the emotions of their people and she needed to exude calm, like the dog expert guy on TV advised doing during thunderstorms and fireworks displays.

The three days Biscuit spent at the clinic would be the hardest to get through, and so Hope deliberately planned activities—tedious outings she would normally avoid—just to get away from the empty house. Thankfully, Asher and Jesse's quote-unquote band had a gig on Wednesday.

For a couple of guys who could maybe scare up about four guitar chords between them, Apeshit enjoyed an abounding popularity in the local underground music scene. When they'd started out four years earlier, Hope had supported the endeavor with a zeal that now seemed embarrassing in hindsight. Her primary motive in producing all those fliers, which she did by Xeroxing collages of cut-up comic books, was to give Asher a reason to stay in San Lazaro. But as their popularity grew, so did her relief at not having to attend any more of those rowdy and obnoxious testosterone-fests.

Apeshit took gigs wherever they could, often accepting beer as payment to entertain a small handful of inebriated revelers. Hope assumed this to be the arrangement at Barracuda Vespa, the new scooter shop who'd just booked them to play at their grand opening. But Wednesday night, as she circled the block looking for parking, the crowd already gathered on the sidewalk defied her expectations. They looked like real concertgoers. The proliferation of cute mod-style fashions outside the balloon-adorned storefront nearly compelled her to go home and change; she'd worn plaid and ripped denim in order to blend into what was usually a coarse and uncivilized scene. The group's diversity came as a welcome twist. She could play the role of an ordinary passerby stopping to listen, bob her head to a couple of numbers, and then mosey on.

As she approached the venue, though, she found it hard to stay in character; those redundant screeching and grinding sounds would definitely repel an unsuspecting ambler. This particular aural assault—a migraine-inducing stream of complaints called "A Million Times"—held the distinction of being her least favorite of the dozen or so original songs in Apeshit's repertoire.

"A million times I walked the plank . . . a million times so vile and rank . . . a million times your blood was stale . . . a million times a rusty nail . . . a million times a heart attack . . . a million times we fade to black . . . "

And so it went, on and on, never arriving at a chorus or bridge or getting to any sort of point whatsoever. The stage antics didn't help either, Asher pacing back and forth like a gorilla in a cage and then pausing between each shouted phrase to have a violent fistfight with an invisible man. He must have come up with those moves back when he was a young hooligan in the prison for wayward boys.

"A million times I've heard this song," said a pretty girl with a sleek red bob who was smoking a cigarette and leaning against a newspaper box, " . . . and it never gets any better." Hope laughed out loud at the comment, and the girl turned, gave her a nod, and said. "Oh, hey, Hope."

"My thoughts exactly," Hope said, slowly recognizing the girl as Jillian Diaz, Jesse's wife, an individual for whom she was supposed to harbor deep contempt but could never quite manage to.

"Isn't that the definition of insanity?" Hope said, "I mean, doing the same thing over and over and expecting a different result?"

"Yeah," Jillian chuckled. "I guess it is."

Mrs. Jesse proved the perfect companion to take in the show with. She played along with Hope's pseudo-intellectual commentary on each song, pausing occasionally to nod along to Jesse's frantic drum solos. She agreed with Hope about finding a glimmer of ironic humor in "A Million Times" despite its awfulness, but both favored other songs for their stronger concepts and more memorable lyrics. Hope cited "Drunk at Disneyland" as her number one, while Jillian preferred the title track from their latest album, "Fat Guys with Hot Wives."

"I do see why this one's the most popular, though," Hope admitted during the final number, watching a miniature mosh pit form as Jesse and Asher jumped up and down pogo-style to the dizzying and tuneless tune of "Frusterbation." "This one makes *me* feel like going out and committing murder, and *I* don't even kill bugs."

Jillian nodded and laughed, then threw Hope a peace sign and vanished into the dissipating crowd as the lights came on and various employees began scurrying to help the boys clear out their gear.

Hope knew better than to approach Asher during this phase. He was always distracted and testy after a show until everything reached its official put-away and wrapped-up end. Instead she wandered through the shop pretending to browse the glossy information booklets attached to each pastel and chrome Vespa, and when she saw her brother in relaxed chatting mode with some buddies near the back exit, she made her way over to greet him.

She hadn't talked to him in a few weeks, so it surprised her to see a large square patch of gauze taped to one of his knees. "Dude," she called, her voice loud and hoarse at the same time. "Why's your knee all jacked up?"

He looked down sheepishly. "Oh, I . . . injured it," he said.

"Tell her how," Jillian urged, as Jesse tried to stifle a laugh.

"Not important," Asher snapped back with mock indignation. Then he waved at someone behind her and slipped away from the group, leaving Jillian to rat him out.

"He was being a jackass," she said. "He bet Jesse he could jump over a four-foot hedge at one of those office building courtyards, but his foot caught on a branch and he landed on the corner of a concrete bench."

Hope nodded along to the story, not the slightest bit alarmed by it. "But wait, what was he doing at an *office building*?" she asked after a pause, watching him in the background as he exchanged fist-bumps with the out-of-place stranger who'd just come in the door. She then pointed at the man, who looked like a severely jet-lagged computer salesman. "And who's Mr. Business Casual over there?"

Jillian raised her hands in a "beats me" gesture and looked at Jesse, who mimicked his wife's movement with one hand while pulling her into a sideways embrace with the other.

Suddenly it felt like Hope hadn't been spending enough time with her brother. She waited for the right moment, studying the black-and-white movie stills on the walls until she saw him alone in a corner, playing a game on his cell phone and muttering "fuck" to himself every other second.

"What are you doing tomorrow, bro?" she asked.

"I have a doctor's appointment at eleven," he said, lifting his knee and pointing at it with his head so he wouldn't have to take his hands off the phone.

"Want me to drive you?" she asked. "We could have lunch after."

"Uh . . . " He slammed the phone shut in defeat and put it in his pocket. "Don't you have to work?"

"I'll call in sick. Fuck those guys." She'd planned to take the day off to worry about Biscuit anyway, but she thought it would be a nice gesture to pretend she was playing hooky for him.

"Okay, sure," he said. "Call me in the morning."

"Cool."

On her way out, a guy with Buddy Holly glasses and a tattoo of a wolf on his arm bowed his head at Hope in sweet polite acknowledgement. A memory returned to her with a sting; this was the cable repair guy who'd nervously asked her out for coffee in the lobby of her apartment building last year. She'd turned him down despite his obvious fitness as a potential companion, citing her involvement with someone, and this fact now infuriated her. She owed no loyalty to Rush whatsoever, but she'd gone and given him allegiance anyway.

Or maybe not; maybe her mind had simply been such a toxic subterfuge of conflicting emotions at the time that she couldn't find room for one more complication, not even a pleasant one. Maybe she'd gotten so used to half-loves that the prospect of a whole one terrified her.

Or maybe Buddy Holly glasses only looked good now, in hindsight, because she sensed a storm that would bring unprecedented loneliness rustling outside her door.

* * *

STUDIES HAVE SHOWN DOCTORS' OFFICES LOSE more money each year through magazine theft than from health care fraud. The most pinch-prone titles are the gossip rags; sports journals and so-called "women's interest" glossies run a close second. Apparently, many clinics defend themselves against such pilferage by stocking their drab waiting rooms with the kind of reading materials only dull rich people would find interesting, stuff like *Comfort Quarterly*, *Economics Today*, and *Livelihoods*, texts deemed free from the faintest hint of sex appeal. The state-run clinic where Asher was being treated offered the same predictable selection to its bedraggled clientele. At least she could safely assume these pages didn't have many sick-people germs on them, Hope thought as she picked up the least spiritless of the available options. This one even looked mildly interesting. She had stopped despising the guy on its cover a while back. Sure, he was still a thundering bullshit artist, but at least he had something original to say.

REPUTATION REBOOT OR CAREER SUICIDE?
An Analytical Discourse on Brooks Nixon's Latest Offering

The cover showed the subject in a black turtleneck, pressing two fingers into his right temple and looking upward with pursed lips as though pondering an existential riddle like an aged beatnik poet. Hope flipped to the article and immediately found a more flattering image, to her tastes anyway: eccentric uncle Brooks, reclining in a lawn chair surrounded by whimsical metal sculptures. In both portraits, his hair was gray and shoulder-length. In the second one, it also looked slept in. The article began:

> Let's say you're a best-selling self-help author. You make your fortune helping lonely single ladies find lasting love, but something about your work has always felt artificial to you. You've been talking down to your audience, presuming them incomplete beings and not giving them credit for being able to have rich fulfilling lives while remaining single. You release a book to express these feelings but alienate more than half your audience in the process. What do you do next? Declare you were "just kidding" and revert to your old ways? Give up writing altogether? If you're Brooks Nixon, the answer is neither of these. You write a follow-up to the misunderstood work—something even more controversial—something guaranteed to inflame your disapprovers. And maybe, if you're lucky, you incite a revolution.

The next section showed a series of pictures of vandalized books in bookstores, their pages ripped out and words like "homewrecker" scrawled across the front. Apparently, many stores were pulling copies of the recent release off the shelves for their protection and others had stopped selling them altogether, viewing them as a liability.

Hope skimmed past this section. If memory served her correctly, getting stitches taken out was expedient business. In eighth grade, after a long, arduous recovery from a tree-climbing mishap, she remembered looking at the doctor with disbelief after her sutures' instantaneous removal. She didn't have time to read the whole article, so she needed to quickly confirm her suspicion of it as a whole lot of hype over nothing. What harmless collection of words had ruffled feathers this time?

> . . . *Veiled Misery* is being called a "handbook for breaking up other people's marriages." Its basic premise asserts that any married individual, be they male or female, is inherently living a lie. If you have your eye on one of them, Nixon claims, all you have to do is coax your target into rediscovering their authentic selves and—presto—you'll free them from their tortured imprisonment. The legal details and other messy logistics will take care of themselves thereupon, having become mere formalities in the face of your hurricane-like passion.

On the bench next to Hope, a toddler in a Spiderman shirt puked all over himself and his mother pulled a diaper from her overstuffed bag to mop it up. As Hope diverted her eyes from the spectacle, Asher emerged from the double doors looking like a brand-new man.

"Where do you wanna have lunch?" he asked. "I'm in the mood for Mexican."

"Sure," Hope said, dropping the magazine on the side table and ushering him out of the lobby quickly.

Once they reached the car, the discussion of restaurant choice became the same old overplayed schtick it always did. After letting him choose the general category of food, Hope shot down all his suggestions of corporate chains and called him an "uppity gringo." Then, as a childish retaliation to this, Asher agreed to her authentic hole-in-the-wall pick only to declare his intentions of ordering the most disgusting meat-laden item on the menu.

"Okay, I'll go to Ay Chihuahua," he said, clapping his hands and then rubbing them together like a scheming villain. "Maybe I'll get the pickled pig's feet."

The lunch conversation followed its usual predictable course, too. Across a ceramic tile table adorned with paper flowers, he updated her on the three women he'd dated over the past six months ("two whore-bags and one ice queen"), and eventually circled back to venting about his number one rival, Jillian Diaz. His latest beef with the latter concerned the roomy Spanish Colonial style home she and Jesse shared and her attempts to control its uses.

"Bitch wants to turn the garage into another bedroom just so we won't have any place to practice."

"Why do they need another bedroom? Is she pregnant or something?"

"No, thank God. Not yet anyway. She's just selfish and anal and doesn't like Jesse to have any fun."

To introduce a much-needed change of subject, Hope brought up the mysterious-looking yuppie guy from the night before.

"It looked like you guys were doing a drug deal," she half-joked.

Asher shook his head as he pushed a pile of flesh swimming in red sauce around his plate with a tortilla. "Nah," he said. "Actually, Desmond was my drug counselor in prison. He's a cool guy." His phone made a noise and he stopped playing with his food for a minute to frown at it, holding it in his lap under the table. "Not much to tell there."

After lunch, she dropped him off at the small studio he rented, an illegal attachment on the house across from Jesse and Jillian's.

She'd helped him move in three years ago and couldn't believe he still lived there. To get from the kitchen to the bedroom, you literally had to climb over the pile of clothes on his bed. It made him look like a giant in a doll's house; she'd told him as much once and he hadn't invited her back since.

From the street, she could see the Diaz's kitchen window and for a second she thought she glimpsed Jillian's burst of red hair at the sink. This living situation really did seem a tiny step up from the one where he'd crashed in the RV in Jesse's parents' driveway, and Hope could imagine easily how bad Jillian must want to get rid of him. What a parasite he must seem to her.

"Whaddya got planned for the rest of the day?" she asked as he climbed out of the car and stretched his back.

"Pop the rest of my hospital-strength pain killers and pass the fuck out," he answered with a long, contented exhale. "What about you?"

The first thing she planned to do was call the vet to check on Biscuit, of course. But she decided not to tell Asher this. At an earlier mention of her beloved companion's plight, he'd made crass inquiries about the cost of the surgery and Biscuit's age, implying she should opt for the unthinkable. Instead she began telling him about another possible plan, to visit Chapterhouse and check out Brooks Nixon's "handbook for breaking up other people's marriages." But the roar of a low-flying plane cut her off, giving her time to come up with a different answer. This, she decided, was for the best. As little as she cared about how others might judge her, Asher or anyone else, some ideas were simply better left unspoken.

"Maybe I'll try to clean my apartment," she lied.

* * *

Human minds—animal minds, too, Hope liked to think—have certain built-in defenses against their most feared states. Adrenaline kicks in when physical suffering and death become imminent possibilities, and when our delicate emotional balance is upset by the terror of living, our spiritual instinct—nature's perfect hypnotist—arrives to soften the blow.

After her eighth-grade tree smashup, when Hope failed to answer simple questions in the ER, a boyish doctor with freckles and buck teeth strapped her into a machine that felt like a coffin inside the eye of a hurricane. Claustrophobic and cold inside that weird mechanical hum, desperate for any relief from the confusion and fear of it, her injured intellect took a blind leap of trust into the Abyss of the Unknown, a place she'd recently heard about in a Wasted Grave song. The song, called "Hollow," had made a believer out of her with far less effort than the myths offered by her parents' Episcopal Church.

> *Pushed, swallowed*
> *Into the velvet door*
> *Pale whispers in the mist as we surrender*
> *Floating, dreamless*
> *The Abyss of the Unknown*
> *We're hollow*
> *Melted lights for ever after*

To her surprise, she'd found the Abyss of the Unknown almost pleasant. She'd discovered a benign silence on the other side. It was not exactly luminous there, but not dark, either; just a harmless clarity, an immaculate absence the color of sea breezes.

Since then she'd tried to recall the benevolence of the Abyss whenever she could, whenever any emotional disruption came near her. But she could never feel it with the same certainty as when it had come to her on its own.

She did stop at Chapterhouse after dropping off Asher, and she did pick up a copy of *Veiled Misery*. But it wasn't because she had any intention of ever reading a word of it. Buying it just felt like a deed in need of doing, a procedure required of her before she could carry on living. Having made it out of the store, goods in hand, she sat in her car clutching the brown paper bag like an alcoholic. Staring out the window and breathing heavily, she began to feel her chest hollowing out as the mist of pale whispers floated in. Recognizing the feeling did cause some trepidation, but only a little; mostly she felt comforted, assured, and safe.

She opened her phone's contact list and pressed the number for Good Shepherd Animal Clinic.

Speaking softly, her voice hollow as a melted light behind a velvet door, she requested a status update on her fifteen-year-old German Shepherd-Lab mix.

"I'm sorry," the vet tech said with a careful, professional balance of sympathy and detachment. "He went into cardiac arrest this morning. We did all we could, but he didn't make it."

She didn't fall apart. In fact, from the outside, she thought she must have sounded like a regular ice queen. Those pale whispers were strong medicine, it turned out. Numbed her brain's pain receptors like Novocain.

"Well," she said, "at least he doesn't have to fight anymore."

The spell didn't last long. At a stoplight, she glanced down and noticed a golf ball sized tuft of fur on the car's floor among the pine needles and unopened mail. She would retrieve it as soon as she got home, then search for more fur balls under the seat and between the car's various plastic crevices. In the apartment she would find infinitely more fur balls to add to the assemblage, along with a towering pile of half-gnawed rawhides, and she would pile them all atop Biscuit's fluff-covered fleece bed. And then she would finally break down, crying her way through three boxes of tissues and half a roll of paper towels.

A comforting ritual of memorial-making comprised the next day; she placed the artifacts in a potted fern which featured a cartoon bone and the words "it's a ruff life" painted on the side. She later enshrined Biscuit's ashes and collar there after retrieving them from the vet's office. Finally, at dusk, she placed the pot on the balcony alongside similar memorials for Peaches, Beatrix the Rabbit, and a pair of newts named Figgy and Sir Isaac. Edith the parakeet was still alive as far as she knew—living with a hairdresser named Beverly who kept her in a sunroom filled with Jesus statues—and was probably still calling everyone a turdwad. As the sky went black, she lit candles and continued to sit silently, awash in gratitude for all their little animal spirits.

By the time she returned to work, the puffiness around her eyes was no longer noticeable. She figured she could pull off any brand of mindless small talk with ease—then she ran into Shawna in the hallway.

Having spent the past four years emerging as the highest earning psychic on Mystic Partners' payroll, Shawna Van Belle also maintained a fervent personal crusade aimed at Hope, a mission designed to help her overcome her "barriers of negativity" and restore her "true nature as a spiritual Being." The advice was constant, never solicited, and often redundant, but due to the sheer supply of it, occasionally accurate.

"I have a message for you," Shawna said, stopping midstride and raising her shawl-winged arms to convey a sense of urgency. No matter the area of her proclamations, she always delivered them with the same wide-eyed conviction, like someone discovering the straightforward solution to a complex riddle.

"Lay it on me," Hope said.

Shawna turned sideways and framed the air with her hands, like a screenwriter pitching a movie title: "Grief is just another word for love."

Hope swallowed, took a step back, and collapsed onto the waiting room bench. "Wow," she said. "That's pretty, um . . . my dog just died."

Five minutes later Rush found the two of them there in the hallway, Hope still weeping in Shawna's arms. When she told him the reason for her tears, he responded by describing his wife's despondence when their cat got run over by a garbage truck. *Not helpful at all, dickhead,* she thought.

"I've actually got some kinda sad news of my own," he said.

"Oh?"

He wasn't going to be the building's maintenance man anymore, he told them. His employers/in-laws required his services at a different strip mall, anchored by a different Butter House, in a different part of town. He must have felt relieved to get that little gob of information off his chest, and grateful for not having to tell Hope in private, because he appeared much lighter as he walked away.

Shawna clearly sensed Hope's additional layer of distress following the exchange, though she'd missed countless clues about the affair's primary existence since the day it began.

"Nice guy," Shawna said, handing Hope a tissue from her purse. "But he's kinda dense, isn't he?"

Hope laughed. "Very," she agreed.

When they parted, Shawna gave Hope a special magic rock for communicating with bygone spirits. Hope kept it warm in her palms for the rest of the day and deposited it in the fern-urn when she got home.

Later, in a text message, Hope asked Rush what this change in circumstance would mean for them. The answer came instantaneously, free of any mood-hinting punctuation.

haven't really thought about it

In a flash of clarity, Hope knew Rush had no emotional investment in her whatsoever, zero, never had and never would. The epiphany didn't hurt much, though. It was almost a relief. She pictured Rush himself dissolving into a fine, benign, whispering mist. More specifically, she pictured herself pushing him through a velvet door. His absence barely made a difference.

EIGHT

The crisp, white light of reality hovered at a comfortable distance from the safe darkness below. This was Hope's favorite place to visit in her dreams; colorful coral statues delighted her eyes as the rest of her swam in easy, graceful summersaults.

Something shook her, and she grabbed the pool noodle tightly as if it could keep her tethered to the illusion. A voice echoed with tactile vibration in her right ear. "Where are we?" it demanded, and she wondered how on Earth she was supposed to answer such a vast inquiry. But the voice refused to stop pestering her. "Where are we?" it asked again, and she knew the only way to stop it was to loosen her grip and begin her ascent.

The closer she got to the crystal-glowing surface, the louder her breathing became. Each inhalation offered further proof; people couldn't breathe underwater in real life, so this wasn't real life. Embarrassment followed. *Once again, I've forgotten the fundamental facts of existence.*

Soon the voice dissolved into its real form, not a human voice but an animal one—not speaking but barking. She felt something cold and spongy on her ear, and against all the gravitational forces in her body she opened her eyes. Piggy, her new mini Australian Shepherd-Poodle mix, was standing on the pillow next to her head, wagging her tail and nudging her into coherence.

"Well, good morning, precious," Hope said, rubbing the crusty discharge from her eyes and rolling over to read the red glare of the clock. "Guess you're ready to get up, huh? Okay, just give me a minute."

The dog ran to the foot of the bed where she grabbed a plush hot dog with a squeaker inside, darted off, and ran in three consecutive circles, then returned seconds later still chomping the toy with impatience.

"Okay, I'm coming," Hope groaned. "Geez, you're kind of obnoxious sometimes." She swung her feet to the floor and grudgingly began slapping the blood flow into her own cheeks. "I love you anyway though."

7:45 was the crack of dawn to Hope but it wasn't too early for Piggy, so she was grateful her foul-breathed bedmate had let her sleep in. She started the coffeemaker and pulled on the jeans she only wore for dog-walking, a paint-splattered pair she'd owned since Peaches was the one waking her up. She mistakenly called Piggy "Peaches" from time to time, as they shared the same incessantly frantic energy. Piggy even answered to the misnomer, which proved what she'd always known about animals; they don't care who they are. They're made of pure, egoless spirit, plain and simple.

After Biscuit's death, Hope had lived a dogless existence for two weeks—the amount of time it took for her loneliness to reach critical mass. She'd wanted to make a trip to the pound the very next day to fill the void but resisted for what now seemed like ridiculous reasons. Somehow, she would have felt tacky, like those frowned-upon people who remarry weeks after their spouses die. But you can't betray someone who's dead, as the millions of animals languishing in shelters would certainly agree. Stupid humans, always getting worked up over nothing.

She still missed Biscuit, especially on these chilly mornings, getting dragged through several blocks' worth of dewy grass before the caffeine began kicking in. Even in his younger days, Biscuit would let her sleep until noon if she wanted. And in the later years, his walks consisted of no more than a lazy stroll to the vacant lot on the corner and back.

When no other life forms occupied the apartment but her own, Hope's proclivity for hoarding tended to increase exponentially. She could endure the quiet restlessness only so long before running to the thrift store for joy-tickling knickknacks. It was a craving for such useless doodads that led her to a yard sale clear over in the South Valley the day she first saw Piggy.

As soon as she parked in the gravel driveway, she feared the way her visit to the house would play out. Something about the empty fast-food wrappers stuck in the chain link fence made her doubt the homeowners would share her eclectic decorating taste. Sure enough, a quick browse along the crap-laden strip of grass comprising the house's side yard and she was already preparing to give her standard let-them-down-easy-speech ("Well I didn't find anything I can't live without today, you've got some great stuff though, I'll spread the word," etc.).

But before she could begin her spiel, a leather-faced woman emerged from a back door wearing a stained housecoat and wreaking of cigarettes, inciting an obese and filthy animal to commence yapping from a kennel Hope hadn't yet noticed.

"Shut up, Pig-dog!" the woman yelled, erasing all traces of hospitality from her face as she walked toward Hope, straightening the army jackets slung over the fence on her way. "You wouldn't be looking for a dog, would you? This one's the last of the litter. No one wants her 'cause she's too fat. We call her Miss Piggy."

The Universe can behave in tricky and enigmatic ways, but sometimes it makes its intentions known plainly. Paying attention to such moments is a skill one develops intentionally through careful practice. So went the line Hope taught phone psychics to use whenever someone challenged their insight about karmic destiny.

She hesitated, half expecting a catch. Yes, she was looking for a dog. In fact, it was all she thought about lately. And the ones no one else wanted happened to be her favorite variety.

"Um, well . . . I . . . "

A twenty-something guy in an oversized football jersey and pants fastened well below his butt emerged from the house talking on a cell phone. "The lord gave me another chance," he said. "It took me almost dyin' to see what a dirty drug meth is, know what I'm sayin'?"

Hope squatted down and peered inside the kennel at the bone-dry water dish, soggy brown kibbles, and half-eaten chicken bones. From under a mop of dreadlocks, a pointy black nose poked out through a warped spot in the cage wires while a fanned tail wagged reluctantly in the background.

"I suppose I am," she admitted. "Yes. I am looking for one of these. I'll take her."

She was glad she'd kept the name Piggy, she reflected now with pride, letting the animal take an extravagant amount of time to sniff a telephone pole in the shivery wind. It would always remind her of her companion's humble beginnings. These days Hope felt like the assistant to a canine supermodel; they couldn't go anywhere without someone saying, "What a beautiful dog," and asking Hope what breed she was. And Hope never missed a chance to brag about her own role in Piggy's transformation, especially how she'd started her on a homemade vegan diet with the help of a local canine nutritionist. It was ironic; if she saw Piggy at a shelter today, she would probably pass her by in favor of some less conventionally adorable prospect.

The humans in Hope's life also tended to be of the "not wanted by anyone else" variety. Speculating about possible reasons for this incited all kinds of knotty analytical unpleasantness; she hated to think of herself as one of those martyr-like do-gooders who sees every relationship as a project. More than likely, she related to outcasts because she'd always felt like one herself. But is it fair to call yourself an outcast when you exile yourself from social groups intentionally? Perhaps her affinity for rejects stemmed from the same character trait moving her to only shop in thrift stores; she just hated to see anything go to waste.

When it came to eldercare work, her part-time status at Enchanted Hands meant she often got stuck with the clients whose caregivers cancelled on them a lot—in other words, the geriatrics no one else wanted. On her way to these gigs, she would mentally prepare by imagining herself encased in bulletproof glass. Meanwhile, she would maintain an earnest aspiration for a miraculous breakthrough, a chance to prove herself a prodigy of human connection. Like her other noble daydreams, this one frequently led to imaginary talk show appearances.

They'd warned her about Gwendola Andersen. Colleagues had armed her with a useful bag of tricks for dealing with her many eccentricities. "Don't ever call her Gwen or Gwendolyn," they'd said. "*Gwendola* is a made-up name she gave herself ten years ago after it came to her in a dream. It means strength reaped from sorrow or something, and if you screw it up she thinks it puts a curse on her day." Calling her the right name sounded easy enough. But then you also had to intercept her mail and throw away anything addressed to her pre-dream name. You couldn't just throw it in the trash either, you had to take it all the way out of the building and off the property because if she found it she would completely lose her shit.

Saying "Gwendola" also worked as a soothing mechanism, and looking her in the eye and delivering a firm "Okay, Gwendola" could buy a minute of silence in the midst of one of her frequent meltdowns. This Hope figured out herself the first time she worked with the woman, now over a year ago, after Gwendola went all wacky over a missing can opener and blamed the former caregiver.

She owned several other can openers, Hope had made the mistake of pointing out. But each one was assigned to a specific type of food vessel, Gwendola had explained, her agitation escalating. This prevented cross-contamination. Such rules were a product of her obsessive-compulsive disorder. "When my household harmony gets disrupted, I can't function!"

"Okay, Gwendola."

Obsessive compulsives were supposed to be immaculate housekeepers, or at least that's what Hope had always thought, but Gwendola's apartment looked like a post-apocalyptic flea market. She made art from found objects, and evidence of her manic creative spirts lined every exposed surface, remnants of them floating through the air in sneeze-inducing fairy poofs. "Not all OCD sufferers are anal-retentive clean freaks," she snapped at Hope once, apropos of nothing. "My Fibromyalgia makes daily cleaning tasks a challenge for me."

For someone who looked fine, Gwendola boasted an impressive list of medical conditions, all of them hard to prove and each providing a convenient excuse for some peculiar want or character defect. Acknowledging these illnesses was another effective negotiation tool, one Hope excelled at using. But the main reason Gwendola consistently requested Hope over all other caregivers was this: Hope knew underneath it all, the woman just wanted to be listened to. Listening to people makes them feel valued. If there was one piece of wisdom fifteen years of horsecrap psychic practices at a place like Mystic Partners could teach a person, it was that.

Mystic Partners also deserved credit for helping Hope develop a thick skin and a high tolerance for other peoples' suffering. But even bullet-proof glass isn't totally impenetrable. Gwendola finally broke through hers one gray November afternoon during a planned bathroom-cleaning frenzy.

They were going through her extensive collection of toiletries one by one and separating them into three boxes: keep, toss, and donate. The "donate" box was intended for products received as gifts and never opened, products which Gwendola claimed to have many of. But midway through the second drawer, unopened containers were ending up in the "toss" box because of a sticky film smelling of rancid vanilla saturating all their paper labels. In the rear depths of the top right drawer, Hope discovered the culprit; a shampoo-sized red plastic bottle with "Sweet Love" printed on it, the font reminiscent of 80s home perms. She studied it for a moment, reckoning it to be some sort of sexual lubricant. Apparently, it came from a time when marketing pros thought romance-infused labelling would lure in their sexually liberated consumers; nowadays they know the opposite to be true. Nowadays such items bore names like EZ-Grind.

Gwendola said to put it in the "keep" box, then snapped "Don't you dare look at me like that!" as soon as Hope's eyes met hers. "I'm entitled to a private life, you know."

"Okay, Gwendola."

"I may not have had sex for a couple of years . . . okay, maybe twenty years, but it doesn't mean I'm celibate for life. In fact, a nice-looking man approached me at the bus stop the other day. He asked for my phone number, and I would have given it to him, but the problem, you see, is . . . " She rubbed her eyes and then threw two clenched fists in the air, shaking. "Dammit! Why do you insist on making me justify myself! The problem, if you can try to understand it, if you're capable of understanding anything at all outside of your own privileged little self-centered universe, is it's hard to work a sex life in with the constraints imposed by my—"

"Chronic Fatigue Syndrome?" Hope ventured.

"Chronic fatigue is a small part of it, yes," Gwendola said, a calm veneer barely masking half her rage. "You know my red dress, Hope? The one in my closet with the purple sequins? The one you're always eyeing and are for sure gonna steal the minute I turn my goddamned back? I used to love to go dancing and—" Suddenly she stopped shaking and the veins in her forehead subsided. She looked like she was about to burst into guttural sobs, and Hope steeled herself for the consoling hug she'd soon be expected to administer.

Instead of the outburst, there came a resigned sideways smile—a sort of "Oh, well" expression—and instead of a deluge, only one single tear.

"I might still go dancing," she shrugged.

"Okay, Gwendola."

Leaving Gwendola's apartment after her shift that night, Hope did not feel pride over the unlikely connection she'd forged with her client. What she felt was horror, sheer horror at having glimpsed a possible future version of herself. She knew about Chronic Fatigue Syndrome not from Gwendola, but from a recent late-night internet search she'd conducted on her own mélange of mysterious symptoms. And come to think of it, she probably did have a half-used bottle of EZ-Grind gunking up a long-ignored drawer at this very moment.

She walked briskly to her car which happened to be in the darkest corner of the parking garage, a sufficiently dungeon-like atmosphere for her spooked mindset. In the car she sat for several minutes, clutching her cell phone as if it were a space-age gizmo able to beam her into another dimension. She turned on the engine and cranked the roaring heater to the widest part of its red indicator line; she wasn't cold, just craving warmth. From the glove compartment, she retrieved her vile of homebrewed herbal anti-anxiety tincture. As several droppers of it fell on her eager tongue, she considered how if ever such medicinal flora were found to cause cancer, she probably wouldn't give them up.

The entire drive home she worked diligently on composing the text message she would send when she got there. Contact with Nathan having gone silent for over a year now, the note would have to be a masterpiece: playfully affectionate, inciting a response without coming off as too needy. She pictured him stopping to read it in the middle of a busy day as he ran several hotel kitchens simultaneously, juggling clipboards while harried wait staff swooshed by him in white uniforms. Then again, he might also hear the ping while playing a video game in pizza-stained sweatpants; she didn't actually know what his life looked like these days. Increasing work demands had been blamed for the decline in phone call frequency over the years, by both sides; she'd made her workload sound bigger than it really was, perhaps he'd done the same. She now looked back with deep regret at the times she'd let his calls go to voicemail while preening herself in the mirror, preparing for Rush's quick and disgusting maintenance calls.

At the tree-lined curb of her own building, she rolled down the window and leaned back in her seat. The crisp air from outside tickled her face and she sensed her optimism slowly returning. But she couldn't leave the car before sending the message; if she let this moment's urgency pass, she might put off the important deed forever. She scrolled through her photo gallery and selected a priceless shot of Piggy looking comically reluctant in a silver dragon costume she'd found at a yard sale.

Psychic head-honchos say I have to get a webcam, she typed beneath the image. *Any suggestions what kind? I don't trust those orange-shirted fools at Computer City. Thought I'd ask a real tech wiz—*

The mechanical ding shook her phone sooner than expected, just after she'd thrown her red plaid poncho on the floor and sunk into a pile of clean laundry on the couch. But her excitement faded when she saw the screen: Rush's name, along with the symbol indicating a photo attachment.

Just woke up from a dream about you, it read, and she opened the photo tentatively; she'd learned never to open pictures from him without a quick glance over her shoulder to make sure no one else could see it, and the habit stuck even when she was alone. Just as expected, it showed him lying back proudly with his swollen cock in his hand, smiling as if it were a bouquet.

Must have been some dream, she typed back. She couldn't help but chuckle a little at his coincidental timing. Putting one's intentions out into the Universe can result in frightfully scrambled signals sometimes.

Will you send me an artistic picture back? Pleeeease?

"Artistic" was a code word for naked the two used back when their affair was in full swing, and Rush continued to treat her to his artistic offerings on a regular basis even though she hadn't reciprocated in over two years. It had become somewhat of a comedy routine between them, her remaining aloof and out-of-reach while he pestered her with ever-increasing determination. She knew she would never give in but still hoped he would never give up.

Okay, she replied, *just a minute.*

Again she scrolled through her photo gallery, this time selecting a selfie she'd taken in a fluorescent-lit kitchenette wearing a homemade Jackelope costume she'd put together for the office Halloween party.

Ooh, baby, he responded after she'd sent it. *They should give you a raise. I'm sure getting one.*

Showing him her Halloween costume referenced another of their inside jokes. He and his wife did corny couple costumes every year and Hope always mocked him relentlessly about them. ("What's it gonna be this year? Peanut butter and jelly? Mickey and Minnie? The right shoe and the left shoe? Cause you're such a perfect match?") If he showed her any pictures, she would smile and nod approvingly, feigning genuine appreciation for a second. "That's actually kinda cute," she would say, right before excusing herself and making dramatized puking sounds. He always had a ready comeback though, a rebound so easy it almost wasn't fair; he would inquire as to which obscure outfit she'd spent hours creating only to scrap all the party plans and stay home with her dog.

The rest of the exchange played out the way they always did; Rush reminded her of his enduring availability should her "equipment" ever need "servicing," and Hope assured him that, while she'd gotten pretty good at maintaining the equipment herself, she might still require his services someday. He never seemed to mind the constant rejection. In fact, she got the feeling if she ever became so pathetically horny as to call him on one of his bluffs, he would probably shrink away from the offer. Desire, she'd read in some ridiculous self-help book once, needs distance in order to thrive.

The phone went on the charger then, its volume turned off with a vow from Hope not to look at it again until morning. For now, she no longer felt panicked. Leave it to Rush to show up with a temporary ego fix. In transactions like these, negotiations involving delicate emotions like desire and self-worth, it makes sense to quit while you're ahead.

She fed Piggy and then turned on the TV and clicked straight to her favorite guilty pleasure, a raunchy true-crime show called *Deadly*

Longings. She'd seen tonight's episode before at least three times, so she knew it was a good one; a sociopathic high school teacher poisons the slutty cheerleader who has seduced her awkward football coach lover. This show never failed to act as a healing salve for moods like this. It eased Hope's suffering tremendously to know her own longings—no matter how unpleasant—still fell far from the category of deadly.

When Nathan did respond three days later, he asked her to call him on the following Sunday afternoon when he would have "fewer distractions," and by the time the designated hour rolled around, she'd all but forgotten why she reached out to him in the first place. She knew she was a bundle of nerves but didn't know why. Nothing was at stake, after all. She prepared for the call by slipping into a tee shirt he'd left at her old duplex ten years earlier, just before he moved to Seattle. It featured an armband rimmed with native Northwestern tribal art, and she liked to pretend it still smelled like him. A quote popped into her mind as she began entering his number into her phone. She attributed this quote to Brooks Nixon for some reason, though it could have just as easily come from a fortune cookie: "Love, like death, is no big deal."

"Hey, Crotch Rocket."

"What's up, Pool Noodle."

It was a good thing she didn't have to feign interest in his webcam advice for too long. She'd forgotten all about the pretense, and her lack of readiness to discuss image sensors and microphone circuitry probably showed. Answers to the questions she really cared about— like how much he'd thought about her in recent years—were dealt with in sublimely short order.

Five minutes in, he started reminiscing about the first time he'd noticed her, more than a decade ago now. She'd been sitting on a bench eating curly fries from a greasy paper bag and lazily allowing her two leashed dogs to lick the salt and residue from her fingers. "A scruffy-ass girl with two scruffy-ass dogs," he said, "just rockin' out with her headphones on, oblivious to the world and not giving a fuck about anything. I thought, man, I gotta meet this human."

Midway through the call, he started cursing at what he explained to be an army of tiny ants swarming a piece of croissant he'd dropped on the floor. "Sorry, little fellas," he said over the hissing sound of aerosol bug spray. "Don't take it personally, it's just—you irritate me. But your next life will be much better. I promise."

"Since when do you apologize to ants?" Hope asked.

"I don't usually," he confessed, chuckling. "I just didn't want you to think I'm a heartless S.O.B."

"I wouldn't harbor a preposterous belief like that for one second," she assured him.

His idea for her to drive up to Washington for a visit came up with alarming breeziness. He told her he was catering a wedding at the hotel's newest location—south of Seattle in a town called Fort Brandon—and he thought the venue would provide a perfect setting for their long-overdue reunion. "I love it down there," he said. "It's free of . . . you know, distractions."

She stopped biting her nails when she heard this, stood up and smiled into the sun-framed mirror in her dresser. "I'll consult my pendulum," she said, reviving an old joke from her early days as a phony psychic-in-training.

* * *

HOPE STILL HADN'T READ *VEILED MISERY*, at least not in its entirety. Bits of chapters had gotten absorbed in the process of sorting through her bookshelf and deciding which titles to purge. She would pick it up and open it at random, deciding after a few sentences not to toss it just yet. It might come in handy someday, she would reason.

Countless self-help gurus, including this one, have burnt themselves out trying to give people a magic formula for winning another's devotion. What if, instead of worrying about controlling one another, we each focused more on our own levels of commitment? When I use the word commitment here, I'm not talking about making hollow promises borne out of a sense of obligation. I am talking about something I call "Super Star Excellence." What is Super Star Excellence, you ask? Bear with me while I explain myself.

I once spent several months visiting some relatives of my mother's in Sapporo, Japan, and an uncle I'd just met there introduced me to his complex new high-tech karaoke system. The Song Joy 8,000 had a fascinating scoring system; there was one measurement for pitch, one for lyrical accuracy, and a third for commitment. At the end of your performance, one of four messages would flash across the screen: *need more effort, not bad, great job, or super star excellent.* Now, I'm barely vocally competent enough to sing happy birthday to someone, much less to belt out the Whitney Houston number my uncle Enji cued up for me. But after an afternoon's practice, I eventually reached Super Star Excellence level with my wildly shrill rendition of "I Wanna Dance with Somebody." It was a revelation. I found the experience so instructive that I had Enji order me my own Song Joy 8,000. I needed this technology in my life.

You see, the machine had taught me something important. Singing—like many endeavors, writing self-help books among them—is ninety percent listening. As Uncle Enji put it, "Instead of thinking about how you sound, simply unite with the music." He paraphrased a Zen saying for me. "When you can't control something, relax and become one with it."

When you experience new love, try approaching it in this manner; pretend it's a song you've started involuntarily tapping your feet to. Forget society's illusory constraints. Ignore the moralizing of the fear-hearted masses. Focus on the music you're hearing right here, right now. Practice Super Star Excellence, no matter how foolish you feel doing so. I can't predict the outcome, but I will promise you one thing: you'll never settle for Needs More Effort again.

* * *

GETTING THREE DAYS OFF WORK WOULD have been so much easier if Delma was still her boss. The woman never failed to accept Hope's flimsy excuses without questioning them, and probably would've even encouraged her plan to visit an old boyfriend knowing it was the same old boyfriend who'd given her rides to the nursing home all those years ago. The two of them could have reminisced about the old days. But Delma was semi-retired now and only showed up for the important meetings. The rest of the time she oversaw the remodeling of a palatial Malibu house bought with the tears of desperate believers.

Delma's replacement, Connie Chi, was all business. "She doesn't fuck around," Hope warned Nathan. "If I'm gonna take three days off without putting in an official request for it, I'd better have a damn good reason."

"*Connie Chi?*" Nathan repeated, apparently finding humor in the name. "Sounds like Cottage Cheese." Then he drew from his own experience as a manager to advise her on how to deal with the situation. "Just tell Cottage Cheese you're visiting a decade-long client who's sick," he said. "It's not a lie; you've done readings on me before, and I *did* have a pretty bad case of the sniffles earlier. It'll look like you're going the extra mile for customer loyalty. Managers love that."

"What if she wants more details?"

"She won't. Trust me."

Looking back now as she drove up the Pacific Coast Highway, with Piggy riding shotgun and a homemade CD mix labeled "Cruisin'" blaring away from the stereo, she couldn't believe how easily Connie Chi bought it. All the events leading to this weirdly exhilarating time and place were hard to believe, come to think of it. Why now, she wondered, after all these years of his never mentioning a visit in anything but the most abstract terms? Since his grandparents' quick successive deaths eight years ago, he'd lacked any reason to come to San Lazaro except to see her, and he always claimed work demands made this impossible. She'd brought up her coming to Seattle once or twice, but his less-than-warm welcomes had scared her from ever mentioning it again. "Sure," he'd said, "You'll love it here if you like paying eight dollars for a cup of coffee."

Hope didn't know what she'd done right to make him act this way, but she didn't care. It felt so good to be speeding toward the center of the riddle. She reached over to give Piggy a scratch behind the ears as the beginning notes of her favorite song on the CD—"Thousand Pepper Love" by Wasted Grave—began to play.

> *Your crystal eyes remind me*
> *Of another lost soul I knew*
> *The memory burns like a thousand fiery peppers*
> *Each time I look at you*

The tempo tripled for the chorus and Hope always began bobbing her head to it automatically despite knowing how stupid she looked doing so. Then it spiraled into weird jazzy configurations for the bridge. This was the best part of the song:

> *A thousand swollen noises shattering*
> *like bleak red hungry throw-pillows*

But the ending was where it all came together. This is where lead singer Victor Vex's pure songwriting genius really shone through.

> *Yeah yeah I close my eyes*
> *And the face emerges*
> *That thousand-pepper love*
> *I saw it only once*
> *Long ago*
> *Reflected in the silvery pool*

Funny how you can hear the same song a billion times and always interpret it a different way. Her father always managed to find veiled drug references in Wasted Grave music when she was a teenager, and sometimes even now she wondered if he could have been onto something—even though he knew even less about drug culture than Hope herself did. But then sometimes a song speaks to you on such an intimate level it's hard to believe its author didn't have your every nuanced emotion from that exact moment in time in mind when they wrote it. If she ever did meet Victor Vex, she decided as she coasted down a hill and through a thickening fog, she would like to ask him about the reflection in the silvery pool and what it meant.

*   *   *

THE TOWN OF FORT BRANDON WAS lush and rustic with old-growth evergreens and cute log cabins. She didn't know what to expect with the hotel; the one Nathan worked at in San Lazaro offered little in the way of character. This one featured a totem pole with a bear at the top in the large circle drive, an encouraging sign; bears symbolize renewal, as well as fierce protection of the things one holds dear. The only advance research she'd done on the place was to make sure they allowed dogs, and as she parked the car it hit her just how little about this whole trip she'd made clear in advance. She didn't know, for example, whether she and Nathan would stay in the same room or not. Come to think of it, she didn't even know whether to expect an amorous reunion or a platonic one. She assumed the former, but when she searched her mind for proof, she could think of none. Piggy barked to announce their arrival as they approached the front desk. It was made of reclaimed wood and there were bookshelves made of vintage suit-cases lining the wall next to it. She took an instant liking to the laid-back vibe.

The minute they got to the room, as Piggy ruffled the patchwork bedspread with her muddy paws, Nathan called.

"I'm here" she said. "Room 511. Where are you?"

"512."

"No way!"

"Way."

She thought her head might explode from the serendipity of it. "Do you wanna come here or should I go there?" she asked him. "Never mind. I'll go there. If you come here, the dog will freak out and I won't get to hug you."

He'd put on weight since she last saw him, but also bulked up in the shoulders. His shaved head admitted to a receding hairline. She smiled approvingly at the changes.

His cell phone started ringing, the ringtone set on the theme from Miami Vice.

"Do you need to get that?"

"Nah. Fuck 'em."

She could see the screen said Heather.

"It's Heather," she informed him flatly, and he jumped back and looked at her like he'd seen a ghost. He promptly took the call, disappeared onto the balcony and shut the door. When he came back he was saying, "Uh-huh. Okay. You, too. Bye."

Hope didn't say another word about the call because she knew he didn't like being bugged about stuff like that. He raised his eyebrows and clasped his hands together as if he'd just gone through some kind of total system reset. "Wanna go for a walk?" he asked.

Piggy's floppy ears perked up at the familiar words.

"You got *someone's* attention," Hope giggled. "Sure. Sounds fun."

Mountain bikes whizzed by them as they traversed the edge of a moss-covered pond. Nathan's side of the conversation contained very few specifics, but the overall tone of it was one of overwhelming frustration. There was so much to do and so little time, and he admitted to feeling "trapped like a lab rat." He seemed to want her to free him somehow, but all she could do was reach into her back catalogue of stock lines and pull one out.

"Well, you don't really *have* to do anything in life except die and pay taxes," she said. "And the taxes part is open to debate. I know many people who've gotten around that one." It was one of many unsuccessful attempts she made to change the subject.

Eventually the path wound up at a misty gray beach where, in a small patch of sand, some previous visitor had built a teepee out of tie-died sheets. "Come in," read a small sign taped above the entrance. Nathan was the first one brave enough to crawl inside. Two minutes later, he came out smiling.

Hope handed over the dog leash and took her turn; inside the tie-dye light prism lay several sheets of paper on a clipboard, along with a pen wrapped with crystals and a big feather. The top of the page said "Thoughts?" And there was a note in Nathan's hand-writing, a quote from some dead philosopher, followed by a compliment for the project's architect. ("Cool Idea. Wish I'd thought of it.")

After struggling in vain to come up with something original, Hope wrote "A thousand swollen noises shattering like bleak red hungry throw-pillows."

By the time they got back, a brilliant blue spotlight brightened the suddenly bewitching totem pole. Nathan had spent much of the walk hyping up the vegan dinner he planned to have made—he'd even arranged to the have the night off so they could have room service and eat together on the balcony. *Super Star Excellence*, she had heard herself think.

But as she fussed with the key card at the door to her room, he made a short, pained grunting sound. She turned around to see him looking at his cell phone and rubbing his temples. "I'm sorry," he said. "I'm gonna hafta bail on dinner. Apparently, being married means you're not supposed to have a life of your own."

"Wait, you're married?" she asked with far less alarm than the situation merited.

"Looks that way," he offered with a pathetic shrug and a weird sideways smile.

Why she didn't punch him in the face right then would forever haunt her as one of life's great unanswerable questions. Fortunately, she didn't have any girlfriends in whom she regularly confided the details of her intimate relationships; they would've surely made her feel like a betrayer of all womankind for her wimpy reaction. But Nathan had never actually lied to her. He'd simply omitted a fact. He'd spoken to her in vague terms and allowed her to believe whatever she wanted to believe, just like a highly skilled phone psychic would.

"I see," she said, trying not to act crestfallen. "Well, do I still get the butter squash quinoa casserole and asparagus with cashew sauce?"

He smiled with relief. "Of course," he said. "I'll have them sent up right away."

Eating alone was much more relaxing anyway. She savored the sumptuous feast—which Nathan paid for—from a precarious table made of the pillows on the bed, tossing bits of bread into Piggy's bowl as she rewatched an old episode of *Murderous Yearnings* on the true crime channel. In this episode, a widowed stockbroker kills himself and his two young children after discovering the Ukrainian long-distance lover he'd been sending money to didn't actually exist. Hope was glad she didn't have any murderous yearnings. She prided herself on her ability to discern fantasy from reality, and thankfully, her reality contained just enough simple pleasures not to arouse relentless soul-screams of lack from inside her.

What made less sense though—what would be harder to explain to her imaginary girlfriends at their imaginary champagne breakfast tomorrow—was why she still slept with him later that night. Why she let him in when he knocked on her door just before 1 a.m. with whiskey on his breath, just as she'd settled into a comfortable half-sleep beneath the tightly tucked hotel blankets. Why she listened to his tedious and questionable tale of woe—how his wife, a British national, had tricked him by claiming she only needed a marriage certificate for work status purposes and then used it to make claims on his affection, how she'd threatened to expose him for seducing her when she worked as a waitress under his command, how good waitresses were hard to come by and blah, blah, blah.

After all this unburdening, Nathan admitted to still having fantasized about Hope on a regular basis for the last ten plus years, even during long periods of no contact. And Hope responded— God knows why—by placing her forefinger under his chin and pulling him toward her for a high-octane, open-mouthed kiss.

Married people cheat on their spouses every day, according to statistics. The most recent study Hope had seen showed more than a third of them did, and that was just the ones who would admit to it. Why did everyone always act so freaking appalled by something so commonplace? This is what Hope would say to her outwardly shocked girlfriends, and they'd probably laugh and high-five her in the moment and then call her a slut the minute her back was turned. Good thing she didn't have real girlfriends.

But the biggest rationale was something much simpler. Not having sex for almost two years will cause a woman in the prime of her life to panic and make less-than-stellar choices. "Born again virgin" is a label no one wants to carry around with them for long, and no one should have to.

"It's like going to a Mexican Restaurant," she told Asher three days later as they wandered around a discount home-décor store looking for rugs for his new apartment, borrowing Jack Cohen's old metaphor. "When you're all hungry and your food hasn't come yet and they put those chips on the table in front of you. It's impossible not to eat them, you know?"

"Makes perfect sense to me," her brother nodded, squinting at the price tag of a ceramic vase he'd just grabbed from a shelf. After reading it he shook his head in disbelief and placed the vessel back delicately.

"Let's face it," he said. "We're both cursed in the sex department."

Hope laughed out loud at his remark, recalling the story of the last date he'd tried to bring home. As soon as she'd seen his old efficiency apartment, the girl had gone all pale. She'd then made a show of looking at her phone, which wasn't even turned on, taken a couple of steps backward, said something about needing some air, and never returned. In consequence, he'd resigned himself to moving, enlisting Hope's help to find more "adult" accommodation.

"Aw, it's not that bad," Hope said. "Once you get the new place fixed up, you'll be a regular chick magnet."

"Speaking of which," Asher said, pausing and pointing at a staged bedroom display, "why do women always have so damn many pillows on their beds?"

"I don't know."

He furrowed his brow. "So, if I put a ton of pillows on my bed, would more women sleep with me?"

She pretended to consider the question for a second. "Hmm . . . I'm going to say no on that one. Anyway, we're here for rugs, so let's focus. I think they're on the second floor."

On the escalator, as the Muzak version of a 70s funk jam tried to pipe in a sense of whimsy, Hope saw a familiar face pass them on the downward stair lane. After running through her mind's database of images, it hit her: the out-of-place preppy dude from the Apeshit show at the scooter shop. He looked a little scruffier around the edges now, but it was doubtlessly him. She nudged Asher and pointed at the back of the man's descending head just as he, too, did a double-take. "Hey isn't that your drug counselor from—"

Asher quickly looked away. "I don't talk to him anymore," he said flatly.

He seemed distracted all through the rug selection process—they settled on a flashy faux sheepskin and two generic Orientals—and when they got to the car and started loading their purchases into the hatchback, she broached the subject again.

"So why don't you talk to what's-his-nuts anymore?" she asked.

He made a revolting throat sound and spit into the corner of the parking garage. "Who, Desmond? It's a long story." Once in the car he clapped his hands together and rubbed them vigorously, conveying his firm determination not to tell the long story now.

"What ya got going on this weekend?" he asked her.

She turned around to push down the fluffy plush rug so she could see out the back while she reversed. "I'm going to a book signing at Blankenship Brothers, remember? Victor Vex's memoir!"

He rolled his eyes. "Oh, yeah."

Luminous Doom was the only book Hope ever bought on the day of its release and read in a single one-night sitting. Though the book itself proved an abysmal disappointment—little more than a bitter rehashing of old record industry grudges—she still jumped at the chance to meet her favorite teen idol in person.

"You sure you don't wanna come?"

He rolled down the window and shook his head. "Sounds depressing, man," he said.

She reached for the radio but switched it off immediately after it hissed a burst of ear-splitting punk-rock through a shitstorm of static.

"Hey, that sounded good," Asher joked. "Why'd ya turn it off?"

"Here," she said, handing him some discarded tinfoil from an old piece of carrot cake. "Chew on this instead."

Outside the garage they drove straight into a downpour, and as Hope struggled with her car's half-gnarled windshield wiper control, she asked him what he planned to do with his weekend.

"Oh, I'll probably just get a bucket of fried chicken and watch porn," he said.

She nodded with deadpan acceptance. "That doesn't sound depressing at all."

When Hope first learned Blankenship Brothers' Books would be taking over the sad shell of a defunct Jordan Marsh store on the outskirts of town, she signed a petition against it. "Big Brother Censorship," as some called it, represented everything she despised about corporate America and she'd feared how its presence would affect her beloved Chapterhouse. But eight years later, she'd made peace with the soulless, capitalism-driven behemoth. They had an awesome clearance bin. She'd once got a green satin journal with art nouveaux fairies on the pages for two dollars. And now she could cite a new reason not to hate them: they'd used their corporate clout for good by getting Victor Vex to do a book signing there.

She arrived an hour before the advertised time, clutching her copy of *Luminous Doom* and expecting to fight her way through an eager crowd of black-shrouded fans. But she was surprised to see the place looking no busier than it would any other Saturday night. She walked around the store's perimeter, trying to act casual but feeling foolish, like the first guest to show up at a party. At last she found the gift-paper wrapped table she presumed would soon host the guest of honor. Keeping it safely in her peripheral vision, she headed to the knickknack section to read all the snarky fridge magnets.

Across the aisle from her in the horror section, she spotted the back of an olive-green jacket and instantly recognized it as belonging to Asher's mysterious frenemy from the home décor store and the scooter shop. Desmond was chuckling to himself while skimming a graphic novel called *Dumpster Fetus Returns*. There was something comfortingly familiar about his peculiar kind of gawkiness; he reminded her of a theater geek she knew in high school who used to help her cheat on her algebra tests.

In the store's center, where all the aisles met, there stood a round desk with a tall plastic lamppost in the center and the word "Information" circling its parameter. A young woman with a tight mousy-brown ponytail stood inside it, looking half asleep as she scrolled down a computerized stock list taking notes. From out of nowhere a stalky man in a tight black suit approached. His too-short trousers curtained a surprising pair of bright red socks that flashed when he leaned over the desk to ask a question; when the salesgirl pointed in Hope's direction—the direction of the giftwrapped table—his matching red ascot also announced itself. Something about him reminded Hope of a circus freak. He looked at his watch, nodded, then meandered—more like strutted—to the children's book section.

Desmond appeared intrigued by the man, too; he watched him all the way to the plastic play cube and then put down his book and approached the information desk.

"Is that Victor Vex?" he asked, his voice a little bit louder and more urgent than those normally heard in bookstores.

The salesgirl picked up a clipboard and frowned over it before answering, matching his inappropriate decibel level. "Um, I didn't catch his name . . . he's tonight's guest author and . . . yes."

Hope's belly erupted in a fit of ticklish joy. "Oh, my god," she blurted out involuntarily in a voice louder than both of theirs combined. Then, embarrassed, she tiptoed over to them as if moving stealthily would make up for the outburst. "I didn't recognize him," she said in a near-whisper to Desmond, "without all his makeup and hair product."

"I'm friends with him on MyFacade," Desmond beamed. Hope had only vague knowledge of the social media platform—she barely knew what a social media platform was in general—but the idea of Desmond's being "friends" with such a legend in any capacity impressed her regardless.

"I found out he has a personal page under his real name," Desmond explained, still not clarifying anything. "His real name isn't Victor Vex, it's—"

"Jax Williams," Hope interrupted, not to be out-fanned. He'd released a solo project independently under the name Jax Williams in 1998. Copies of *Shimmering Choke Dance* were rare, but she owned two.

"That's what most people think," Desmond said, coughing into his fist. "But I got to know him through a horror film chat room. His *real* real name is William French."

"Cool," Hope said, leaning on the info desk with both forearms, suddenly painfully aware of what every single part of her body was doing. She shifted her gaze over to Victor, whose nose was now buried in a large colorful pop-up book called *Bunny Likes to Run*. "There's something about him, isn't there," she said. "I mean, even before I recognized him. He's just got a certain . . . "

"Irreverence?" Desmond offered.

"Totally," Hope said, adding, "His spirit animal must be skunk."

Desmond looked puzzled for a second, then nodded as if he completely understood her. They both moved slowly to a bench near the wall, watching him closely as if he might suddenly flee like an antelope.

"I've loved his music since I was 13," Hope said. "It's kinda hard to believe he wrote that book though."

"Indeed," Desmond agreed. "So bitter and petty. Holding grudges is such a terrible way to waste one's energy. But then, he *didn't* write it, did he? A ghostwriter did. He probably just needed the income. I mean, Wasted Grave haven't put out an album or toured since—"

"1997," Home chimed in, eager to prove she could carry her end of the conversation.

Two bookstore employees emerged from a camouflaged door carrying large cardboard boxes, and Desmond's posture sprang into alertness. "It's almost go time," he said as copies of *Luminous Doom* were stacked on the table and a maze of velvet ropes was set up to direct the queue formation. He didn't wait to receive permission; as soon as Victor sauntered up to his post behind the table, he took two giant steps over the ropes and extended his hand in introduction.

"Hello, William," he said. "It's me, Billy Bloodlust 71. Your old pal from the Slasherfans chatrooms. I brought you a gift." He opened his blazer and for a split-second Hope feared he might pull out a gun and execute the guy; given the surreal implausibility of this whole evening, it wouldn't have shocked her much at all. He pulled out an old VHS tape and placed it on the table. Hope couldn't make heads or tails of the words on its cover—they appeared to be in German—but whatever it was, it made Victor's tired eyes brighten like sunflowers.

"Aw, that's brilliant," he beamed. "Thanks a lot, mate."

Desmond returned his hands to his pants pockets, clearly pleased with himself. "Now, I know you didn't write this appalling drivel," he said, pointing to the stack on the table, "But I'd be honored if you'd sign a copy for me anyway."

"Sure thing, friend."

Victor—or William, or Jax, or whatever his name was—sat nodding and smiling at the video in his hand for a couple of seconds more before grabbing a hardcover from the top of the stack. Then he leaned back in his chair and tapped the pen against his cheek, looking at the ceiling. After some forethought he began scribbling, keeping most of his face hidden by the book but raising his eyebrows coyly from behind it.

When he finished, he pulled the book down over his chest and held it there for a couple of seconds, grinning to build suspense before placing it on the table.

"Voila!"

Hope leaned in behind Desmond but could barely make out the image: some type of animal with a huge belly, wearing a crown and sitting upright—human style—with two smaller animals at his side. He'd signed the masterpiece in his nom de plume, Victor Vex.

"It's my cat, Sherman," he explained, his vivid imagination churning behind his eyes like a child's. "He's the king of his feral domain and those are his loyal cat-toy servants."

"Brilliant," Desmond said, nodding with his whole upper body as he moved aside to let Hope have her turn.

As Hope took a tentative step forward, everything she'd planned to ask him vanished from her mind. All her brain's resources converged on the task of not staring; seeing him in person was like seeing every mythical creature populating the ether—a unicorn, a Yeti, the tooth fairy—all rolled into one.

"It's an honor to meet you, sir," she said, handing over her book. "I've loved your music since I was thirteen years old."

He bowed to her in thanks, then said, "That makes me feel bloody ancient!" as he waved his pen in the air for dramatic effect.

"You look exactly the same as you did then," Hope offered, giggling nervously.

He took almost as long to sign her book as he did Desmond's, and when he gave it back to her she could hardly believe her luck; he'd drawn the same cat, sans crown, holding a mirror and gazing pensively at his own reflection. "The fairest of the feral cats," he beamed.

She pressed her hands together in a praying gesture. "He sure is," she said. "I love him. Thank you."

By now a decent-sized line snaked out from behind them, so Hope and Desmond took their prized doodles and returned to the bench by the wall to marvel quietly.

"Well, that was amazing," Hope stated in a drab tone meant to mock the comment's obviousness.

"A little bit," Desmond chuckled.

She'd wondered this whole time if he recognized her—knew of her association with Asher—and whether she should mention her recognizing of him. To her relief he made the first move and introduced himself, writing is phone number on a Blankenship Brothers events calendar he'd picked up. He said he could show her William French's MyFacade page, which featured photographs of Sherman the cat. His computer sucked right now, he demurred, blaming viruses from illegal file sharing, but they could use the one at his job.

"Where do you work?"

"Maxine's. It's a café on Fourth and Vine. I wait tables there part-time."

Hope's stomach dropped. She knew the place well—she'd passed it at least a dozen times in the past month in fact—as Asher's new apartment building faced its entrance from one side. For a second she clung to the faint possibility of this not being the same dude from the escalator and the scooter shop, but the chances of his having a doppelgänger with the same first name were too remote. If she were to see him again, which she wanted to, she might have to betray her own flesh and blood.

But she'd cross that bridge when she came to it. For now, she thanked her new friend with a heart-felt hug. No point in ruining the strange perfection of this night by creating unnecessary worry; after all, maybe the reason for the rift between the two men wasn't too serious. Maybe they'd simply drifted apart.

Two days later she got a phone call at 10 p.m. from the county jail. It was Asher asking meekly if she could come bail him out. He was being held on an assault charge. She drove to the jail first thing the next morning, no questions asked.

"Remember my old drug counselor from the state penitentiary?" he asked her as they went through a fast-food drive-through on the way home.

"You assaulted *him?*"

"Him first, then another guy who tried to stop me. That's who pressed charges. Shoulda just quit while I was ahead."

"Jesus Christ, bro," Hope sighed, hanging her head in a carefully measured show of disappointment. She wanted to ask about the severity of Desmond's injuries but stopped herself short; if she let him tell the whole story without judging him, he would get there eventually. She pulled into a parking lot next to the burger joint and cut the engine but left the heat on.

"All right," she said, turning to face him as he scarfed down a smelly chicken sandwich. "Tell me the story. What do you have against this ex-counselor of yours?"

"Not much to tell," he said, pausing to suck the straw of an over-sized soda cup and wipe his mouth. "Buddy broke the code."

She kept on watching him, refusing to lessen the interrogating expression on her face.

"All right," he said. "Desmond was my counselor, but he also helped me and my buddies get stuff we needed from the outside. He made a shitload of money off us, smuggling cell phones and weed and shit. But the feds caught up with him a few years after I got out, right after he came to the Apeshit show. He ratted out a couple of my friends, so he got a lighter sentence and they got time added on theirs. Dude's a snitch. That's all there is to it, man."

She nodded. "I see," she said. "So even though you've been out of trouble for a decade and have a normal job and everything, part of you still thinks you're some kind of hot shit gangster thug. I get it. So, is there ever a time when it gets old? I mean, I'm just curious." Under normal circumstances she would never talk to him in such condemnatory terms, but she had the upper hand now.

He shrugged. "I guess so."

"When?" she persisted. "When one of these punks pulls a gun on you?"

He sighed and squirmed in his seat. "It's already old, man," he conceded. "Bein' in that cell last night reminded me how awful it was and how I never wanna go back. I've been stressed lately, and I guess seeing homeboy just triggered something. That's all."

She looked away and reached for the ignition. "So do you have any more unfinished business? Any more scores you gotta settle?"

"Nah, man," he said. "I got it out of my system."

"Good," she said, adding, "'cause I might not bail you out next time." Though inside she knew otherwise.

They rode in semi-uncomfortable silence for a few minutes until Asher straightened in his seat and broke the tension. "Hey, you'll like this," he said, gathering all his fast-food refuse and crumpling it together in one bag. "There was this dude in the holding cell with me who just got transferred from Oregon, and guess who he was locked up with? The crazy self-help motherfucker. What's his name? Brooks Nixon."

"No way," Hope chuckled, shutting the heat off and rolling down her window. "What did *he* do?"

"Possession of stolen material. They caught him with like ten grand worth of scrap metal they say got jacked from an old amusement park up there. He says he legit bought it from some dude—which makes sense to me cause the guy's got plenty of money—but . . . anyway. That was kinda interesting."

"Yeah," Hope agreed. "Hmm. Wonder if they'll convict him."

She got the answer two months later when she picked up the free alternative weekly from the aromatherapy store. In a section titled "News from Bizarro Land," she came across the headline, "Brooks 'Narcissus' Nixon found guilty; Critics Accuse Judge Of Bias."

According to the article—which she skimmed at the store before returning the paper to its wire holder—the female judge who'd found Brooks guilty and given him the maximum two-year sentence once authored an article titled "Brooks Nixon Destroyed my Marriage." A civil lawsuit had already been filed against her alleging bias.

Holding grudges is such a terrible way to waste one's energy, Hope thought when she got home, recalling with perfect accuracy the statement made by Desmond at the bookstore on the night they met. She'd never called him—the prospect of doing so felt about as easy as opening a box of rattlesnakes—but she knew exactly where his number was. She'd kept it folded inside a hand carved Cherrywood box, a gift from one of her elderly clients years earlier. If you'd asked her where her car keys were right then, she wouldn't have been able to tell you, even though she'd held them in her hand mere minutes ago. But she could determine that little piece of paper's location with razor-sharp precision.

NINE

"The older you get, the faster time slips away." Hope's dad had told her this once in her senior year of high school—his tone way too casual for such horrifying news—as he peered over a newspaper from his recliner. "It makes perfect sense if you think about it. I mean, every year takes up a smaller percentage of your whole life than the last one, right?"

Frank Townsend had no way of knowing how poorly timed his remark was. At eighteen, Hope already found herself struggling with one profound existential crisis after another. His comment freaked her out so much that she immediately sought counsel from her mother, who welcomed the conversation as she stood peeling potatoes over the sink.

"I suppose it does speed up," Maybel Townsend said, "but in my experience, something else happens with each passing year. You grow into yourself a little more. You become a tad more secure about your place in the Universe. It's pretty neat, actually." That was during Mom's hippie phase, when she'd taken up yoga and started using words like "Universe."

As it turned out, they were both right; Hope's 40th birthday now loomed on the horizon, and even though her existence felt as ephemeral as a gnat's, she rarely stewed about her place in the Universe for long.

Flashes of a vague fear did overcome her at times, usually after she woke from a deep, lavender-induced sleep. A weird temporary amnesia would set in, making her think she was still a fresh-faced student in Mrs. Schlesinger's homeroom class. When the reality of her chronological age returned on those mornings, the shock of it could be unsettling. But the angst never lasted more than a few seconds.

She reflected on this fact with gratitude as she climbed the back stairs to her brother's top floor apartment on 4th street, arrived at the entrance, and lifted the straw mat to retrieve his spare key. Apparently, it was Asher's turn to torment himself now. Sensing a lack of real purpose in his life, he had gone to help their aging parents renovate their summer house in Colorado.

She inserted the key, jiggled it in the precise manner he'd shown her, and the door swung open to reveal an environment stale enough to make the staunchest optimist crave a new beginning.

Her initial mockery of his crisis might have been a little harsh, she thought now, but she'd had good reason for it; there are few things more irritating than someone younger than you whining about how old they feel. It's simply poor manners. *Cry me a fucking river,* she'd snapped at him. *So you're 35 and not a homeowner yet. I'm almost 40 and haven't had a real boyfriend since high school. We've all gotta adjust our expectations.*

This place did have more cheer than his former digs—aided in no small part by the sprinkling of decorative touches she'd helped him pick out when he first moved in—but it also lacked an unidentifiable something. She considered this as she threw her coat on the futon couch and read the list of instructions he'd left for her on a side table.

"Think of them as pets," he'd told her about the sad triad of three-inch marijuana plants sprouting on the windowsill by the kitchen. When he showed her the closet where he planned to move the plants once they reached a conspicuous height—an elaborate configuration of lights, fans, and reflective insulation—she'd expressed doubt over whether the whole endeavor would ever pay off. He wasn't even that big a user, after all.

But she'd relented once he explained how much his new hobby meant to him. Growing his own weed had already taught him more about horticulture than all his years in the landscaping business, he claimed. He also convinced her—falsely or not—that it carried far less risk than buying it from one of those shady characters who were always lurking near the library's marble steps.

"It's just that everything's changing so fast," he'd lamented to her in that troubling phone call a week earlier, the phone call that started it all. "Jesse drives a goddamned Suburban now. Some old buddies of ours played a gig at Wolfgang's a couple of weeks ago, but he said he couldn't go cause he had to get up early to take Jillian to, wait for it—the *fertility clinic*. I remember when we all used to talk about going on tour together, man. Nothing cool like that even seems possible anymore."

Cohesion. That was what was missing from this apartment, Hope decided as she felt the soil of the meekest plant for dampness. She ran a precise amount of water into a measuring cup, adding in plant food with a dropper as per the directions. "Here ya go, dude," she said as she saturated the dirt, recalling that plants like it when you talk to them.

Returning the cup to a shelf, she surveyed the items scattered across the table: a pair of dice, a box of Q-Tips, a washcloth, and a fly swatter. There was no central identity tying these objects together, nothing to give you a clear picture of the person who lived here. Maybe this time away would help him find one.

" . . . and Mom and dad seem *so fucking old* all of a sudden," he had gone on to say. "Mom's got a hearing aid now and Dad almost forgot my name the other day. I think he might have Alzheimer's. Seriously."

"You should hope so," Hope said. "Maybe he'll forget about all the hell you put him through. Not to mention the money you owe him."

A noticeable silence followed, and Hope knew exactly what this meant. Years of teaching people how to talk to sad sacks on the phone made her a qualified expert at knowing when something touched a nerve.

"I was a pretty shitty son, wasn't I," Asher had said.

The idea for the trip had actually come to Hope first. "Well, maybe you can make up for it now," she'd urged. "They're not dead yet. They just got that new place in Colorado. You can go help them fix it up."

To her surprise, he'd not only warmed right up to the idea but had tried to guilt her into coming with him, making less-than-subtle hypothetical comments about how bad she would feel if they dropped dead and she hadn't visited in over a year.

Hope didn't flinch at all at the suggestion. She'd seen enough people for whom death was not just in the mail but at the door, and she knew her parents weren't even close to that stage yet. She also knew that when they were, she would be the one out of all her siblings who would wind up spoon-feeding them and changing their diapers. Somehow, she'd carried this inevitability since before Asher was born, maybe even before she opened her own eyes. Resisting it never even occurred to her.

She needed to check her email from his computer, as she did from any computer away from home since ninety percent of the population's internet connection surpassed hers. So she sat at Asher's desk, a piece of plywood atop six cinder blocks, and pushed aside another bunch of random objects: a stick of deodorant, a toy car, a hand fan, and a cork. The machine had a visible split along the seam on one side, an injury from when Asher threw it across the room in reaction to its poor downloading speed. With timid fingers, she turned it on tentatively, trying not to worsen the damage.

Against her better judgement, Hope always expected something life-changing to happen each time she signed into her email account. She skipped past the first three items in her inbox, pleas from various animal rights organizations she had donated to in the past. She didn't even open them because she knew the horrible images of emaciated horses and blinded kittens would ruin her day if she even glanced at them. These organizations would reap all her disposable money if she had any. But her twenty-year-old car was falling apart piece by piece in a manner that reminded her of slapstick silent movies; recently the sunroof had blown off on the highway, startling both her and Piggy to such a degree that she'd had to pull over so they could comfort each other. And this morning when she opened the driver's side door, the handle had come off in her hand.

The next email she ignored bore the name Shawna Van Belle in the "from" field and "meeting" as the subject. This would be the second forum to discuss the new video chat initiative spearheaded by Shawna; at first, Hope had paid the minimum amount of attention necessary, stifling a level of contempt reminiscent of those mandatory school assemblies on topics like Self Image and Leadership.

After signing out of her account without opening anything, she noticed a sidebar story that caught her eye. The picture showed a middle-aged woman with a tight blonde ponytail wagging a finger at the camera. Hope felt with startling certainty that she recognized the woman; it resembled a former downstairs neighbor of hers who'd once left a passive-aggressive note on her door about the noise caused by her boots. ("Wearing slippers would not only be less noisy, it would also be more comfortable for you and cause less floor damage.") But then she saw the headline:

Judge In Brooks Nixon Stolen Scrap Metal Case Settles Defamation Suit

The judge who sentenced controversial self-help author Brooks Nixon to two years in prison for possession of stolen property in 2006 has settled a lawsuit filed against her by the author, the associated press said. The lawsuit pertained to comments she made about the case in an interview for *Rebel Magazine* in 2007. Nixon's supporters had accused Judge Ellen Thomas of bias in the case, citing a blog post she'd once written titled "Brooks Nixon Broke up my Marriage." The lawsuit alleged that Thomas's response to questions about bias amounted to "intentional insult of character and infliction of emotional distress."

"My job was to rule on the case presented to me," Thomas said in the interview. "As for Mr. Nixon's many crimes against good taste, family values, and basic human decency, that's a matter best settled in higher court."

Judicial immunity prevents any judge from being sued over a ruling, Law Professor Mitchell Silverman explained, but this settlement basically equates an admission of bias by Thomas.

Neither party would release the amount, but a spokesman for Nixon has described it as "satisfactory," adding, "it is more than enough for him to legally buy all the scrap metal in Thrillville."

That was a colossal waste of time, Hope said to herself as she powered off the computer, fully understanding why a person might throw such a machine across a room.

When you work at an office job for fifteen years, you develop a high tolerance for the kind of irritation that necessitates the destruction of property. As Mystic Partners increased in size, so did its penchant for corporate oppression, and Hope had taught herself a few tricks over the years: get extra sleep before meetings, plan rewarding activities to engage in after difficult situations, and remember the affirmation *no one can force me to do or think a damn thing if I don't want to.* By the time Friday's meeting came around, she felt amply prepared.

As the head of the new webcam reading division, Shawna carried more clout than before, but Hope struggled to take her seriously as she wore her new authority with artificially played-down arrogance. She strolled into the conference room on the day of the second meeting wearing a corseted floral blouse pulled painfully tight over a black pencil skirt, smiled at everyone she passed, then cleared her throat like a famous tenor about to perform an aria.

"No one knows for sure why certain people receive the gift of psychic ability," she began. "What is known is that we who have the gift have an obligation—encouraged by our spirit guides—to share the gift with others."

Half the room nodded at her opening statement, the other half sank into their chairs with embarrassment.

"Many clairvoyants—myself included—feel called to spread their gifts around the world. We are on a mission to find the specific souls who need our help, and physical distance does nothing to quell our robust determination. Today, the use of modern technology enables us to answer this calling like never before."

The last line had a ring of familiarity to it, Hope thought; it might have come straight out of one of the company's radio commercials. Or maybe she recognized it from the old instructional pamphlet from the 90s, the one she'd snickered at with Nathan on the night before her first day.

"What is perhaps the most impressive part about webcam psychic readings is the ability to communicate face-to-face with your client. These readings will be very personal. You will be able to interact with your client in a manner that conveys empathy and spiritual bliss. Clients will have the opportunity to witness firsthand the physical experience that occurs when the spirit guide enters the psychic's body to reveal their messages."

One trick Hope sometimes employed for enduring Shawna's high-flying BS sessions was to imagine how her brother Asher would react to them. She quoted her colleague often in his presence, and she never got tired of watching his deadpan responses. "I'm sorry," he would say, shaking his head and rubbing his eyebrows with his palms. "I'm gonna have to blow that place up."

"Another benefit unique to webcam readings is the healing that occurs. Both parties, regardless of the miles that separate them, can feel a restorative spiritual bond taking place."

Someone in the room—a guy in a poncho who Hope didn't recognize—raised his hand to ask a refreshingly blunt question about sales targets and minimum session length requirements.

"A webcam reading may be conducted over several sessions," Shawna bluffed, clearly unprepared, "or advice may be delivered in a single event. This will depend on what the client is searching for and what the spirit guide is willing to reveal at that time."

The vague and patronizing answer didn't seem to satisfy the poncho-wearer. His inquisitive expression turned confused and three or four other hands went up around him.

"In other words," Hope blurted out, "drag that shit out as long as possible." The quip brought a welcome eruption of laughter into the stifling room. She leaned back in her chair contentedly; for the second time that day, her timing had been impeccable. The first time was when a car rounded a corner nearly hitting her and the driver yelled, "Ever hear of looking before you cross the street, bitch?"

"Ever hear of using a turn signal, asshole?" she'd retorted promptly, adrenaline surging through her entire body. She was on a roll, she thought; it would be a good time to buy a lottery ticket.

The laughter dissolved, and Shawna inhaled deeply, gripping the crystal pendant in the crepe-paper skin of her bosom with such force that Hope could see a knuckle turning white from ten feet away. "Believe in limits and you'll only create them," she said, closing her eyes as if channeling the words from a higher source. "We should strive to detach ourselves from such illusions. Conditions and qualifications don't exist—only spirit exists, and spirit has no end."

"Ugh. I just want to cunt-punt that woman sometimes," Hope would say later when she told Asher about the meeting. To emphasize her annoyance, she would raise her right knee in a pantomime of the imagined fighting maneuver. "Thwack," she would say. "Right in the third eye."

A typical rewarding activity after a brutal day like today would involve a trip to the Century Mall for a giant soft pretzel and a diet cherry soda, two of her worst guilty pleasures. Depending on the level of the day's brutality, she might also pay the extra 50 cents for a packet of gooey electric orange crap called Ezee Cheez whose list of ingredients read more like that on a tube of jock itch medicine than any earthly dairy product. Not all vegan food is healthy, it turns out. Tonight, she thought she might also pay a visit to Acid Tongue, the horrendous chain store for depressed teenagers where one could dig through cardboard boxes of clearance-priced tee shirts with slogans like *I hate the world* on them.

Also, this time she would stop by the Trophy Bee to see Desmond. That was one guilty pleasure she wouldn't have to feel guilty about now, not with Asher out of town.

Not that she should feel guilty. The guy had paid his debt to society; he'd lost his counseling license and spent a year and a half locked up, he'd been forced to cough up thousands in fees, and just when he'd gotten his life together he'd also had to give up his little café job thanks to Asher's childish vendetta. He deserved companionship just as much as anyone else, maybe even more so after all he'd suffered through.

And besides that, she deserved the company of a guy like him. Despite his bad-boy streak, Desmond lacked the "inconsiderate bastard" quality of the men she usually attracted. He answered all her calls promptly. She'd only had to wait to hear back from him once—after the first tentative voicemail she left him, right after Asher busted his jaw. But he'd invited her to dinner and confessed his whole sordid history to her just as soon as he recovered from his reconstructive surgery. She'd responded by confessing her relation to the cause of his hurt, and they'd enjoyed an undefined but mutually beneficial friendship ever since.

The line in front of the Trophy Bee contained an unusually high number of squirmy children tonight, so Hope took her pretzel and Ezee Cheez to a nearby cluster of benches to wait it out. She stood on her toes to wave to Desmond from behind a large potted palm, and he responded by grinning widely, then rolling his eyes and making a gun-to-head gesture with his hand.

As she sat back and watched him working the engraver in his tight black tee shirt, she considered what a great catch he seemed like from a distance. They shared other interests besides the secret life of Victor Vex; Desmond, too, would drive miles out of his way if the prospect of a good yard sale, flea market, or thrift store beckoned. He had an unhealthy obsession with collecting old VHS tapes—unhealthy because the debt it caused had led to his decision to make cash by smuggling years ago—but everyone had their vices. His movie tastes tended toward the outrageously gory, and some might consider this a red flag. Then again, Hope herself found true crime shows relaxing, so who was she to judge? He had two pet rats that he treated like children, and she was pretty sure he wasn't a serial killer. And he looked great in a tight black tee shirt.

The line dwindled to one frantic mother and her young son, so Hope tossed her pretzel bag and strolled up behind them, winking at Desmond over the mom's shoulder. The boy looked about eight, had gorgeous shoulder-length brown hair, and kept tugging at his genitals and swinging his head around as though watching a miniature airplane do figure eights.

"Are you all right, honey?" the mother asked, stuffing a water bottle and tiny sweater into her tote bag so she could kneel to his level. "Do you have to pee? We can go pee in just a minute. We gotta pick up your trophy first, though. You won a trophy for being so good at reading! Remember that? Your teacher gave you a trophy because she loves you so much. Remember?"

The boy stood still for a second and a smile lit up his face.

"Yeah," the mother continued. "Maria said you rock." She made a fist and held it in the air, emphasizing the word "rock," and the young boy imitated her, giggling. Then he started to pull down his pants.

"Oh, no honey, not here," the mom said. She turned around and flashed Hope an embarrassed grin. "My son has autism," she explained. "He's very smart, but he struggles with social expectations."

Hope smiled at the boy. "I know *exactly* how he feels," she said.

"Me too," Desmond chimed in from behind the counter.

Neither Hope nor Desmond were faking it to make the harried mother feel better. They talked about struggling to meet social expectations—a challenge they both faced—often. It probably explained why the conversation between them always went down so effortlessly, and it might've explained why the sex did not. They'd slept together only three times in the five years since they met, and it always felt like the minute their clothes came off, both forgot what was expected of them. By now Hope had concluded, sadly, that she probably needed a "smooth operator" type to take charge when it came to such matters.

If it weren't for that one problem, Desmond might have made a fine life partner for Hope. Well, there was one other drawback: any time she mentioned his name around her brother he still shot her sideways glares and groaned his disapproval.

Maybe she liked this obstacle, though. Maybe it placed Desmond just outside the scope of her reach, allowing enough room for some longing. Desire needs distance in order to thrive. It made sense. If you ate constantly all day long, you would never be hungry enough for the food's savory flavors to make a difference. The pleasure receptors would go numb after a while.

At the now empty counter of the Trophy Bee, Hope chatted up Desmond for a few more minutes about special needs children just to hear him talk. Every one of his thoughts on the subject delighted her. He said he liked working at the trophy shop better than the café because here he could make a difference in people's lives, so he didn't have to miss counseling as much. Sometimes his sweetness almost made him feel unreachable to her, like an itch in the dead center of her spine.

He allowed her to unload about her workday, about the meeting and Shawna, though she spared him the catty "third eye" comment. At the end of the visit he came out from behind the counter, wrapped his long arms all the way around her, then kissed her on the cheek. "You have yourself a wonderful evening," he said.

"You, too."

She turned to leave, feeling more than rewarded for her day's irritations. She didn't need to go buy a ridiculously juvenile tee-shirt from Acid Tongue. She didn't hate the world anymore. At least not as much.

"Don't work too hard," she called back to him over her shoulder.

"I won't."

Maybe Desmond was gay. That's what one of her imaginary girlfriends would probably have said. Each time she pictured those bitches, they had a different setting going on around them; in this one, they were all lounging in someone's off-white living room, it was dark outside, they were listening to a compilation CD called something like *Fizzy Electric Chill,* and one of them was flipping through a magazine.

In the parking lot, steps before reaching her car, she stopped and froze with dread; the front tire she'd kept meaning to fill at the gas station lay limp like a dead balloon. She made a quick calculation of her cell phone's battery life; ten hours since she last charged it would leave it at approximately zero.

Of course, she thought, collapsing internally as she turned to go back in the mall. How naive to think her day could have ended on a perfectly pleasant note. Now she would have to ruin the mood by returning to Desmond as a whiney little damsel in distress. She pulled her black sweater tight around her shoulders as the wind kicked up and a cyclone of leaves crossed her path.

"Hope?"

The familiar voice made her muscles tense and slacken almost simultaneously; it was Shawna, striding out of the mall with her arms full of department store bags. Evidently, the day's events had left her with the same urge to reward herself as they had Hope.

"Are you all right? You look sort of lost."

"I have a flat tire and my cell phone's dead."

"Poor thing. Let me see what I can do." She set down the bags and Hope could see the corner of a shoe box with a glaring orange price tag: $149.99. Shawna pulled a cellphone from her purse and pressed a couple of buttons.

"Hello, Henry? It's Shawna. Are you available to change a flat tire? At the Century Mall . . . it's one of my associates . . . "

Every few seconds she paused to cover the phone's mouthpiece and ask Hope a question ("Is there a spare? Make? Model? Which section of the parking lot?") before peppering Henry with compliments and hanging up on him.

"He'll be here in twenty minutes," she announced with an impressively casual air. "My car's right over here. Let me put these things in the trunk and I'll wait with you 'til he gets here."

Shawna's car, a newer model Mercedes, smelled oddly of wine coolers and nail polish. The specific mélange carried a distinct olfactory association with it, reminding Hope of a stuck-up girl from Boston with whom she'd hung out exactly three times in the ninth grade.

"Sweet ride," she said, curling into the slick blue leather of the passenger seat.

Shawna brushed the compliment off, her bracelets creating an orchestra of jingles as she pulled down its duct-tape-free visor to check her lipstick in the mirror. Then she sighed with something like exasperation and shook her head. The car had been a gift from one of her "benefactors," she explained, and, "It serves its purpose . . . . for now."

"Well, I don't have any benefactors," Hope said. "My car is 25 years old and the door handle fell off in my hand the other day. I'll tell you what, though; I love the shit out of that thing."

With that, Shawna pursed her lips and nodded knowingly. "Well, if you believe in limitation, then that's what you will end up with."

Hope repressed the urge to come up with a clever comeback this time, as her annoying colleague had the upper hand.

HENRY ARRIVED LOOKING LIKE HE'D BEEN on his way to a much more interesting appointment; the handsome fifty-something wore a tight black button-up and had his peppery hair slicked-back with mousse. He changed Hope's tire with astonishing efficiency, waving off her attempt to pay him. When Shawna hugged him goodbye, he closed his eyes and made an extended "mmm" sound, and as he drove away, Hope gave Shawna an inquisitive head tilt.

"Seems like a nice fellow," Hope observed. "Is he, like . . . a *benefactor with benefits?*"

Shawna laughed heartily at this, more heartily than Hope knew the woman was capable of. "No, but now I have something new to manifest," she said, seeming almost earthbound for a second. "Henry's an old friend," she explained. "I help him clear his chakras."

Hope rubbed her chin and nodded, squinting suspiciously. "I see. Is that what they're calling it these days?"

Shawna held the corners of her mouth down for a second. "I didn't mention *how* I was helping him," she said before tossing her head back in a fit of defeated hysterics. This made Hope crack up, too, though she wasn't entirely sure she got the joke.

"Ah, this is nice," Shawna said, sighing and wiping her eyes when her chest finally stopped bouncing. "Listen, Hope. I've been meditating on the importance of kinship to divine feminine energy. What would you say to grabbing a coffee this weekend? I think it would do us both some good."

"Sure," Hope said, fighting a surge of reluctance that made her shoulders tighten and her fingers twist and curl. "Why not? I'm down with divine feminine energy."

*   *   *

THE OLD HONDA INCHED FORWARD BEHIND a lemon-yellow hotel van in the airport's circle drive as Hope scanned the haggard faces of waiting passengers. Asher had warned her that she might not recognize him; he'd lost weight, gotten a haircut, and started wearing his plaid button-up shirts buttoned instead of draping them over tee shirts. "I look like I belong in a goddamn granola bar commercial," he'd said.

The two-week trip to Holden, Colorado—their parents' new summer home—had turned into a six-month sabbatical. He'd gotten a job in one of the tiny villages nearby, someplace named after a pine tree—Cottonwood, Spruce, or Pinyon—and decided to "try out this mountain man thing for a while." But the real basis for his sudden change of plans, as he'd finally revealed to Hope a month earlier, was a girl.

Well, not exactly a girl, he'd clarified—she was 47, a former contract lawyer who'd given up the rat race and now flipped houses full time. From what Hope could tell, the relationship sounded promising so far; Asher hadn't made a single derogatory comment about Lucinda yet, unless you counted his calling her his "hot cougar MILF" in emails, which he did without a hint of shame, surrounding the phrase with emojis as if he were shouting it from the rooftops.

Lucinda had a son, a ten-year-old named Zeus who had Asperger's syndrome and ADD and was "a real cool kid." Picturing Asher in a stepfather-type role was like imagining him in high heels and a ruffled bonnet, but he seemed happy so she didn't question it.

On the fourth pass through the circle drive, Asher emerged. He wore a new leather messenger bag strapped across his chest and was struggling to pull the trolley carrying his other luggage while eating a floppy slice of pizza from a box.

"Hey, aren't you the guy from the granola bar commercial?" Hope called to him through the window, leaning on the horn so long it made the other travelers turn and look.

"Yep, that's me," he said.

The first thing he wanted to talk about were his marijuana plants, and thankfully Hope bore nothing but good news on the subject; through an incredible stroke of luck, she'd found a neighbor, a green-thumbed teacher from Jamaica, to take over the job for the past four months. "You might want to let Althea move in there permanently," she said now. "No, seriously. I'm not kidding at all."

He rolled down the window and lit a cigarette. "Well, if things go my way, I might be living in a condo on Ridgecrest Avenue soon anyway."

Hope laughed. In San Lazaro terms, Ridgecrest Avenue equated Rodeo Drive; any time either of them drove its Rolls-Royce-lined streets, they would return with harrowing stories of being gawked at with suspicion, if not tailed by cops, for their obvious outsider status.

"Wait," Hope said when he failed to laugh with her. "What?"

"My girlfriend lives there. Things are getting serious."

"You mean Lucinda? I thought she lived in Colorado."

"Just in the summers. She's actually from here."

"No shit? That's cool."

Asher had an awkward favor to ask of Hope, and he waited until she dropped him at his apartment to bring it up, emphasizing his discomfort at mentioning it as if to underline its importance.

"Lucinda believes in psychics and shit like that," he said. "I know, I know, but—I kind of told her my sister did tarot cards. Do you think you could give her a freebee and put in a good word for me? Kind of drop a few hints about the man in her life being *the one*? I really don't want to fuck this up."

"Won't she get suspicious?"

"Not if you're subtle about it."

"Well, I haven't done a reading in years, but I guess I could BS my way through—"

"Great. She'll be here on Tuesday."

One week later, Hope overcame her reluctance and was pacing nervously outside a small square building with bars on its window watching for Lucinda's white Prius. The place looked more like a payday loan store than a laid-back coffee house, and she didn't want her esteemed guest to miss it.

She'd chosen the In-Focus Café for the meeting because of its proximity to her office. The business doubled as the headquarters of an indie film company who'd come to do a documentary on Mystic Partners once. "Telepathic Telemarketing" never made its way to completion, as it seemed most of their projects didn't, so they opened the café as a way to make ends meet. The café used impractical beanbag chairs for seating, kept lots of books and games around and let people draw on the floor with chalk, making it a good option for someone with a high-maintenance kid in tow.

Bruce, the owner/director of In-Focus, stuck his head out the door and whistled inquiringly in Hope's direction. "You doin' all right there?"

"Waiting for someone," she hollered back.

Bruce's username for the social media platform where he posted all his video endeavors was Protaginis Interruptous. He had tried to hit on Hope by showing her some of his stuff, mostly depressing interviews with drug-addicted old jazz musicians. His username sounded kind of like a species of dinosaur, she'd told him. She didn't tell him she also thought it sounded like a technical name for premature ejaculation.

In-focus was also where she'd met Shawna for the obligatory coffee date following her parking lot rescue a few months back, but their friendship had never made it off the ground.

"Finding suitable comradery presents a unique set of challenges for me," Shawna had told her. "I can't turn off my ability to read auras, you see. It's hard to concentrate on what someone is saying when all you want to do is burn tree-sized bundles of sage around their heart."

"Makes sense," Hope had said.

The sky turned dark and a large wet raindrop hit Hope on the arm, convincing her to move inside. As she waited in one of the beanbags, the Protaganis Interruptus stood with his hands on his hips and one leg on a footstool telling her about his various stalled projects.

" . . . and I'm also working on a documentary about Brooks Nixon," he babbled on after apprising her of his other six ideas. "You know how he won the defamation lawsuit against the judge, right? Well, he bought that old run-down amusement park property. He said he was gonna fix it up and turn it into a museum, but instead he's just living there. Dude's in terrible health, he's a total recluse and compulsive hoarder. My idea is to interview him, find out what made him, ya know, turn his back on everything."

"Sounds fun," Hope said. "Does the documentary have a name yet?"

"Narcissus Nobody," Bruce beamed, seeming pleased with the question. "My scriptwriter thinks we might scare him off by calling it that, but my ex-girlfriend used to know his publicist's daughter, and she said he probably wouldn't give a shit."

Hope's curiosity escalated a little, momentarily outweighing her general opinion of Bruce as a huge dufus. "So did he build a house in there or what?" she asked. "I mean is he just, like, camping out in one of the ticket booths or something?"

"Well, the project's kinda stalled right now," Bruce said. "Funding issues. But our new one's really starting to generate a buzz. It's about people who get headaches from living near cell phone towers."

At long last, the front door swung open with a jingle and a tall brunette stood in it looking around as though lost, a little blond boy at her side.

"Lucinda?" Hope called from the coffee-stained beanbag. Through her eyes, she tried to convey apologies for having suggested such a dumb place along with pleas for a rescue from this absurd conversation.

"Oh, good," Lucinda said. "I thought I was in the wrong place. Sorry I'm late." She had a funny, hard-to-place accent. Brazilian, she would reveal later, leaving Hope to wonder why Asher hadn't mentioned it. Didn't it add another layer of gratification to his twisted MILF fantasy?

"You're fine."

She wore knee-high tan suede boots over jeans and a coral-colored cashmere sweater. She was indeed beautiful—a knockout—way out of Asher's league, and Hope pictured an idealized version of the couple to stop herself from saying so out loud. Maybe with his landscaping skills they could become one of those house-flipping dream teams on the home decorating channel. The cougar/boy-toy dynamic might even help stir up ratings.

And Hope was immediately smitten with Zeus, who walked up and presented her with an origami frog he'd just made.

"Are you dying of cuteness right now?" he asked.

"Yes, I am," she said.

He proceeded to kneel to the floor and tear into a cauldron of colored chalk, drawing what looked like fire-shooting cats doing the mambo along the base of a bookcase.

Hope gave Lucinda what she estimated to be one of the great BS tarot readings of all time. Her tactic, which she'd come up with days in advance, involved appearing surprised—even shocked—by the information each individual card conveyed. At one point she confessed to having feared her brother's less-than-stellar history with women might cause the cards to go an entirely different way. She finished it off with a line she stole from a horoscope she'd gotten a few years back.

"You don't have to perform for anyone. Open your heart and let its light guide you."

Lucinda loved the reading so much she insisted on paying for Hope's coffee and chickpea chips, and when she left, she kissed her on the cheek in the same way Hope always kissed misplaced objects upon finding them.

ONE NICE THING ABOUT SOCIAL ENGAGEMENTS: they refresh your appetite for solitude. When Hope returned home from her adventures at the In-Focus Café, she locked the door behind her as though shutting out a pack of angry hyenas. Her phone was sounding an assortment of muffled melodies from the unreachable depths of her handbag, but she stopped the intrusion by tossing the whole bag in a kitchen cupboard and slamming it shut. Piggy jumped toward her, an eager front paw getting tangled in the loose knit of her sweater, and she scratched the dog's head as she gently freed her. She removed her ankle boots and sat on the hard linoleum, pacified by the vibrating hum of the refrigerator.

For the next two days, she didn't have to answer to anyone; she savored this knowledge like a sip of heavenly nectar. No one expected a thing from her except for Piggy, who currently knelt on her front elbows and wedged a cold nose under her hand. They could go for a drive up the coast. She could collect some more beach glass for that tabletop she'd found behind a church and planned to turn into a mosaic.

On the refrigerator door, pinned beneath a dream-catcher magnet, a flier announced further motivation to leave town: a giant fundraising walk for skin cancer awareness whose route passed right in front of her building and straight through the dog park. A neighbor had given her the flier a week ago, asking her if she might want to participate, prompting Hope to tack it up and write AVOID across the top of it with a red sharpie. She couldn't participate, she would tell the neighbor if she saw her again. She was going out of town.

Aimless road trips are nature's antidote to social wariness. With no commitments and no one to impress, Hope could masquerade as a different person. She could listen to conservative talk radio stations and even take in the occasional raving Jesus spiel, observing these foreign ways of thinking with the noncommittal pity of a tourist. She could skip the eyeliner and wear clothes she'd originally purchased as pajamas because of their comfort: wide-legged rayon pants and a hoodie with some 90s cartoon character on it. She filled an old vinyl airline bag with enough supplies to get her through the weekend in case she went too far and couldn't make it back before nightfall. She put away the used dishes, clothing items, and dog toys strewn about the apartment, giving the place just enough superficial shine as to welcome her return. She drank her sleep-inducing tea early, ensuring she could leave at the first sliver of dawn.

Morning came, a crisp wind blew the leaves off all the plants on her balcony, and Hope hit the road with the determination of a long-distance runner. She passed all the beaches without stopping. She passed a new farmer's market she'd wanted to check out ever since it opened six months ago. She even passed Kapp's Diner, the friendly grease-bucket whose owner took such a liking to Piggy on their last road trip that he allowed the dog to sit inside with her. To this day, a picture of the two of them smiling from the orange pleather booth provided her computer's desktop background. But she didn't stop for Kapp's. She didn't even slow down, so strong was the sudden urge to see something outside her everyday realm. Like elusive sunbursts on a cloudy day, every new mile marker teased her.

A destination finally presented itself as she crossed the border into Oregon. She passed one of those route confirmation signs that lists names of towns and their distances; Belua 12, Ashbrook 35, Portland 79. If she drove for just half an hour longer, she could see the infamous Thrillville and satisfy the needling curiosity created by Bruce with his maddeningly half-told tale. She would have to stop driving eventually; this spot sounded just as good as any.

With nothing like nostalgia, she remembered her family's singular outing to Thrillville. It must have been about 1985, the last year all of them lived at home. She would have been thirteen, which is why her memory of it still stung with the all-encompassing pain of a person who doesn't fit in their body right. Her older siblings had fallen right into line, going on all the rides in order of popularity: first the Death Spiral, then the Wheel of Screams, followed by Earthquake Mountain. For Hope, most of the day consisted of walking around with her arms folded across her chest, certain—like most thirteen-year-olds—that the world would cave in on her at any second.

The low-key rides she remembered as mildly pleasurable, lifting her above everything and giving her a superior perspective on it all. She also liked the Mirror Maze because viewing her new lopsided haircut from all directions accentuated its avant-garde freakish appeal. Asher, who was seven at the time, had spent the whole drive up blabbering maniacally about all the rides he planned to go on but chickened out the minute he saw them up close. He spent half the day lurking behind Hope like a shadow, the other half tethered to their parents, poking everyone they passed with a sword made of twisted balloons.

He'd cried the whole way home.

What she remembered most about Thrillville was the way it dominated headlines in the months leading up to its closing around 1987. First, some exchange student from Germany snuck in after hours, climbed to the top of the Death Spiral drunk on grain alcohol, lost his balance, and plummeted. Then an 80-year-old man suffered a heart attack on Earthquake Mountain. Finally, a toddler drowned in the duck pond while her young parents had a screaming match just a few feet away.

Even after investigators cleared the park of any wrongdoing in all three deaths, the public turned away from it in droves. One commentator likened their reaction to her own aversion to certain foods during pregnancy; knowing the egg salad didn't directly cause her suffering didn't stop her from gagging at the smell of it.

Ten minutes past Belua, the trailers and billboards started appearing in tighter clusters, a hopeful indication of Ashbrook's proximity. She had no clue how to get to Thrillville from Ashbrook, whether the not-so-fun park could be reached at all for that matter. Then she went over a hill and saw something promising in the distance: a graveyard of broken-down rocket ships jutting out above the dirty fog. She pulled into a gas station to make one final pit stop before zeroing in.

The gas station's pumps looked like they'd been around since Thrillville's heyday, and so did the attached convenience store; the words "Easy Mart" hung over its entrance like party decorations someone forgot to take down. Hope approached the glass door, flinched at the paper *No Public Restrooms* sign, but went inside anyway. Several seconds passed as she stood there recalculating her plan, the idea to revisit a childhood disappointment sounding less and less appealing.

"Can I help you, miss?" a woman in a polyester smock asked.

"Um, well, maybe. Is that the road to Thrillville?"

"Yep." The woman wore thick bifocals and her name tag said Marcie. "It's not open, though."

"I know," Hope said. "Thanks."

Marcie frowned over the top of her bifocals. "Why on Earth do you want to go *there*?"

"Just curious."

Marcie shook her head, expressing—Hope guessed—befuddlement with the quirky interests of big-city folk. "I'd be careful," she said. "The new owner's not a very nice guy. He doesn't take kindly to people snooping around out there. Last week he chased away two TV reporters and spat at them."

"I just want to drive by it," Hope said. "I mean, I probably won't even get out of the car . . . Childhood memories and stuff."

"All right. Have fun," Marcie said with a dismissive wave.

A few minutes later Hope found herself traipsing through the world's itchiest weeds, Piggy trotting along dutifully behind her. They both squatted behind a bush, Hope using a paper towel from the car as toilet paper. As she stood and began plucking the pointed grass barbs from her pants, Piggy's whole body stiffened. Her animal eyes and ears became fixated on something beyond the next bush.

In a flash of blurry blackness, a large cat darted into an old metal shed. Only the shed wasn't a shed, Hope noticed upon closer inspection; it was an old carousel cart in the shape of a swan.

Hope smiled at the sight; the cat's now tiny head peeking out from beneath a rusty, once-white wing. The image could have all kinds of gorgeous symbolism if she wanted it to; life goes on, even amidst the deadest of fantasies. She pulled her phone from the pocket of her sweatshirt. If this photo worked out, she decided—if it ended up being the only thing she had to show for this entire weekend foray into pointlessness—the trip would not be wasted.

A meow unlike any feline song Hope had ever heard started creeping up from behind her. As it got closer, the ghostly catcall became less cat-like, morphing into a strange, anxious half-growl.

"Eeeowrrr, eeeowrrr, eeeowrrr . . . "

After glancing once furtively over her shoulder, Hope swiveled around and stopped, stunned, in her tracks; an obese figure in a black hoodie and jeans was trudging by her, his neglected gray mustache trying in vain to hide the still-compelling presence beneath it.

The realization hit her with a jolt of astonishment. *Whoa, I guess we're here*, she said to herself, feeling herself mouth the words and hoping they didn't make a sound.

He didn't notice her but started massaging his temples with his mitt-like hands as he paced back and forth along the barbed wire fence. Hope sensed the source of his angst and felt an obligation to speak up.

"Are you missing a black cat?" she asked.

He turned, startled. "Oh, um, yeah," he said, zipping up the hoodie to hide the lower half of his face. "Why? Have you seen one?"

She raised her eyebrows and nodded toward the swan cart. "I think he's in there." Piggy still had the animal cornered in a comically dramatized standoff.

He glanced over, and his shoulders collapsed with relief. "Oh, eeoowrr," he said, walking over and scooping the frightened black tuft in his arms, repeating the sound as he stroked its fur. "Thank you," he said to Hope without making eye contact as he headed toward an old, rusty pickup truck parked a few feet away.

"Don't thank me, thank my copilot here," she said, scratching Piggy behind the ears.

Without another word, he ducked into the cab of his truck and pulled out a small pet carrier.

This, she figured, was the end of a great little humorous anecdote. She would tell this story for years to come, anytime she found someone worth telling it to. She began mentally rewinding the tape—back to the Easy Mart and Marcie—to watch it again, adding a bit of color and shading to build narrative tension. Perhaps she'd give Marcie a thick southern drawl. No one would ever know.

But Brooks didn't drive away. He sat in the front seat with the door open and the pet carrier on his lap, uttering muted sweet nothings into it, then looked back up at Hope, perplexed.

"Are you lost?" he asked.

"No," she said. "Just wandering." She laughed and pointed to a bumper sticker on her back windshield that read, *Not all who wander are lost.*

"I see."

An uncomfortable air of suspicion still lingered between them. She wondered if he knew he'd been recognized. Did he think she was recording him right now on a high-tech camera hidden in the pattern on her sweatshirt? To put him at ease, she embarked on a long-winded explanation of how she'd needed to make a pit stop, how the gas station up the road didn't have a restroom, things she clearly wouldn't have told him if she thought he was a celebrity. Then, in the one moment she would always leave out of the story in future retellings, she held up the wad of paper towels as evidence.

He didn't react, so she pointed at the cluster of shapes in the distance and let her mouth continue talking without seeking permission from her brain.

"Good old Thrillville," she said, staring wistfully into the fog. "I used to go there with my family when I was little. I hope they never tear it down. It'll make way more interesting ruins for people a thousand years from now than some stupid mall or whatever."

"Mm," he said, his hand pausing mid-stroke to consider her words. A gust of wind blew his hood away from his eyes for a second, enough time for her to glimpse a trace of that old bedeviling ambition she remembered from the glossy 3M book jacket.

She picked Piggy up and, clutching the dog's paw in her hand, moved it up and down in a waving gesture. "Well," she said, "it was nice meeting you, Meow-meow."

"Yower," Brooks said.

"What?"

He lifted one tiny black paw from the crate. "Yower. My cat's name is Yower."

"Oh. Okay. Bye, Yower."

She exhaled for what felt like the first time in an hour upon returning to the Honda. As her breathing became normalized, she pulled the keys from her pocket and implored the Universe in all its wisdom to let the car start on the first crank this time.

Her starter had been on a death spiral for about three weeks now. The last mechanic to see it had advised waiting no more than two months before having it replaced. She sat back and tried to remember every piece of car advice she had ever heard in her life, including the unserious ones; Nathan once told her if you think too hard while you turn the ignition, it makes the engine flood.

Then she swallowed, tried to forget it all, turned the key, and winced as it clicked into silence.

Standard protocol for this situation required her to sit and slowly count to a hundred before trying again. But Hope's panicked mind was incapable of doing anything slowly right now. She tried again after about twenty seconds, again after another ten, then leaned forward with her forehead to the steering wheel, said "fuck" under her breath, and tried to disappear.

When that didn't work, she opened the car door and swung her legs out into the dandelions and pretended to do something with her phone, even though she'd already noticed it had no reception.

She looked up to see Brooks—still leaning against his truck cab with his hand in the crate—tilting his head with a mostly annoyed but marginally concerned look.

"Well, this is awkward," Hope said, a fizzy panic moving from her feet up to her flushed cheeks. "Say, you wouldn't know where I can find a land line, would you?"

He nodded and set the crate and Yower on the cab's passenger seat. "I'll let you use mine," he said without looking at her, unhitching the tailgate and gesturing for her to climb in the back.

For the first time, Hope noticed what a striking resemblance Brooks Nixon bore to Buster Diggs, the famous porn producer.

Based on appearance alone, he was someone she would never get into a car with in a million years.

"I guess my battery's dead or something," she babbled, shrugging and giggling uncontrollably. "I don't know anything about cars . . . I have roadside assistance through my insurance . . . but there's no cell service out here . . . I'm so sorry to inconvenience you . . . I hope it won't be any trouble . . . you can just drop me back at the gas station if you want."

"They would make you buy something," he grunted.

"Whatever's easier then." She boosted Piggy into the truck bed and climbed in after her.

The ride was bumpy, the misty air bracing. Within minutes they entered the old park. They drove past a devilish-looking clown, his mouth a ten-foot cave with hanging moss covering the entrance. They passed a pile of broken fiberglass horses that looked like one of those depressing pictures Hope's animal rights newsletters always stuck in. The dark side of horse racing, the caption would have read. The most awe-inspiring sight was a splintery wooden roller coaster that leaned sideways like a Tower of Pisa made of toothpicks. Hope pulled her phone from her sweatshirt pocket to steal a picture, but in her rattled state, she set the camera to self-facing and snapped an unflattering portrait of her own scrunched up face.

They pulled up to a building covered with psychedelic rainbows and a sign that read "House of Illusions." Her host got out of the cab and slammed the door.

"You *live* here?" she asked, feigning surprise.

He chuckled. "In a manner of speaking, yes."

She deleted the horrendous accidental photo as he keyed the padlock on the door, a massive warehouse gate that reminded her of ancient Egypt with its solemn pronouncement of long entombed mysteries.

"So are you, like, the caretaker then?"

"For now."

The door swung open to reveal a thrift store junkie's paradise: several lives' worth of unclaimed memorabilia stacked in towers that almost scraped the twenty-five-foot ceiling.

"I don't usually have people in here," he warned her, his tone more informative than apologetic.

"I'm the same way at home," she said as two orange cats darted out across her feet. Their appearance caused a delayed reaction in Piggy, who lurched toward them seconds too late. "You're talking to a lifelong dust bunny breeder here."

The dust bunny line was one she used frequently on her homecare clients when they apologized for clutter, and it probably worked because of its truthfulness; she really did feel more at home in disorganized settings than in tidy ones. The messier the place— the more organic and natural its arrangement of stuff—the less likely she could get in trouble for mucking it up with her presence.

Admitting to her slovenly ways usually put clients at ease, but Brooks' breathing became shallower and more rapid as he heaved a pile of boxes aside and directed her to an old office phone atop a desk strewn with manila envelopes. He clearly wanted her out of there as soon as possible. It was time to can the chit-chat and get straight down to business.

The phone number on her roadside assistance card led to a recording which asked her to enter her nine-digit policy number. The number, of course, occupied the only area of the card with coffee spilled on it. She pressed zero instead, then groaned when the recording informed her of her invalid entry. Experience showed to repeat this cycle three or four times would eventually connect her to a human, so she waited, surveying the space discreetly between each exasperated poke.

As far as hoarding situations went, she'd seen far worse than this. Sure, the guy had more reading materials than any one person could consume in a lifetime, but it looked like he was trying to get through it. Philosophy books sat open on surfaces with passages in them highlighted. Periodicals filled boxes with their date of issue marked on the side. His knickknacks weren't museum-worthy but there wasn't any actual garbage anywhere. And unlike her brother's apartment, this room's disarray had a cohesiveness to it. You could tell the person who owned it liked Japanese art, for example, as well as hot-air balloons, seagulls, rockets, and rainbows. You could also tell he enjoyed messing around with art supplies, like Hope herself. Random rolls of ribbon spilled out of drawers and cans of paintbrushes soaking in muddy swirling liquids created tripping hazards on the floor.

At last, a representative picked up the line. Before she could explain her problem, she had to spell out her full name and address twice. Brooks was looking more agitated as he weaved around through the piled-up boxes flipping on lamps around every corner. He appeared to be looking for some misplaced object, an event she figured must happen hourly in this Bermuda Triangle of human interest. By the time she reached the point in the phone call where she needed him to give directions to the location of her vehicle, he couldn't get any words out. The part of his mouth she could see beneath his mustache had acquired a bluish tint. It reminded her of her dark plum lipstick, the one she liked because it underlined everything she said, the one she would throw out as soon as she got home.

"Um, sir?" she called to him, barely avoiding a major faux pas by calling him by his name, which she wasn't supposed to know.

He looked at her with a terrifying panic, the look of someone being suffocated by his own body.

"Are you asthmatic? Do you have an inhaler?"

He nodded twice and sat on an end table. A ceramic mug fell to the concrete floor and shattered.

"Miss, are you gonna be needing an ambulance, too?" the woman on the other end of the line asked.

"Maybe," Hope said. "Just a minute." She covered the receiver and repeated the question to Brooks, but then mirrored his response when he shook his head no. She tried to convey a tranquil message of safety to him through her eyes. Keeping the asthma sufferer calm was job number one, she remembered from her first aid training.

Another thing she knew from experience; people whose homes had this little floor space usually had one nesting spot, a place where they spent most of their time. Nine times out of ten, any every-day item that went missing could be found there, the forgetter having looked right past it in their frantic search. Hope dropped the phone and dog leash and made a beeline toward a filthy recliner about ten feet from where they stood. A bowl of spaghetti balanced on the chair's arm. Next to it, wedged into the cushion, she saw what looked like pharmaceutical typing on a small plastic canaster.

"Oh, wait, hang on. Is this it?"

As soon as she placed the medicine in his waiting hands, he grabbed onto it and sucked greedily. When he opened his eyes again, they looked miraculously restored. *Could she finish her phone call now?* she asked him wordlessly, pointing at the receiver and tilting her head a little. He nodded his unspoken permission.

"They'll be here in thirty minutes," she said after finally getting across all the relevant information and hanging up. "Are you going to be able to drive me back out to my car?"

"Sure," he said. "I'm fine now." He did look better, though "fine" seemed like a stretch.

To help him recover a sense of normalcy, Hope tried to make small talk by commenting on some of the items in her line of view. Right across from her, an industrial-sized clothing rack housed elaborately patterned shirts in every combination of colors. Hope reached for one of the sleeves and pulled it out admiringly. "I wish more men would wear stuff like this," she said.

He nodded. "I've always believed—"

He paused to puff on his inhaler again before finishing his thought, like a stoner drawing on a spliff. The action gave weight to whatever words would come after it. Hope waited, expecting some grand pronouncement.

"The only respectable answer to the question, 'Are you *really* gonna wear *that?*' is 'Yes.'"

She laughed. "Words to live by."

From a piano bench she kept him company with sporadic small talk for about ten more minutes, squirming awkwardly like the single front-row viewer of an intimate piece of performance art. The oxygen and adrenalin had boosted his ability to put words together, pushing him briefly into performance mode, and for a twinkle or two he revived his old eloquent media star persona from all those interviews. But much of what he said in those spurts failed to register in her overstimulated mind. She kept up appearances by nodding in the appropriate places—or trying to, anyway—while inwardly rewinding the entire tape to watch it again.

She broke out of her trance when she noticed a black square box with speakers and an assortment of dials on it, much too big for a CD player.

"Hey, is that a karaoke machine?" she asked, noticing the telltale microphone.

"Yep," he said. "I use it to practice my honesty."

She nodded at the cryptic comment as though she completely understood it.

"It's like my mother always said," he added, "Never open your mouth until you're prepared to speak a full sentence you can stand behind.'"

"Good advice," she said, smiling.

She pulled out her cell phone to make a show of checking the time. "Well, I suppose we'd better get going. They'll be at the car soon."

"Sure."

As they left the House of Illusions, she noticed for the first time that one of the window panels twenty feet above them had no glass in it.

"Wow. It must kinda suck in here when it rains," she observed.

He stopped, arched his back and considered the gaping, jagged hole and the sky beyond it.

"I have safety and room to breathe," he said. "That's all anybody really needs."

On the drive back, he let her and Piggy ride in the front. She thanked him again, profusely, mostly to fill the uncomfortable silence. Finally, as they pulled up next to the swan car, he turned to her and almost smiled.

"No trouble. It was just one of those things," he said. "Wrong place, right time, know what I'm sayin'?"

She laughed. "Sorry, it's just—the way you said that. The way you said *know what I'm sayin'*. That's how people in prison talk. When my brother first got out of—"

She stopped herself, realizing that she'd just used a move straight out of a psychic cold-reading handbook: "Try to get a subject to open up by dropping suggestive hints." It was becoming her natural method of communication.

"Never mind."

He chuckled, and from this point on, she wondered if he saw through her naivete ruse, if he knew she'd been aware of his whole backstory from the start.

"I can see that," he said, his eyes widening a little. "Not being understood was probably what got them in there in the first place."

"Hmm."

The next suggestive hint she dropped was completely intentional.

"Somebody should write a book about that."

He laughed again, a heartier and more genuine laugh this time. "Well, with the tripe that gets published nowadays, any idiot can write a book. All you need is a catchy title and a good hook."

At the first sight of the assistance vehicle's headlights, he hurried her out of his truck. Apparently, he'd suffered through enough social interaction for one day.

The driver, a long-haired dreamboat who looked about fifteen, adjusted her starter by tapping on it a few times with a hammer. The fix would get her to the nearest mechanic, he said, where she would find several motels within walking distance. As she watched him work, she noticed a shiny gold object on the ground and reached for it. Turned out it was a hand mirror for a doll. She put it in her pocket to keep as a souvenir.

Another day and three hundred and fifty dollars later, Hope returned home. She tried to remember what she'd been so vexed about as to require the escape in the first place, but decided if she couldn't remember, it probably didn't matter.

TEN

SAYING "NO" TO PUSHY SALESPEOPLE GETS easier the older you get. The hormonal changes that turned you from a carefree little spaz into a mopey, sensitive teenager linger into early adulthood, causing an excess of pointless empathy. But after life kicks you around a bit, you realize the receiver of the rejection will live to see another day if you turn them down. Not everyone will reject them, and someone might even give them a "yes" at some point, as improbable as that may seem. Looking back now, Hope wondered: would she even have started working at Mystic Partners in the first place if it weren't for the dangerous combination of her youth and Delma's savvy salesmanship?

Delma lived in Malibu permanently now—and was quite senile, gathering from numerous accounts—but Hope still harbored a ridiculous sense of responsibility toward her. On the subconsciously ingrained level where such absurd thoughts dwell, she believed she couldn't quit without hurting the old bird's feelings. Not that she thought about quitting. Not every day, anyway. Not very seriously. At least not before that afternoon in Connie Chi's office.

As a side hustle, Connie represented a multi-level marketing outfit called Pink Box Accessories, and with blatant impropriety she sometimes leveraged her authority to gain new customers and recruits. Hope was already on high alert, having noticed her coworkers getting sucked into their boss's whitewash with alarming frequency lately.

Connie worked subtly, wearing different pieces of overpriced costume jewelry every day and making deliberate, casual-looking hand gestures designed to bring attention to the trinkets and elicit compliments. As soon as one unsuspecting victim would say, "Cool bracelet," Connie would swoop in with a barrage of cultish direct sales jargon. "I've become a part of this amazing company that has totally changed my life," she would say. "They empower women by putting us in charge of our own income. I get to travel and go to cool parties with games and prizes and stuff. There's one at the Holiday Inn this Saturday. You would love it. I'll put you on the guest list."

Hope first learned of the con game indirectly after an appropriately laughable misunderstanding. Noticing the glossy fuchsia booklet on Shawna's desk, she read the words *Pink Box Accessories* aloud and asked, in all seriousness, what on earth would make a woman want to have her vagina bedazzled?

Shawna had just taken a sip from her water bottle at the time and had to swallow hard to avoid laughing through her nose.

"I guess it is an unfortunate brand name, isn't it?" she said. "No, this is Connie's latest business venture. I told her I'd take a catalogue and show it around for her. I can't buy anything though because cheap metal interferes with my body chemistry. It has to be sterling silver or 14 karat gold or I'll break out in hives."

"Oh, dear," Hope said, widening her eyes on the first photograph she opened to, an elaborate floral bib necklace with tear-shaped plastic pearls dangling from it. "Yeah, that would give me hives too. Thanks for the warning."

Since then Hope had taken a defensive stance against Connie. That afternoon in the hallway, when the woman handed her a file using an awkward and unnatural claw-like hand configuration—to make sure Hope caught sight of the baubles on her fingers—she decided to launch a preemptive strike.

"Is something wrong with your hand?" she asked.

Connie faked an inquisitive head tilt. "No, why?"

"Why are you holding the paper all weird like that?"

Connie retracted her hand and hid it behind her back, using the other one to tuck her short hair behind her ear and reveal a Ritz-cracker-sized earring covered in paisley rhinestones. "I didn't feel like I was holding the paper in any unusual way."

"Okay," Hope said, maintaining her suspicious gaze as Connie brought out the ringed hand again to comb through the turquoise strands on yet another statement piece, this one a woven Cleopatra-style number. "Well, was there anything else?"

Connie's neck flushed. "Actually, I was wondering why you didn't respond to my email invitation. You're the only one who hasn't."

Hope's pulse quickened in readiness for confrontation.

"Oh, you mean that jewelry thing? It looked like spam so I deleted it. I thought your email got hacked."

Connie stepped back and smoothed out her white linen shirt. "Actually," she said, "It's an event I've been working *very* hard on for a company that I'm *very* proud to have partnered with, and I would *really* appreciate it if you'd give it a read."

"Oh, I did," Hope said. "I won't be able to make it, sorry. It's just not my kind of thing." She smiled and started walking away. "Thanks for thinking of me, though."

Shortly after she returned to her desk, Connie summoned her to her office.

"Hope, do you recall the mission statement of Mystic Partners?"

Hope turned her face toward the ceiling. "Um . . . to guide seekers in discovering—no, reaching—their true destinies, and, um

. . . help them—no, enable them—to achieve balance and happiness in their lives?"

"You got most of it," Connie said. "And we take that aim seriously, Hope. We take it just as seriously with our team members as we do with our clients. Do you know why I invited you to the Pink Box Adornment Gala?"

"Uh . . . to try and sell me stuff I guess?"

Connie frowned, straightened some folders in a wire basket, then took off her glasses and exhaled loudly. "It's because I care about your success," she said.

Success at what, Hope wondered, watching the light refractions from Connie's endless multifaceted nuggets skate across the walls like stars.

"At the Gala, you'll have the chance to enrich yourself with quality products and empowering opportunities. You're one of my senior team members, Hope, and frankly, I'm a bit troubled to hear such an opportunity doesn't interest you at all."

Hope folded her hands on her lap, trying to draw attention to the conversation's stupidity by treating it with a solemnity it didn't deserve.

"I guess I don't think I need enriching," she said. "Not by crap jewelry and a shady pyramid scheme, anyway. That's all. No offense. And besides, if I wear anything except 24 karat gold, I'll get nasty little warts all over my body."

Connie appeared to deflate before Hope's eyes, as if a tiny puncture in her skin were splintering off in all directions.

"Here's the thing, Hope. I'm getting the feeling that you aren't really fitting in around here anymore. Are you willing to try and work on that?"

"No."

For a word with such a straightforward definition, "no" is rarely interpreted as "an expression of dissent in response to a question"

—except, apparently, when "no" is the asker's desired answer. After more than fifteen years, Hope swiftly found herself cleaning out her desk, barely registering the moment as different from any other. The desk contained little in the way of items she cared about. The valuable things had made their way home with her one at a time for months now, as if they knew this day would come before she did. The real severing from her job had probably taken place right around the time she began training team members for webcam work: showing them how to not look like they were bored to tears, telling them not to calculate the minutes while they spoke, showing them how to decorate their workspace to make it look "mystical." As she passed through the lobby for the final time, she felt almost nothing. Just the faintest hint of sadness at something ending, like throwing dead flowers in the trash.

"Life isn't as serious as the human mind makes it." So read the paper tab on the end of the "tranquil moments" tea bag Hope pulled out as soon as she got home. She tended to put more stock in these manufactured words of wisdom than she should, and today she clung to the printed catchphrase like gospel. Her pantry contained boxes of tea designed to deliver any possible mental state one could want—from "alert and focused" to "libido lift" and "blues chaser"—and each bag held its own little corny inspirational quote like a kite. She pulled down her latest favorite thrift store mug, a black one emblazoned with the words "Psycho Bitch from Hell," popped in one tea bag from each box and laid their corresponding tabs in front of her like tarot cards.

As fucked up as the Universe is, it never stops imagining ways to take care of itself.

She grabbed her phone and opened Desmond's last text, a *how's it going* from the day before which she hadn't bothered to answer yet.

Dude, I just quit Mystic Partners
Awesome. What r u gonna do next?
No idea. Any suggestions?
Maybe you should start a blog
What's a blog?

Truth be told, Hope wasn't unfamiliar with the term; she just wanted to rid herself of its previous associations. During their ill-fated coffee date, Shawna had droned on and on about a blog called "Manifesting Riches," forcing Hope to look it up on In-Focus's communal computer and refusing to shut up until she acknowledged its greatness. As a result, Hope now thought "blog" was one of those words that sounds like a perfect phonetic imitation of what it describes; a combination of "blah" and "ugh." But Desmond's take on the subject would probably make it less disagreeable to her, as his take on most subjects did.

You get your own webpage and write about what-
ever you want

What's the point?

To get stuff off your chest. You can make money
from it if you're good

'Blog' sounds like a throw-up sound

Haha well you asked for suggestions and I gave
you one

Thanks. I'll give it some thought. Later

You're welcome. Onward and upward. xo

After staring at the wall and scratching Piggy's head for forty minutes, she rose to pull one of the many half-used journals from a shelf in her bedroom. The cover featured an introspective-looking teddy bear with a pencil behind his ear and the words *penny for your thoughts* in a bubble above his head. It took ten more minutes for her to find one half-functioning pen among the scores of dried-up ballpoints dirtying every surface in the apartment like cigarette butts. Finally, she settled into an easy chair facing the window, as the light gray sky began its slow final curtain into blackness.

ENRICHING LIES

CONFESSIONS OF A PROFESSIONAL BULLSHIT ARTIST

A decent start, she decided, and good enough for now. She still had 45 minutes before the thrift stores closed, and she could use a pick-me-up. A perky new throw pillow, maybe, or a comfy sweater so ugly she would never wear it out of the house. Anything would do, as long as it made her likely new reality as a shut-in sound more appealing.

The car radio hissed and whined as she searched the dial for anything she could stand. Eventually she stumbled on a station playing "Fantastic Dream," Wasted Grave's one and only top forty hit and the only one she didn't exactly love. In fact, she kind of hated it. It sounded better to her now, though—maybe due to her newfound freedom. Like how music sounds better after a breakup.

Oh, oh, oh! Take me there, fantastic dream!
Oh, oh, oh! Take me there, fantastic dream!

Hope kept singing after the song ended, and when the DJ started talking, she almost didn't hear what he said.

"Breaking news from Ashbrook, Oregon: Author and lecturer Brooks Nixon is dead at age 62. Local authorities say the reclusive Nixon was found by his lawyer Tuesday morning, apparently having suffered a massive heart attack."

Hope pulled into the parking lot of the Glory and Grace Thrift Store and turned the ignition off, but kept the radio on and listened. What she thought she would hear next she wasn't sure; it seemed entirely possible that Brooks would make some weird contentious declaration from beyond the grave, some head-scratching little quip that explained nothing but kept her tethered to the radio far longer than she needed to be there. That his body had given out she could believe easily; that he didn't have anything to say about it seemed like the most outrageous crock of hooey she'd ever heard. And she'd heard her share of tall fables.

" . . . Nixon rose to fame in 1986," the DJ continued, "with his book *Manage, Manipulate, and Maneuver; How to get your Noncommittal Man Hooked in Three Easy Steps.* But in later years, he became an outspoken opponent of monogamous partnerships. 'Narcissus Nixon'—as he was called by some—spent two years in federal prison on a larceny charge and later won a lawsuit against the judge in his case. He lived alone in a converted theme park attraction formerly known as the House of Illusions."

The DJ's voice switched from solemn news reader to relaxed entertainment commentator with jarring ease. "Well, rest in peace, Narcissus Nixon. Like my Irish grandfather used to say, 'May you be in Heaven half an hour before the devil knows you're dead.' And we've got more of your favorite hits coming right up."

Just a minute, Hope thought. That was all she needed to pull herself together. Maybe two, but no more. In two minutes, she'd be ready to face the world.

After five minutes she emerged from the car, and she hoped her red eyes wouldn't make the church ladies at Glory Grace mistake her for a drug addict.

She wouldn't ever tell anyone she cried when she learned of his death. How could she? She'd spent half her life rolling her eyes at the mere mention of the guy's name. There were *real* things in the world worth crying about, after all.

Nearly a year had passed since her surreal visit to Thrillville, and it had been the shortest year of her life. Not only because it was a smaller fraction of the whole thing, but because up until today, so little movement had occurred within it.

The humorous anecdote of meeting him had played out a thousand times in her mind, but in this new light, it transformed into a different story altogether. It had been a tale of poetic justice before. She'd focused on the squalor of his surroundings, taking secret pleasure in the messy humanness of him. She had ignored the parts where his celebrity persona came to the surface, as his voice had taken on a didactic tone then, and nothing compelled her to tune out more than sensing arrogance. *Here he goes*, she had thought, *mansplaining the nature of existence to me.*

But now she found herself re-examining those sections, pulling them up like polished rocks from the bottom of a riverbed. The pitiful rantings of a sad, old has-been now presented themselves as a previously undiscovered historical manuscript, something she alone was privy to. She almost wished she had paid closer attention.

She opened the glass door to the Glory and Grace Thrift Store; as the mechanical bell completed its high-pitched whine, a folksy chorus of acoustic hallelujahs greeted her from a boombox on the counter. Some guy who sounded vaguely like Jerry Garcia was singing about redemption, and the song provided the perfect backdrop to the images of Narcissus Nixon flickering like an old home movie across her memory's ripped screen.

"One can never have too many books, right?" she had lied to him, commenting on the first thing in her line of vision—the bountifully stuffed bookshelf—as the only means she could think of to fill the silence.

This got Narcissus going, propping him up on his soap box, and that's when Hope tuned out, focusing on the fact that he had bookshelves made of cinder blocks and plywood, just like her brother did before Lucinda entered the picture. *Wait til I tell Asher about this,* she had thought. *This is so insane.*

Narcissus Nixon then told her these days he only learned things in order to unlearn them. He said most people grab on to easy answers and their curiosity stops there. But just past every realization lies a complete obliteration of it. This axing out of awareness can be terrifying when you first encounter it, and it deepens your curiosity tenfold. But eventually you learn to love the obliteration itself. He then told her he planned to keep on reading until there was no more curiosity left. Nothing but a sweet, merciful silence.

The knickknack section at the Glory and Grace Thrift Store contained an inordinate number of shell sculptures today. Someone must have donated their entire collection of frogs and owls with clamshell mouths and plastic googly eyes, and whoever did the merchandising here had decided to place these ridiculous creatures next to more serious shell offerings like macramé planters, picture frames, and jewelry boxes. Hope eyed a shell-coated journal with pulpy unrefined paper inside but dropped it when she remembered a horrible video she'd seen once about seashell harvesting in the Philippines. She left the grotesque sea cemetery and moved on to the stationary section. There, in a blue milk crate, she found unused journals and notebooks of every size and color and scooped them up, overcome by a zealous urge to fill all of them. It didn't even matter what they had on the covers. Things like Bible verses, babies in adult clothing, and American flags would've normally turned her off, but if they had blank pages, she added them to the pile. Likely their destinies contained nothing more groundbreaking than grocery lists, passwords, and phone numbers, but for now it didn't matter. For now, they contained possibility.

The folksy man on the boombox sang something about

"stumbling in the darkness and calling out His name"; one of the church ladies let out an unexpected chortle.

"Every time I hear 'stumbling in the darkness,'" she said to her friend, "I think about stubbing my toe when I get up in the middle of the night to go pee."

Her friend laughed. "I'm pretty sure it would be a sin to call His name then," she said.

Hope smiled at the church ladies above a display of Styrofoam wreath forms, wanting to acknowledge their genuinely funny joke. But the church ladies didn't notice her.

Back in the House of Illusions, on top of a piano with several missing keys, there sat a cardboard box labeled "love letters." Hope made the same observation about the love letters she had made about the books, that she supposed a person could never have too many of them.

Narcissus told her the letters weren't from one person but from many, most of whom he had never met. Then he kept talking, and Hope tuned out. She focused instead on the box itself, a shipping box for a brand of inexpensive toilet paper.

Narcissus Nixon said he didn't understand why people fear dying alone. There's no such thing as dying alone, he said. Even when someone dies indigent and doesn't have anyone to do their funeral, the state buries them using prison labor and the prisoners sing hymns and say prayers for the dead person. He told her he had witnessed one of these funerals firsthand once. He said the prisoners cried, and he said in his whole life he had never seen grief so pure, so uncomplicated. Narcissus Nixon then said none of us are ever really alone, no matter how hard we try. And he said he had tried.

"Lord knows," he said, "I've tried."

A bunch of rainbow-colored yarn went into Hope's shopping

basket, followed by some knitting needles and a book on how to crochet. What the hell, she thought, she'd have plenty of free time on her hands. Might as well develop a skill. Bust out a few scarves. Send them out as Christmas presents to all her extended family. Maybe make herself a big gaudy afghan while she was at it. When she pulled out her wallet to pay for everything, something in the bottom of her purse caught the light. Between the hand sanitizer, old receipts, and melted lipstick, she rediscovered the doll mirror she'd found in Ashbrook.

In the fluorescent ceiling light, she saw for the first time the elaborate pattern of swirls on its tiny handle. It might look pretty cool as a necklace, she thought. Or hanging from her rear-view mirror.

Clichéd things people say about the dearly departed aren't universally applicable. Not every dead woman was the kind who "would light up the room" when she walked into it, and not every dead guy "would give you the shirt off his back." Brooks Nixon would likely do neither of those things. But, given the right set of circumstances, he might have let you use his phone. And if, in his relatively brief time on Earth, he managed to gain some insight he thought others might find useful, he was the kind of guy who would share it rather than keep it all to himself.

* * *

THE REST OF THE WEEKEND PASSED at the lethargic speed of volcanic lava. At the start of her next shift with Gwendola Andersen, the familiar beige walls of her client's apartment complex seemed darker than usual. She stepped into the elevator with its framed ads for hair salons and breakfast joints, and the weight of her undetermined future nearly crushed her. Could this be what eternity felt like, she wondered? Pressing a button against every instinct in your body to reach the floor where you would cocoon yourself in apathy just to face the day's trials, slogging away for a pittance doing the work you got by default because no one else wanted it? No, this couldn't be it, she told herself, and the words repeated themselves and got louder in her head as she approached the apartment and gave Gwendola the secret knock. *This can't be all there is.*

"Yeah," called the voice from inside—instead of "come in"—and Hope could tell from her client's curt and pissy tone that she would have to start the day apologizing for nonexistent trespasses.

Gwendola stood two feet from the door, fisted hands on her hips, her orange floral shirt buttoned incorrectly so the right tail hung lower than the left. "What did you do with my fruit can opener," she said matter-of-factly, with no inquisitive uplift at the end of the sentence.

"I . . . didn't—"

"You know I always have canned applesauce with toaster waffles on Monday mornings. But I can't have canned applesauce without a can opener, now, can I? Do you know what happens when one part of my routine gets botched, Hope? Do you?"

Hope scanned her memory for the polite way to say "you go all apeshit," but the words momentarily escaped her.

"I can't function, that's what!"

"Right," Hope said, taking a tentative step forward. "Okay, Gwendola. I know. I understand how frustrating this is for you. I'm going to do everything I can to get you back on track, okay? But you're going to have to cooperate with me."

The disheveled woman expelled a burst of air through her gritted teeth.

"I lose stuff all the time at home," Hope said, not realizing that her effort to find common ground left her wide open to attack.

"I'm sure you do," Gwendola snarked.

"I mean, everyone knows the feeling," Hope clarified. "It feels like someone *must* have taken it to mess with you, right? Stuff doesn't just grow legs and walk away."

"Oh, it doesn't, huh?"

Hope hung her bag on the rack by the door and stepped into the center of the room with purpose. "No, it doesn't. Now the first step here is to calm down. So I want you to take a seat over there by the window. Go on."

Gwendola waddled over to the assigned position, shaking her head and mumbling the whole way.

"Now I'm going to go back through all the most likely places. Sometimes all it takes is a set of fresh eyes."

Almost immediately she spotted a set of white plastic handles out of the corner of her eye; the utensil in question was resting open on a TV tray—among some wadded-up napkins and olive pits—in front of the dusty-rose couch. This tableau surrounded the end of the sofa with the most dirt—the side where the cushion had become permanently dented—the place where its owner spent most of her time.

She could have declared victory right then, but to do so would've been too easy. Gwendola would've probably accused her of having just produced the can opener from her pocket. Something similar had happened with a hair scrunchie once, and suspicion of Hope had been the final outcome of that fiasco. ("Next time *ask* before you steal something," Gwendola had said after Hope quickly found the leopard-print accessory wrapped in the twisted sheets of the bed.)

"Seen any good TV shows lately?" Hope called from the messy kitchen now, trying to pass the question off as an aimless conversation starter while she picked through a pile of dirty dishes in the sink. Gwendola shared her penchant for true crime docu-dramas; discussing them might steer her mind in the direction of the couch.

Gwendola thought for a second, then her face brightened as much as it could under the circumstances. "I saw one about a rich guy who killed his neighbors and burned their house down because their kid's treehouse blocked his view."

"Oh, yeah," Hope said, chuckling. "Last night's episode of *Suburban Sociopaths*. That was a good one." On the counter next to her sat a half-eaten can of peaches, a thin layer of dust coating the brine. "Except it was gross when he put the wife in the woodchipper . . . Say. Are these generic peaches any good? I usually buy the local organic ones at Health Max, but they're expensive."

Gwendola shrugged. "I eat 'em like potato chips," she said. "Did you find the can opener yet?"

Hope turned and flashed her a calm smile. "Not yet," she said, "but bear with me for a minute. I have a hunch." She then strolled to the TV tray, picked up the truant object and held it in the air with a triumphant, "Eureka!"

The look on Gwendola's face switched quickly from impatience to complete bafflement. "What the hell was it doing *there?*"

Hope regarded her with authority and a measured dose of playfulness. "Don't ask me," she said. "I'm not the one eating peaches in front of the TV like potato chips." She then touched the tip of the can opener to her temple and grinned. "Fresh eyes," she said. "That's why they pay me the big bucks. Should I make you a waffle now?"

Gwendola turned away, conceding the argument with a good-natured wave of her hand. "Well, you seem to know everything. Why don't you decide?"

"One waffle with applesauce, coming right up."

After saving the morning with such suave efficiency, it would be hard to get in trouble for much else; Hope figured she could probably sail through the day on these laurels. They watched the local news together and then Gwendola went to work on a sculpture in the spare bedroom while Hope washed dishes and put a weeks' worth of minestrone into little Tupperware containers. No can opener required. As long as no crafting supplies went missing, another workday would soon end without catastrophe.

"Well, I'm all done in the kitchen," Hope eventually announced, peeking around the corner into Gwendola's spectacular craft room. "What's next on your priority list?" A six-foot bulletin board hung on one wall of the craft room with at least a dozen photographs of raccoons in every possible position. Some crouched in waiting, some munched on discarded pizza crusts, some rolled on their backs in mischievous reverie and others slept curled up like kittens. Hope loved raccoons. She'd once told Gwendola—who'd listened attentively—about how people with raccoon totems tend to be clever and courageous truth seekers.

Gwendola lifted her head from behind a large stack of copper objects in various patinas. "Laundry time I guess," she sighed. She steadied herself on a rickety easel and strained to heave her round body to a standing position, knocking several tubes of acrylic paint to the floor in the process.

Hope extended her arms futilely. "You can just keep working in here if you want," she offered, "I know where the dirty clothes are. Just let me take care of it."

Wincing with allover pain, Gwendola shook her head. "No. I have some sweaters with special care instructions. I don't want you ruining them." She arched her back, groaned, and farted loudly. "I'll need to show you the proper way to handle them. Come on."

As they passed the front hallway, a mechanical whistle sounded from the coat rack and Hope's flesh froze. The noise had come from her cell phone, Gwendola's number one pet peeve. "People checking their cell phones while they're working make me furious," she'd declared on their first day together. "So I have one rule: turn the damn thing off. If I hear so much as one little ping while you're working, that's it." The throat-slitting gesture Gwendola had made then still haunted Hope. Her turquoise-rimmed eyes had burned with more intensity than usual, the sting of the phantom blade's slice nearly palpable.

So much for *this* catastrophe-free day.

Before she reached the bedroom door, Gwendola stopped in her tracks; she extended one arm to stop Hope from moving ahead and cupped her ear in the direction of the coat rack. Another whistle sounded, and she faced Hope with her hands on her hips and a toxically smug expression on her face.

"Well? Aren't you gonna answer it?"

Hope's eyes darted back and forth instinctually as though looking for a way out. "I guess I forgot to—sorry. My bad. I'll just turn it off now."

A maniacal laugh sprang from Gwendola's dark soul. "Oh, no, don't do that on my account, dear. Your social life is far more important than your work here. Now, let's see who it is. Go on."

"Okay." Hope stepped toward the coat rack, reached for the black vinyl bag hanging there and undid its turn lock, not about to let this freak her out. If her getting fired was the most original thing the Universe could come up with right now, so be it. She retrieved the phone and opened her text messages. The first one was from Rush, whom she hadn't heard from in six months.

Watching an artistic film right now, can't help thinking of you.

Good thing he used code language, Hope thought. Gwendola looked like she was about to grab the phone and read it aloud mockingly.

With imperceptible thumb movements, Hope deleted the message, opened to the second one, and prayed for some uninteresting spam. Instead she found a greeting from Nathan, whom she hadn't heard from in almost as long.

Hey there. It's been a while. Whatcha been up to?

"Well?" Gwendola probed, tapping her foot.

Hope didn't say anything out loud, but her imaginary girlfriends got treated to a deliciously snarky line as they all strolled beside her down an imaginary city street, imaginary chai lattes and shopping bags in hand. *It's raining douchebags,* she quipped to them. *Where's my umbrella?*

Her face must have betrayed something, because Gwendola contorted her own ruby-lined lips into a sadistic smile and raised her eyebrows. "What is it, dear? Is it your boyfriend? Is he lonely without you?" She made a sad puppy-dog face.

"Yeah," Hope said, slapping the flip phone shut and returning it to her handbag. "They both are." If she was going to go down anyway, she might as well throw some grease on the flames.

"Sucks for them," she added. "Guess they'll have to settle for their wives."

Her confession might well have come out in a cloud of pepper spray the way Gwendola reacted, stepping back and waving her arms as though knocked off balance. Once recovered, she asked Hope, in a much milder tone this time, whether she planned to answer the messages. The expected demands for a humiliating recital never came. When Hope said she didn't, Gwendola shrugged and waddled away to the laundry room.

As Hope followed, a mix of relief and disappointment settled into something like bland acceptance in the bottom of her stomach.

About ten minutes into the tedious sorting of whites, colored, and delicate, Gwendola leaned back on a window ledge and let her hands drop to her sides, two silk robes pooling on the dirty carpet below.

"So you like married men, do ya?" She asked.

"No," Hope answered, honestly. "I hate them. They're the worst." All fears of losing her job had become irrelevant by this point.

Gwendola chuckled a little to herself and nodded, scooping up the robes together and stuffing them in a mesh bag that hung on a closet doorknob. "They are, aren't they," she said.

Without reacting to the comment, Hope gave herself fully to the task of untangling a nest of motley sequined scarves from each other. She couldn't react because she had no way of knowing what kind of reaction Gwendola wanted. Was this old basket case trying to bond here? It sure looked that way. But how do you bond with someone you only know as frightening and unstable? She reached for another laundry pile, which she soon realized was only one enormous pair of jeans with a single enormous bra coiled tightly around it. She decided to keep quiet and let Gwendola do the talking.

"I suppose . . . " Gwendola said with a thoughtful head tilt, "it is kind of nice in a way. I mean, you're the one who's getting all the best they have to offer. Right?"

Hope nodded cautiously, as though having a conversation with a gun-toting hostage taker. She didn't know where Gwendola was going with this. Maybe the woman had been the wife of a cheater long ago and was trying to trap Hope into admitting something, fishing for a valid reason to kill her and chop her body into tiny pieces which she would then dry out and use in one of her sculptures.

"And another nice thing about them," she said, lost in reverie as she lovingly combed the yarn of a latch-hooked vest with her fingers. "They take exactly what they need from you and nothing more."

Hope nodded again, still reluctant to show she had any strong opinions on the matter.

"It's lonely being the other woman though," Gwendola continued. "You can't talk about it even though it's a huge part of your life."

"Nope," Hope said. This was one statement she didn't mind acknowledging as unequivocally true.

"So you become your own best friend and therapist. Lucky for me, I've always been very good at taking care of myself."

"Clearly," Hope said, clearing her throat.

"I have a trick," Gwendola said. "Every night when I go to sleep, I ask for guidance to come to me in my dreams. During my twelve years as Arthur's lover, I unlocked much wisdom there."

There was no doubt about it. Hope had a knack for getting people to unload all their most awkward shit on her. She never sought out the messy entrails of broken human spirits, but somehow, such frailty always found her. As she stood there, literally and figuratively knee deep in dirty laundry, she accepted the role with a massive internal shudder.

And so it began, the slow recounting of Gwendola's decades-old dreams, dreams meticulously edited over the years to create lessons far more coherent than their muddy subconscious source could have imagined.

Before she got started, Gwendola collapsed into a squeaky office chair and sighed, indicating her contribution to the day's manual labor had ended. Something more important was required from her now, a duty she'd always known would present itself one day. She sat up as straight as her diseased frame would let her, an expert witness about to deliver testimony on this most salacious of subjects.

"The night Arthur first made his intentions known," she reminisced, "I dreamt of a beautiful, impoverished town. A place kind of like Tijuana, only English-speaking. In the dream I was walking along, minding my own business, when Arthur came up to me. He pointed at a beat-up bus and told me of a wonderful adventure he thought I should go on. I had nothing else to do, so I hopped on the bus."

A digital alarm clock started beeping somewhere in the room, no doubt the result of some programming mishap the day before, and Gwendola voiced her irritation in a series of mumbled expletives. The directive implied toward Hope couldn't have been clearer; find the damn thing and shut it off—now—so we don't lose the plot.

Hope silenced the errant appliance with the efficient obedience of a genie.

" . . . so I climb aboard and take a seat in the back. In the front, Arthur and his wife are sitting together. He has his arm around her but turns around and winks at me. Cheeky bastard. Anyway, before long we're in the middle of nowhere and I realize I'm barefoot."

"Of course you are," Hope said.

"Yeah . . . so the bus stops, and I tell the driver *I don't have any shoes on and don't know where we're going.* He points me to a little roadside hut full of flip-flops and says not to worry. The bus will make a full circle by the end of the day, so I'll end up back where I started."

The punchline of this dream seemed imminent, so Hope stood in readiness to take the first basket of laundry downstairs, trusting her subtle use of nonverbal cues to speed things along.

" . . . Well, I get my shoes. The bus ends up going to a play in which Arthur's wife stars as the Virgin Mary of all things. The play's an absolute lemon, but instead of being annoyed I just laugh. I can laugh as much as I want, see, because now I have shoes on my feet and I know I'm going home."

After the last sentence, Gwendola looked directly at Hope and made a hand gesture like turning an imaginary key in her brain. Her eyes lit up like pressed-on sweatshirt rhinestones.

"Ah," Hope said. "So . . . the dream told you it would all be fine as long as you took care of your own needs?"

Gwendola nodded slowly, bending her upper body so far it almost descended into a bow.

"Very wise," Hope said as she backed toward the door with the basket in her arms. "Tell you what. Let me take this first load down, and when I get back you can give me the next installment."

"Okay," Gwendola said, squinting at the bundle as though inspecting Hope's sorting skills. "Now, remember to use a quarter cup of fabric softener and set the dial to warm water. If the water's ten degrees too hot or too cold, I'll know."

"Got it."

After piling the clothes in the machine, Hope sat by an open window in the laundry room, massaged her temples and wished she smoked cigarettes. A clock on the wall said 3:10; she could have sworn the digital clock in the craft room had said 3:10 when she fixed its misfiring alarm what felt like hours ago. She waited until it said 3:20, prepared a story about a sticky coin slot to explain her long absence, then dragged her reluctant body back up the stairs.

" . . . The first few years with Arthur were wonderful. He made me feel like the only woman on Earth. And the elicit nature of the affair was . . . exciting." Gwendola hugged herself and shivered when she said the word "exciting," creating a spectacle Hope could foresee taking several weeks to extricate from her visual memory.

"I knew it couldn't last forever though. The first sign that I needed to make a change came the night I dreamt of the Picasso House."

Hope raised her eyebrows. "Picasso House, huh? Do tell."

The Picasso House dream would prove much longer and more detailed than the bus dream, requiring Gwendola to stand at the bathroom door while Hope rinsed out a bucket of queen-sized pantyhose in the sink.

The plot unfolded in a mansion full of original Picasso artwork, and it could have been told far more expediently if the narrator hadn't found it necessary to describe each art piece in detail. At any rate, a voice sounding like Arthur's promised Gwendola she could keep whatever pieces she wanted from the house; after Gwendola eagerly grabbed up a dozen or so of her favorites, she called out to the voice to find it gone. Worse, she was then ordered out of the house by Arthur's wife. ("Who didn't even care a wit about art!")

At that final insult, Hope turned off the faucet and dried her hands. "Wow. That guy sounds like a total jerk," she said. "I don't blame you for dumping him."

But the entire Arthur saga, it turned out, was still far from over. It took three more prophetic dreams for Gwendola to finally break free from the lech. By the end of the final dream—in which her lover's wife appeared as an exterminator and rid her home of cockroaches—Hope had cleared every piece of washable fabric from the bedroom.

"Was that the end?" she called from behind the bamboo screen in the crafts room, where her new job entailed retrieving various paint brushes and solvents from a locker cabinet.

"Or is there a sequel?" she added, realizing her voice might have sounded too hopeful. "You know, where the heroine becomes a famous artist in her own right?"

Gwendola laughed. "I'll have to make something decent first," she said. Her arms relaxed and the paintbrushes dropped to the floor and bounced on the newspapers there with sad little taps.

She then stood up and swept the bamboo screen away with a fierce, determined finality that seemed designed to suggest something laughably anticlimactic was about to happen.

"But . . . I'm afraid, this is as good as it gets," she said.

With no time to craft any kind of a reaction to the finished sculpture other than her most honest one, Hope gasped and braced herself against the wall.

In Hope's entire life as a flea-market junkie, no knickknack had stirred her quite like this one did. The piece was terrifying and adorable at the same time. It gave a visceral warning of ice-cold sharpness, yet it also oozed sensuality and warmth. Undeniably whimsical, one could also imagine it revered as a holy object by some esoteric culture in a far away and far-out land. Cosmic, but earthy. Seriously hilarious. Organically contrived. Cagey and dubious, yet genuine. Cool as hell, in other words. It was the weirdest thing Hope had ever seen and she loved it.

Hope shook her head in lieu of words she couldn't come up with. "I . . . um . . . What the—?"

"It has no symbolic meaning whatsoever," Gwendola insisted, in direct response to the imagined questions. "I call him Lars. So, what do you think?"

Hope smiled and sat down on a stool, relieved at the prospect of being able to speak her mind honestly for the first time that day. She couldn't explain what she thought, exactly, she told Gwendola. But she knew this thing—whatever it was—was a thing she needed to have in her life.

"How much do you want for him?"

Word on the street among the Enchanted Hands homecare set was Gwendola hadn't sold a piece of art in decades. More of a hobbyist, she made things only to deconstruct them and make them into something new. Hope assumed her offer to buy the sculpture would come as a welcome surprise.

At first the artist demurred, but after some back and forth they reached an agreement beneficial to both parties: forty bucks cash, plus rides to the junkyard once a week for the next two months.

When the day's end finally came and Hope started to leave with her purchase, Gwendola stopped her. "Wait just a minute, before you go, I just need—"

"The can opener is in the second drawer from the top next to the fridge," Hope interrupted. She could afford to chide a little now.

Gwendola laughed. "No, I need to fix his mustache."

"Don't touch him!" Hope snapped. "He's perfect just the way he is."

"All right then. If you insist."

Carrying the masterpiece out of the building proved less awkward than Hope expected. She knew she wouldn't mind the looks she got from strangers, but expected more difficulty maneuvering in and out of the elevator and loading him into the hatchback. With the passenger seat down, his head could rest next to her as she drove. The base of the sculpture was a little too big for the back door to close without a bungee cord, but luckily, she kept one in the glove compartment. By the time the sun went down, her new friend was taking up her entire balcony, throwing his funky shadow on everything in the house like an eclectic eclipse.

The next day in the darkened apartment, however, she started to experience the slow drip of buyer's remorse. What she loved most about the sculpture, its utter randomness, seemed to reflect her own lack of direction with a depressing accuracy.

All things considered, this wasn't the worst crisis of Hope's life. Buying everything at thrift stores had helped her amass enough savings to pay rent for almost a year without working. When she ran into Shawna in the middle of a crosswalk one day, she framed her departure from Mystic Partners in positive terms, saying "another opportunity came up." The beauty of this spontaneous and not untrue explanation lied in its vagueness; the "opportunity" which had come up was the opportunity to not work there anymore, and thus to be open to more opportunities.

She spent every morning in those weeks searching job boards and online classes, then made up an errand every afternoon to get out of the house. Chance encounters with Asher and Lucinda were common in those days, as life for them apparently consisted of one big endless shopping expedition. She saw them at the hardware store, the copy place, the flower shop, even the mall. She longed to look as harried as they always did, to have things and services that they needed right away for their purposeful existence. Perhaps out of pity, Lucinda floated the idea of Hope looking after Zeus for a few extra dollars once in a while.

"I'd be honored" Hope said, making a clumsy saluting gesture to indicate her readiness to receive orders. "Let me know when you need me."

It began with a couple of three-hour babysitting stints in the luxury condo while the couple went out to dinner. The visits were fun and stressful at the same time, like being in a fancy hotel room that you can't mess up so you're afraid to touch anything.

Zeus's unique brand of "disorder," as it was called—or difficulty fitting in, as Hope saw it—meant he could get so hyper-focused on something, usually the mixing and matching of different sets of LEGO-type toys to create otherworldly machines, as to literally not hear her when she spoke to him. A solution evolved whereby she would ask him something about his creation and then tie her agenda to his answer.

"So what are all those tubes for?"

"They vacuum up the moon rocks so it can crush them up and use them for energy."

"Interesting. So it's kind of like how a person's teeth crush up sugary snacks and turn them into energy, right?"

"Right."

"So you'd better brush your teeth."

For Lucinda's pristine furniture showroom of a residence to remain so uncluttered with a kid like Zeus around struck Hope as nothing short of miraculous. She asked Asher about this once and learned a housekeeper came twice a week, but that only partially explained the impossible symmetry of everything. Zeus did have free range to mess things up in his bedroom and on the sunporch, and Hope found it easiest to keep their activities contained to those areas. His bedtime reading consisted of massive adult-level tomes on subjects ranging from insects to Colonial architecture, and he frequently made her stop mid-paragraph to look things up on Google. As a result, his bedtime ritual usually managed to fire him up while knocking Hope out like a double dose of cough syrup.

About a month into their arrangement, Lucinda started leaving for longer periods. Once when an out-of-town appointment required a seven-hour absence and Asher was busy at one of her other properties, Hope asked if it would be all right if she brought Zeus with her to her apartment to check on her dog.

When Zeus saw Gwendola's sculpture on her balcony, he called it "gnarly," a bit of surfer lingo Hope thought very fitting because of the way it describes a thing's extreme greatness or its extreme awfulness, or both at the same time. The perfect wave can be "gnarly," as can an infected face tattoo.

At the end of that long day, when Lucinda returned home, Zeus declared, "Hope lives with a gnarly tin raccoon man who makes everything dark."

Looking back, she probably always knew Lars wouldn't remain in her apartment for long. She'd even had what she would later jokingly refer to as a "psychic flash" the first time she saw the statue; she pictured him standing by the roadside surrounded by wildflowers, watching over the expansiveness of it all like an automated prairie dog from the future.

What she hadn't foreseen, though—what no one could have envisioned—was how the artwork would make it to its intended destination. No one could have imagined a trip like that.

When the idea first came to her, she thought she would do it anonymously. That part of the plan veered a bit with her having to explain the whole thing to Desmond so he could engrave the rock for her. He supported her offbeat tribute with unexpected enthusiasm, as only he would.

Asher had ended his years-long feud with Desmond that very week, a stunning development which took place as a result of their running into each other at the liquor store. To hear Asher tell it, "Dude looked rough as shit, and I kinda felt a little bad for him, so I invited him to our party." In Desmond's version, however, Asher had forgotten his ID and Desmond stepped in to help him out.

Whatever forces had conspired to create the truce, Hope owed them a debt of gratitude. The sight of him by the rooftop fire pit at the condo that night shocked, delighted, and slightly sickened her. He poured her a glass of champagne and she spent most of the night there, barely bothering to mingle with any other guests and staying until almost 2 a.m. Asher didn't seem to notice—or if he did, he didn't care—but Hope relished the unexpected relief she felt at not having to hide anymore. You never realize how big a burden is until it's lifted.

She hadn't planned on having Zeus that weekend, but when Lucinda and Asher scored tickets to a couples retreat in Napa Valley, she couldn't say no. The extra responsibility threatened to throw a heavy wrench in her plans—until Desmond offered to drive them all to Oregon together in his truck. "The kid will love it," he said. "It'll be a crazy adventure."

"His mom's gonna kill me," Hope said.

"I'll take all the blame," Desmond offered calmly.

It wasn't until a photographer approached them at Kapps' diner that she truly appreciated what a surprising couple of weeks she'd just had, starting with the day she walked out of Mystic Partners for the last time. The four of them—Piggy included— were lunching in a booth at Hope's favorite roadside haunt, and a stranger approached them to offer a discount on a professional family portrait.

The Universe will go to stunning lengths sometimes to show you how pointless it is to plan things. Hope wouldn't have known where to start had she ever aspired to manage, manipulate, or maneuver anything like this into existence.

"That's lovely, thanks," Desmond said, reaching for the coupon before Hope had a chance to inform the man of his mistake.

As soon as the diner's owner saw Piggy, he brought out a water dish and some biscuits. When he saw Zeus, he returned with a kiddie menu printed on a paper placemat with games and puzzles on it, laying them down before him along with a box of crayons.

"I like the vibe of this place," Desmond said, feeling the leaves of the miniature plastic Christmas tree that sat atop the napkin dispenser.

"What kind of animal has the best vision?" Zeus asked, apropos of nothing.

Desmond leaned back in the booth and rubbed his chin. "Hmm . . . that's an interesting question."

"Definitely not dogs," Hope said, ashamed that it was the best answer she could come up with.

"What about a hawk?" Desmond suggested.

"Correct," Zeus said. "Birds of prey can spot rodents from ten thousand feet in the air." He had turned the placemat over, giving him a blank canvas, and his tongue traced the edges of his mouth while he concentrated on covering it with the beginnings of a drawing. "This animal has the vision that's twice—no, four times as much as a hawk's."

Hope leaned over to admire the page as she blew the steam off her coffee cup. "That's some pretty sharp vision," she said.

"Impressive," Desmond agreed.

Zeus placed a finger over his mouth ponderously while he studied the crayon jar, ultimately deciding on a bright yellow one which he hadn't yet used. "It's also ten times faster than a hummingbird," he boasted. "It can regenerate itself, like an octopus. You can break off one of its legs and it'll grow a new one. And it can see stuff underwater with its eyes shut like a platypus. It has psychic powers, too. It can freeze itself and then come back to life like an Alaskan tree frog. Bet you didn't know an Alaskan tree frog could do that, but it can. It's very resilient."

He sat back and looked over his creation critically, then lined the outer edge of the paper with stars. "This animal has every superpower that all the other animals have, only better. It's like . . . the ultimate power animal."

"Ultimate indeed," Hope said, popping a ketchup-covered French fry in her mouth. "Kinda looks like it could be related to our friend out there." She pointed out the window at Desmond's truck, where one of Lars's metal-spiked knees could be seen through a window in the camper shell.

Zeus shrugged. "That's where I got the idea from, I guess." He held up the paper to show it to them one final time. "He can also walk on water, like a Jesus Lizard." He started to sit back, proud of himself, then remembered something else and his eyes brightened again. "And he *also* can walk on *fire*."

Desmond chuckled. "Nice." He turned and looked at Hope, eyebrows raised. "Guess it's true what they say. A picture *is* worth a thousand words." Then he looked down and squinted at his wristwatch. "Well, we should get back on the road if we wanna make it home before sundown."

"Right," Hope said, waving to get the waiter's attention.

When they got to the truck, Hope realized Zeus held a huge stack of kiddie menus clutched to his chest.

"Dude, what are you doing with all those menus?" she asked him.

He tightened his grip defiantly. "I need them for something."

"Okay." She rolled her eyes as she opened the door and swatted him playfully as she boosted him into the back seat.

"Glad I left a decent tip," Desmond said.

A few miles up the highway, the radio went to static and Desmond popped in a strange banjo CD Hope assumed he meant as a joke. Piggy curled up on Hope's lap, sighing deeply, and Zeus began rustling around in the back seat, probably creating elaborate blueprints for a giant kiddie-menu castle.

"What does this *mean*, anyway?" Zeus asked, and Hope could see in the rearview mirror that he was studying the garden rock she'd had engraved.

"Yeah, what *does* that mean?" Desmond asked with a sly grin on his face.

Hope rolled down the window while she hemmed and hawed, at a loss for words; she hadn't fully explained the purpose of this trip to the kid yet. Well, she hadn't told him anything about paying tribute to a dead guy, anyway. What she had told him was that the tin raccoon man sculpture was too big for her house, so she'd decided to take it to a place where more people could appreciate it. And that was all he needed to know for now, she thought. If she told him anything else, he would do that classic kid thing of repeatedly asking "why" after each answer, and that would be a death spiral if there ever was one. Perhaps there would come a time in the future when she could answer that inevitable maze of whys for him. Until then, she would have to keep his questions contained.

"It's just an expression," she said, turning around to face him. "'Love, like death, is no big deal.' It means life isn't as complicated as people make it."

"It's just a metaphor," Desmond said, trying to help.

Zeus sat up straight in that way he always did when he was about to hold court on something. "That's not a metaphor," he corrected, "it's a simile. We just learned the difference in Language Arts. Similes are expressions that compare two things using 'like' or 'as.' A metaphor is when you say something *is* something else. A metaphor would be if you said, 'Love is . . . '" He looked out the window for inspiration just as they passed a sprawling hotel with a giant water slide in front. "*Love is a giant water slide.* That's a metaphor."

Hope laughed and turned back around in her seat, relieved. "I like that. Sounds like the name of a great song."

"Wet, wild, and over too fast," Desmond sang, improvising a tune with the jangling banjos as background.

"Yeah," Zeus said. "But a *simile* is when you say 'Love is *like* . . . '"

"Almond wine," Hope chimed in, having just noticed a roadside stand selling almond wine. "You know, because they're both really sweet and . . . like . . . kinda make you wanna throw up."

"Correct!" Zeus said, causing Desmond to burst into hysterics, and swerve his steering a little. As he recovered, shaking his head and wiping his eyes while trying to keep them on the road, he held up his hand like an eager student in Language Arts class.

"Ooh, I got one!" he said. "Love is like an Alaskan Tree Frog." He pointed above his head at the back seat. "Zeus?"

"Okay," Zeus said, accepting the challenge graciously. "Um . . . okay. Love is like an Alaskan Tree Frog . . . "

The music got slower and quieter, a single small banjo maintaining the tension.

"It can survive in places you never imagined."

"Whoa," Hope said. "That's deep, man. Good job."

The simile-metaphor game seemed to compress the last span of the trip to Ashbrook into the space of about three breaths. "Oh, wait—there it is," Hope said at the first glimpse of Thrillville's rolling scaffolding hills in the distance.

"So where are we going, exactly?" Desmond asked, hitting the break lightly as a reflex.

"It's somewhere right around . . . " Hope scooted forward in her seat, watching for landmarks she recognized. "Here. Turn at that gas station." Minutes after the turn, she saw the head of that grungy swan cart peeking out from behind a bush. "Stop there, by that bush," she said.

Desmond turned off the car obediently and hopped out to open the tailgate. Hope jumped out too and went to explore the area with Piggy, who stretched and yawned and shook out her ears, jingling metal tags on her collar before making a few preliminary sniffs.

When Hope moved the seat forward to help Zeus out, she saw that the floor was littered with more than a dozen species of origami animals. She picked one up—an elephant—and looked it over admiringly.

"These are awesome," she said. "I can't believe you were making these that whole time." She dug through the rest of the pile: a bear, a frog, a skunk. On some of the animals, he'd even taken time to color the kiddie menu words over with a black crayon—which he'd likely also swiped from the restaurant.

"You know what? I think we should leave these here with the sculpture. That way more people can appreciate them. What do you think?"

"Sure, okay."

It was a good thing she hadn't tried to complete this whole endeavor on her own, Hope thought as the three of them pulled weeds to make room for the sculpture's base. The job was proving more labor-intensive than she'd envisioned.

"Who's Brooks Narcissus Nixon?" Zeus asked, watching Hope brush dirt off the part of the stone with his name on it before she laid it down.

"That's where I got the quote from," she told him.

Zeus nodded. "So is that who the statue is supposed to be?"

"It could be him I guess," Hope said. "But it doesn't have to. It could be . . . the Ultimate Power Animal. Art is kind of neat like that. You can make it be whatever you want."

"Cool."

Hope took one good photo of the finished product and another one right as Piggy squatted at the edge of it to politely pay her respects.

"Well?" Desmond said, looking at his watch again and then pointing at the sky with his eyebrows as though referencing the position of the sun.

"I'm good," Hope said, and the four of them returned to the truck, the banjo music resuming its melancholy twang as Desmond started the engine.

"Goodbye, Gnarly Nixon!" Zeus called out the window as they slowly pulled away.

About the Author

AUTHOR GINA YATES HAS SPENT DECADES honing her craft through an unconventional path of travel and entrepreneurship. After immigrating to Canada on a student visa in the early 90s, she married a Canadian citizen and embarked on months-long backpacking trips with him around Asia, Central America, and Africa, funding their travels by selling handcrafted jewelry at music festivals and at downtown Vancouver kiosks. Following a divorce and a years-long stint on the island of Roatan, Honduras, Gina briefly studied creative writing at the University of Northern Michigan in 2003 before returning to Vancouver and eventually earning a diploma in Fashion Business and Creative Arts. During this period she wrote her first novel, an unpublished fictionalized memoir of her time in Honduras, a time that was marred by the addiction and mental illness she inherited from her father, the late celebrated author Richard Yates. Since moving to New Mexico in 2008, she has owned and operated the eclectic vintage clothing shop Frock Star Vintage in Albuquerque as well as completed her first published novel, *Narcissus Nobody*.

RECENT AND FORTHCOMING BOOKS FROM THREE ROOMS PRESS

FICTION

Rishab Borah
The Door to Inferna

Meagan Brothers
Weird Girl and What's His Name

Christopher Chambers
Scavenger

Ron Dakron
Hello Devilfish!

Robert Duncan
Loudmouth

Michael T. Fournier
Hidden Wheel
Swing State

Aaron Hamburger
Nirvana Is Here

William Least Heat-Moon
Celestial Mechanics

Aimee Herman
Everything Grows

Eamon Loingsigh
Light of the Diddicoy
Exile on Bridge Street

John Marshall
The Greenfather

Aram Saroyan
Still Night in L.A.

Richard Vetere
The Writers Afterlife
Champagne and Cocaine

Julia Watts
Quiver
Needlework

Gina Yates
Narcissus Nobody

MEMOIR & BIOGRAPHY

Nassrine Azimi and Michel Wasserman
Last Boat to Yokohama: The Life and Legacy of Beate Sirota Gordon

William S. Burroughs & Allen Ginsberg
Don't Hide the Madness:
William S. Burroughs in Conversation with Allen Ginsberg
edited by Steven Taylor

James Carr
BAD: The Autobiography of James Carr

Richard Katrovas
Raising Girls in Bohemia:
Meditations of an American Father

Judith Malina
Full Moon Stages:
Personal Notes from
50 Years of The Living Theatre

Phil Marcade
Punk Avenue: Inside the New York City Underground, 1972–1982

Alvin Orloff
Disasterama! Adventures in the Queer Underground 1977–1997

Nicca Ray
Ray by Ray: A Daughter's Take on the Legend of Nicholas Ray

Stephen Spotte
My Watery Self:
Memoirs of a Marine Scientist

PHOTOGRAPHY-MEMOIR

Mike Watt
On & Off Bass

SHORT STORY ANTHOLOGIES

SINGLE AUTHOR

The Alien Archives: Stories
by Robert Silverberg

First-Person Singularities: Stories
by Robert Silverberg
with an introduction by John Scalzi

Tales from the Eternal Café: Stories
by Janet Hamill, with an introduction
by Patti Smith

Time and Time Again:
Sixteen Trips in Time
by Robert Silverberg

Voyagers:
Twelve Journeys in Space and Time
by Robert Silverberg

MULTI-AUTHOR

Crime + Music: Twenty Stories
of Music-Themed Noir
edited by Jim Fusilli

Dark City Lights: New York Stories
edited by Lawrence Block

The Faking of the President: Twenty Stories of White House Noir
edited by Peter Carlaftes

Florida Happens:
Bouchercon 2018 Anthology
edited by Greg Herren

Have a NYC I, II & III:
New York Short Stories;
edited by Peter Carlaftes
& Kat Georges

Songs of My Selfie:
An Anthology of Millennial Stories
edited by Constance Renfrow

The Obama Inheritance:
15 Stories of Conspiracy Noir
edited by Gary Phillips

This Way to the End Times:
Classic and New Stories of
the Apocalypse
edited by Robert Silverberg

MIXED MEDIA

John S. Paul
Sign Language: A Painter's Notebook
(photography, poetry and prose)

FILM & PLAYS

Israel Horovitz
My Old Lady: Complete Stage Play and Screenplay with an Essay on Adaptation

Peter Carlaftes
Triumph For Rent (3 Plays)
Teatrophy (3 More Plays)

Kat Georges
Three Somebodies: Plays about Notorious Dissidents

DADA

Maintenant: A Journal of Contemporary Dada Writing & Art
(Annual, since 2008)

TRANSLATIONS

Thomas Bernhard
On Earth and in Hell
(poems of Thomas Bernhard
with English translations by
Peter Waugh)

Patrizia Gattaceca
Isula d'Anima / Soul Island
(poems by the author
in Corsican with English
translations)

César Vallejo | Gerard Malanga
Malanga Chasing Vallejo
(selected poems of César Vallejo
with English translations
and additional notes by
Gerard Malanga)

George Wallace
EOS: Abductor of Men
(selected poems in Greek & English)

ESSAYS

Far Away From Close to Home
Vanessa Baden Kelly

Womentality: Thirteen Empowering Stories by Everyday Women Who Said Goodbye to the Workplace and Hello to Their Lives
edited by Erin Wildermuth

HUMOR

Peter Carlaftes
A Year on Facebook

POETRY COLLECTIONS

Hala Alyan
Atrium

Peter Carlaftes
DrunkYard Dog
I Fold with the Hand I Was Dealt

Thomas Fucaloro
It Starts from the Belly and Blooms

Kat Georges
Our Lady of the Hunger

Robert Gibbons
Close to the Tree

Israel Horovitz
Heaven and Other Poems

David Lawton
Sharp Blue Stream

Jane LeCroy
Signature Play

Philip Meersman
This Is Belgian Chocolate

Jane Ormerod
Recreational Vehicles on Fire
Welcome to the Museum of Cattle

Lisa Panepinto
On This Borrowed Bike

George Wallace
Poppin' Johnny

THREE ROOMS PRESS

Three Rooms Press | New York, NY | Current Catalog: www.threeroomspress.com
Three Rooms Press books are distributed by PGW/Ingram: www.pgw.com